Joanna Johnson lives in a little village with her husband and too many books. After completing an English degree at university she went on to work in publishing, although she'd always wish she was working on her own books rather than other people's. This dream came true in 2018, when she signed her first contract with Mills & Boon, and she hasn't looked back, spending her time getting lost in mainly Regency history and wishing it was acceptable to write a manuscript using a quill.

Also by Joanna Johnson

The Marriage Rescue
Scandalously Wed to the Captain
His Runaway Lady
A Mistletoe Vow to Lord Lovell
The Return of Her Long-Lost Husband
The Officer's Convenient Proposal
'A Kiss at the Winter Ball'
in *Regency Christmas Parties*

Discover more at millsandboon.co.uk.

HER GRACE'S DARING PROPOSAL

Joanna Johnson

MILLS & BOON

First published in Great Britain 2023
by Mills & Boon, an imprint of HarperCollins*Publishers* Ltd,
1 London Bridge Street, London, SE1 9GF

www.harpercollins.co.uk

HarperCollins*Publishers*, Macken House, 39/40 Mayor Street Upper,
Dublin 1, D01 C9W8, Ireland

This book is produced from independently certified FSC™ paper
to ensure responsible forest management.
For more information visit: www.harpercollins.co.uk/green.

Printed and Bound in the UK using 100% Renewable Electricity
at CPI Group (UK) Ltd, Croydon, CR0 4YY

For (all) my faves.

Chapter One

Enveloped in a fug of stale beer and tobacco smoke, Isabelle Sherborne pulled her hood closer around her face as she wondered—not for the first time—whether she was making a grave mistake. There was little chance of her being recognised in a shabby place like this but she couldn't be too careful. If she was discovered all of society would be ablaze with gossip by morning, and then any hope of discreetly bringing her sister home without a scandal would be dashed.

I can still hardly believe what I'm here to do. How has it come to this?

Seated at the dirty table to her left, a young man was whispering in the ear of his giggling sweetheart, the girl perched on his knee in a manner so intimate Isabelle almost choked on her glass of orgeat, while to her right two labourers were arguing with their voices rough and raised.

More than one pair of eyes had turned in her direction since she'd entered, but she kept hers firmly on the tavern's door, trying to blend into the shadows while praying that *he* would come soon.

Not that I even know what he looks like. I have to trust the landlord will give me a sign.

A glance towards the bar showed the owner leaning against it, his brawny arms crossed over his chest as he surveyed his domain. He'd been reluctant to help, but a handful of coins had gone some way to persuading him, and a vague arrangement now existed between them she could only hope he'd honour. He would signal when her quarry entered, and she would conclude her business quickly—a bargain Isabelle had agreed to at once.

The quicker she could secure the meeting the better. Under any other circumstances she would never have set foot in this murky corner of Bishops Morton, and again she tweaked her hood lower to cover her distinctive golden hair. A woman of her standing ought not to know such a place even existed, only frank desperation making Isabelle risk tarnishing her impeccable name, but what choice did she have?

Little Marina had been just six years old when influenza had stolen their parents and Isabelle had cared for her ever since, throwing herself into the role of mother aged barely eighteen—which made knowing she was responsible for her much younger sister's current danger even more difficult to bear.

She pressed a hand to her forehead, feeling the niggling ache behind it that refused to go away. It had been a near constant presence ever since her letters to Suffolk had begun to go unanswered, and it was made no better by the loud voices and laughter surrounding her. Given the choice she'd get up right that very moment and walk out—but she didn't have that luxury. The stranger she was hoping to meet might be her only chance of saving Marina's reputation, and so Isabelle stayed, with a block of ice sitting in her stomach, and waited tensely for her unwitting saviour to arrive.

'Looking for some company?'

A voice at her shoulder made her jump. A man was standing beside her, leaning down so closely she could smell the hops on his breath, and instinctively she recoiled.

'No, thank you.'

Unfortunately he didn't seem the least bit deterred. A smile spread across his face and he reached for the chair beside her with a slightly unsteady hand.

'No? Why else would you be sitting here all alone? Don't be shy.'

Isabelle stiffened as he tried to pull out the chair, the legs mercifully caught beneath the table. She might have used the delay to escape, but she didn't seem able to move, stark horror running over her like a cold draught.

Had he mistaken her for some kind of...?

The man grunted as he wrestled with the chair and Isabelle's heart began to skip faster. If she left now she'd miss the person she'd come to see, but it might be her only chance to escape, her unwanted new friend probably too drunk to catch up with her if she ran...

'I believe she's waiting for me.'

A different voice at her other shoulder made her flinch again and she turned quickly to see another man towering above her. She couldn't quite make out his face, the newcomer silhouetted against the fireplace behind, although something in it clearly told the first man it was time for him to leave.

Letting go of the chair he slouched away, leaving Isabelle to catch her breath, although not yet ready to feel relieved.

'Are you—? You are Mr Carter?'

She squinted upwards, wishing she could see him properly. Obscured by the orange glow of the fire it was hard to tell anything about him other than he was fearsomely tall, a hulking dark shape, and that he must have entered while she was distracted. There was little chance she would have missed him otherwise, the sheer size of him enough to draw every eye in the room.

She shifted in her seat as he removed his hat and dropped it onto the table.

'I am. Wainwright said you wanted to see me.'

Isabelle snatched what she hoped was a surreptitious glance at the landlord for confirmation, slightly reassured by his brief nod.

'Yes. Would you be so kind as to join me, sir? If you've no other engagements this evening?'

It was an invitation more suited to a marquess's card party than a sticky table in a cheap alehouse and Isabelle grimaced internally. He must be used to far rougher speech—but he sat, at last illuminated by the flames rather than hidden by them, and fresh discomfort knotted her insides.

Not quite what I was expecting—but then again, when have I met a mercenary before?

She hesitated, her carefully rehearsed opening stalling on her tongue. It had taken all her nerve to decide on this plan and it was too late to back out now, even if what she was about to do went against every shred of her better judgement.

For some reason, when she'd overheard a bootblack on the sodden high street telling his customer about an acquaintance just returned from overseas, she had pictured a much older man than the one now sitting before her.

The man the shoeshine boy had spoken of—a Mr Carter, usually to be found lodging at the Drake Tavern when not away on his shadowy business—had sounded like exactly the kind of individual she needed, and if all it would take to secure him was a purse full of gold there seemed little to stop her... apart from principles she could no longer afford. A grizzled old fighter would know just how to deal with the men scheming against her and Isabelle had dropped a few coins into the bootblack's tray as she hurried back to her carriage, hardly caring that the black silk of her widow's mourning clothes would be covered in water spots from the rain still ceaselessly falling.

That had been two days ago and now, as she considered the man in front of her, she realised how wrong her assumptions had been. This Mr Carter wasn't particularly grizzled and he most certainly wasn't old: by the look of him he was only in his early thirties—a few years older than herself—and completely lacking in the disfigurements one might reasonably expect from a hired blade. With his short-cropped dark hair and skin that hinted at time spent in sunnier climes than wintry England, he might be considered almost good looking—but only by those who chose to notice such things, and Isabelle, her mouth dry with apprehension and wondering how to begin, was *not* one of them.

Even so…

As he shrugged off his coat she watched broad shoulders moving beneath a shirt that struggled to contain them, the power of his unsmiling jaw enhanced by stubble that might have made another man look unkempt. On Mr Carter, however, the effect was different. It made him seem dangerous, and if she hadn't already known he made his money through violence it would have come as no surprise. There was something in his hazel eyes that almost made her shiver—a shrewd understanding that spoke of more life experience than she could boast and suggested that he wouldn't shy away from a challenge.

In truth, she'd never encountered such a man before in her entire sheltered life, and sitting opposite him made her feel strangely exposed—a sensation that only intensified when he settled his impressive forearms on the tabletop and fixed her with a direct gaze.

'I could be wrong, madam, but somehow I don't think a place like this is your natural habitat.'

Still hidden beneath her hood, Isabelle swallowed. Was there a hint of dark amusement in his voice? It was certainly deep enough to hold all manner of things, its gravelly pitch like a river so fathomless one couldn't see the bottom. No gentleman would dream of beginning a conversation with anything less than perfect politeness... But then again, she thought uncomfortably, a gentleman was the very opposite of what she'd set out to find.

'No indeed, sir. I would never have ventured in here if I hadn't been looking for you.'

'In that case, I'm flattered.'

The mercenary leaned back in his chair and motioned to the landlord. Clearly he didn't intend to enter into any business negotiations without a drink in his hand, and Isabelle grasped her own glass tighter as a tankard was placed down between them, a thin rivulet of its contents running down one side.

Mr Carter reached out to claim it, drawing the tankard towards him with a hand crowned by a network of scars. His knuckles stood out beneath the patinaed skin—a mountain range roughened by who knew how many fights—and Isabelle's apprehension was just beginning to build when he spoke again.

'So, we've established that you know who *I* am. My question is, who are you?'

He took a sip of his drink, watching her steadily as he raised it to his mouth. His eyes never faltered, their greenish depths lit by the reflection of the dancing fire, and for the briefest moment Isabelle found it difficult to look away. The tavern was busy and yet the bustle seemed to recede into the background, the smoke and noise fading a little as the mercenary's unfamiliar presence forced it back. Something about him made it hard to focus on anything else; perhaps the novelty of a man so far removed from everything she knew, an individual so unlike her late husband they might have been two different species entirely.

Isabelle felt an unpleasant lurch at the unwelcome thought. Poor Edwin had always been frail, bearing his suffering towards the end with a patience she wished she could have shared. Watching his decline had unleashed all her memories of nursing Mama and Papa through their illness, those awful weeks of ten years coming flooding back to drive a skewer into her heart as she'd clung to his cold hand… But he had slipped away despite her willing him to stay, pleading through her tears as she'd knelt beside his bed, and her only comfort had been knowing that Marina hadn't had to watch the man she'd loved almost as a father cough out his final breath.

A dull ache spread through Isabelle's chest and her hand instinctively moved again to her hood to make sure her face was still in shadow. Dwelling on the past wouldn't bring Marina home and she lifted her chin, determined the strength that had arisen from her grief would not abandon her when she needed it most.

'I'd rather not divulge my name just yet. Not until we have an agreement.'

A dark eyebrow raised but Isabelle pressed on.

'I was given your name by an acquaintance of mine. I understand you provide a certain kind of service?'

That wasn't strictly the truth, and her conscience gave a tweak—although the slight tilt of Mr Carter's head was an immediate distraction. The subtle movement threw deep shadows beneath his cheekbones, making his stern face suddenly seem sculpted from tawny stone, and Isabelle felt a flicker of something to realise he was more handsome than she'd originally thought.

'I can't imagine what kind of acquaintance you and I would have in common, but their information is correct. I provide a number of services. Which is it that you want?'

Isabelle looked down into her almost empty glass of orgeat, fresh uncertainty coiling through her.

Where do I start?

Of course she had to tell him what she needed, but

putting her situation into words was a step she could hardly bring herself to take. Until that moment she'd spoken of it to nobody, and she wavered, sensing the mercenary's impatience as he sat back in his chair.

'Come now, Miss Mystery. You'll need to be a bit more forthcoming. Is it a debt to be collected? Some valuables you need me to retrieve?' He glanced at her left hand, where her wedding ring was a distinctive ridge beneath her glove. 'Or perhaps some lover you've grown tired of is still hanging around, needing to be moved on before your husband finds out?'

Isabelle's head snapped up at once. 'Certainly not!'

Mr Carter shrugged. 'You wouldn't be the first well-bred lady wanting me to solve that particular problem. It'll be difficult for me to take your case if I don't know what it is.'

He took another mouthful of ale, his ease the complete opposite of Isabelle's own agitation, and she was glad he couldn't see her face. Her cheeks had flushed pink at his vulgar suggestion and she struggled to keep her composure—a struggle made worse by a rogue thought that wondered if he was referring to anyone she knew.

She took a deep breath. He was easily the least agreeable man she'd ever sat down to converse with. Apparently even the prospect of paid employment wasn't enough to inspire him to attempt good manners, but she had to persevere.

'It's a delicate matter.'

'They always are.'

'Which is why I came here myself,' Isabelle continued, ignoring his interruption. 'I wasn't sure about trusting a servant with this kind of thing.'

The almost black eyebrow flickered again and Isabelle gritted her teeth on another spark of irritation.

'But you don't mind trusting me?'

'As I understand it, your trustworthiness can be purchased.'

To her surprise his lips curved, abruptly transforming the barren planes of his face. It wasn't a kind smile, like the ones Edwin had turned on her for the duration of their comfortable marriage; there was an edge to it, and yet to her horror she felt her pulse pick up speed. With his lips set in that upward tick there was no question that he was attractive, a pair of matching indentations appearing in his cheeks that were more pleasing than they had any right to be.

'That's true enough. Once you've engaged me my mouth becomes yours—along with everything else.'

Mention of his mouth drew her attention to his wolfish smile all the more and Isabelle wrenched her eyes away, too flustered to reply. Thankfully the mercenary didn't seem to notice, more intent on his tankard than on her, but aggravation swept through her all the same.

Did he have to be *quite* so crass? Her sudden unease in his company had to be explained somehow, and Isabelle seized on his manners for an answer, determined not to entertain any alternative. It wasn't the first time she'd been alone with a man—her marriage to Edwin was a testament to that fact—but of course that had been different. Her mild, courteous husband had been the complete opposite of the man she was faced with now, and besides, their relationship had not been quite as it seemed. Encountering someone like Mr Carter, with his rugged looks and broad shoulders, was a new experience entirely, and Isabelle turned away, her frustration mingling with something she couldn't quite name.

There's no hope that I can work with him. I'll have to think of something else.

It was his brusque, disrespectful conduct that made her mind up for her—or so Isabelle told herself as she rose to her feet, gathering her cloak tightly around herself as if it could magic away the last ill-spent hour. It had been folly for her to think he might be the answer to her problem, desperation clearly clouding her judgement. She'd have to place her complete faith in whoever she enlisted to help her and this Mr Carter had done nothing to earn that, making her feel wrong-footed instead of in safe hands.

'This was a mistake. I shouldn't have come. Please forgive the intrusion.'

The mercenary didn't move. He gazed up at her, that damned impertinent smile still lingering, annoying and fascinating in equal measure.

'Ah. So I'm not what you were hoping for after all? I can only apologise that I caused you a wasted journey.'

Unable to think how to respond Isabelle drew back, dipping him the quickest curtsey her own good manners would allow as disappointment and dislike warred to see which would triumph. She'd have to begin all over again in her quest to rescue Marina, but Mr Carter's unpleasantness left her no alternative—a sentiment that only grew when he muttered after her as she turned away.

'A word of advice, ma'am. Next time you want to avoid being noticed in a tavern, choose a less expensive cloak. Silk's a dead giveaway that you don't belong.'

Joseph Carter watched his would-be employer disappear through the door with a single shake of his head. It probably wouldn't have killed him to be more polite—but where was the fun in that?

They were all the same, he thought as he drained the dregs of his ale, these clueless upper classes who expected him to do their bidding with no questions asked, and they wore his patience thin. The pampered lives of his private clients were too fortunate to know any *real* trouble—but then, their self-indulgence had always been his gain. Sorting out the *ton*'s squabbles and tepid love affairs was far easier than going overseas to fight in other people's wars, and as Joseph set down his tankard he wondered how much money he'd just allowed to walk out of the door.

She'd have been a difficult one to please, though. Hiding her face completely and then refusing to give her name—I might have had a lucky escape.

He rubbed the back of his neck, feeling the short hair spiky against his palm. He was used to those who sought his services behaving skittishly, wrestling with the idea of sharing their problems with a man they thought far below them. Occasionally one would deign to ask his origins—more to satisfy their anxiety than out of any real interest—but Joseph had no intention of revealing such private matters to someone who could never understand.

It was nobody's business how he'd managed to drag himself out of the gutter, abandoned as a nameless newborn on the steps of the workhouse but now a man of experience who had travelled to almost every corner of the globe selling his strength to the highest bidder. If those desiring his services considered him beneath them then they were welcome to do so—just as he could never view *them* with much respect, a lifetime of hardship having made it impossible for him to think highly of those who had no idea how fortunate they were.

Women like the one who had just left in an offended flurry knew nothing of struggling, regarding him as little more than a guard dog or messenger boy for their convenience, and he couldn't pretend to be sorry that she hadn't liked the glimpse of the real world that he'd given her.

All the same...

Joseph frowned. She shouldn't have come directly. Usually the well-heeled sent a note or a servant to summon him for a first meeting—and for good reason. A lady like that had no business in a place like the Drake, and she'd stuck out a mile among the labourers and jaded women plying their trade. She'd be jumped by thieves before she could take a dozen steps outside at this time of year, with the February evenings starting early and draping the streets in a cloak just as dark as her own black silk.

As an unfeeling brute for hire he shouldn't have given the mystery woman a second thought, although with a grunt of annoyance he realised he was hesitating.

Damn it. She's not my responsibility...

He scowled down into his empty tankard, ignoring a scuffle that had broken out somewhere behind him. Violence was such an intrinsic part of his life that it barely registered, something he'd been forced to grow used to in the workhouse before he'd even learned to speak. His next lesson had been to show no fear of it, any weakness drawing predators like wolves to a sheep, and the fact that some shadow of decency still lingered behind his uncaring façade was a secret he'd take to his grave.

Ethics were bad for business and yet years of watching the strong prey on the weak had taught him another lesson he held close to his heart. Only a coward made victims of the vulnerable and he would never disgrace himself by doing what he'd witnessed countless times, the pride that even struggle and suffering hadn't managed to beat out of him still guiding his hand. He refused any job that fell short of that strict standard, which meant harming no children and no women—and so knowing he'd just allowed one to stray into certain danger made him get wearily to his feet, pushing himself up from the table with reluctance he didn't bother to hide.

Whoever heard of a mercenary with something so useless as a conscience?

'Going after her, Joe?'

At the sound of his name he turned, midway through pulling on his coat, to see the landlord watching him from behind the bar.

'You know me. Too soft-hearted for my own good.'

The other man scoffed, but Joseph didn't stay to defend himself, heading with long strides to the door. The sooner he steered the woman back to where she belonged the sooner he could forget all about her. The only thing that interested him about her class was their money, everything else about them so removed from reality that to him they seemed to exist in their own separate world, and if she wasn't going to pay him then there was nothing to be gained from his involvement but wasted time.

It was bitterly cold when he emerged onto the street, and he shivered as he pulled his hat down firmly onto his head. Which way had she gone? It wasn't yet nine o'clock, but the chill had driven everyone indoors and the usually crowded street was still, the cobbles stretching out into emptiness and even the moonlight dimmed by heavy clouds.

The woman seemed to have disappeared into thin air, and he was just about to cut his losses and return to the warmth of the Drake's fireside when a scream sliced through the silence—and all at once Joseph knew precisely where to find her.

A narrow alley ran down one side of the tavern, dark and ominous even during the day, and Joseph turned towards it. He'd imagined nobody would be foolish enough to enter that rabbit warren at night but evidently he'd been wrong, the echoing note of the woman's voice drawing him into the shadows with his face set in resignation.

Just as I thought. Barely a dozen steps.

His heart beat a fraction faster as he broke into a run, but he wasn't afraid. It had been years since he'd felt any dread at the prospect of a fight, daily hidings at the hands of boys bigger than him hammering that out until he'd grown strong enough to make them think twice. There had been little point in hoping the workhouse wardens might intervene and Joseph couldn't remember a time when he hadn't known that the only person worth relying on was himself.

Even his own mother hadn't loved or wanted him, the other boys had never tired of reminding him until he'd accepted it as fact, and as he'd grown into a hard, unflinching man he had come to know that his only value to those around him was in the towering frame that meant few dared meet his eye. If brute strength was his sole worth then those in need could have it— for a price. Nobody ever cared for him otherwise and he cared for nobody in return, an untouchable island who hired out the worst parts of himself while keeping the rest locked down tight.

There was only one of them, Joseph saw as he rounded a sharp corner and took in the scene with a single glance. The thief had his prey pushed up against the wall of the alley, one hand at her throat as with the other he tried to rip the small bag she was clinging to from her grasp, and although she twisted and thrashed she had no hope of breaking free.

It was as effortless as breathing for Joseph to hurl the thief to the ground and he stood over him, watching as the man sprawled out on the dirty cobbles mere inches from his boots. Behind him he heard the woman take a rasping gasp, her throat clearly raw from being squeezed so mercilessly, but he didn't turn around, instead addressing the figure at his feet with a contempt that could have blistered iron.

'You'll be leaving now, before I lose my temper.'

The thief didn't need telling twice. Without a word he scrambled back on his hands and knees and then he was up, fleeing down the alley, and Joseph felt his lip curl as he listened to footsteps disappearing into the dark.

Pathetic. Picking on someone weaker and then running when confronted with a fair fight—just the same as every other coward.

He flexed his fingers, allowing them to relax from their tight fists before glancing over his shoulder. The woman was still slumped against the wall, one hand pressed to her throat and her chest rising and falling far too fast, the movement clear even beneath the cover of her cloak. At some point during the struggle her hood had been knocked back and at last Joseph caught sight of her face, a pale oval gleaming in the shadows, but even that indistinct glimpse was enough to make him pause.

She was much younger than he'd thought, her smooth skin silvery in the moonlight and the wide set of her eyes reminding him suddenly of a deer. It was difficult to tell what colour they were, but the thick dark lashes surrounding them contrasted with the fair sheen of her hair—the complete opposite to his own almost black crop. They might have been images in a reverse mirror, everything about them contrary to the other, although in the next moment Joseph dismissed such romanticism as the nonsense it was. He shared no bond with this woman, and a comely face meant nothing—just a countenance belonging to a stranger he would never see again.

'That was pure stupidity. You ought never have walked here alone.'

The mysterious young woman looked back at him, her chin lowered as she fought to regain her breath. She didn't shy away, and Joseph couldn't help a twinge of grudging respect that she hadn't simply given in without a fight.

So she has a thimbleful more mettle than some others I've met.

Her voice was hoarse, her attacker's grip having roughened its cut-glass edges. 'I wanted to reach my carriage as swiftly as possible. I thought perhaps this alley would be a quicker route.'

'You should have brought someone with you. Or why not tell your driver to meet you somewhere closer by?'

'I told you why. I didn't want to trust a servant with this particular task. They're loyal, I'm sure, but they might talk—even if not with malice—and I couldn't risk anyone knowing where I'd gone.'

The woman tentatively rubbed at her throat. Even in the darkness Joseph could see bruises beginning to form on her delicate neck and he looked away again at once, irritated that his eye had been drawn there in the first place.

'You could have been killed. Whatever your trouble is, it can't be worth that. You'd be better off staying at home rather than wandering the streets at night looking for an answer.'

He was mildly surprised when her head came up, her eyes seeking his in the moonlight. In the tavern she'd seemed ill at ease, and then, when her face had been finally revealed, she'd looked afraid. But now as she stared up at him it was with a passion more striking than anything before.

'It *is* worth it. It's the only thing I have left in the world worth sacrificing myself for. And if I don't find an answer nobody else will.'

She shut her mouth with a snap and Joseph saw her jaw tense, perhaps regretting revealing so much to a man she'd already decided she didn't like. She didn't enjoy his company—that much was clear—and for his part Joseph had no desire to waste his time with some prim upper-class miss if he wasn't going to be paid for it…even if she *was* undeniably pretty as she took a cautious step closer, the top of her head hardly reaching his shoulder.

'I must thank you, Mr Carter. If you hadn't come I should have lost my purse, and along with it a very precious miniature. I'm truly grateful for your help.'

She gave him an uncertain smile and Joseph felt something stir low down in his belly. The portrait was of her husband, no doubt, but for a split second that didn't seem to matter. All he could focus on was the sweetness of her smile and the real appreciation in her voice as she thanked him—both things so unfamiliar that he could only respond with a grunt.

'We won't speak of that. I'll take you to your carriage and then we can part.'

He saw her blink at his brusqueness but he didn't wait for a reply. He was tired and hungry and had better things to do than shepherd stray ladies back to their rich husbands, he thought as the sound of silk-slippered feet followed him from the alley towards the relative safety of the main street. She didn't try to engage him again and for that he was thankful, aware of her presence at his elbow and wishing her no closer as they walked in silence through the darkness, her hood once again hiding her face and Joseph trusting to the darkness to do the same for his.

At last the woman spoke. 'That's my carriage.'

Joseph looked up from his study of the pavement. A grand carriage was indeed standing a short distance away, its lamps casting a puddle of light across the ground around it and a fine pair of bay horses patiently waiting to move. At last it seemed he was about to be rid of his unwanted companion, and Joseph almost sighed with relief—although a shadow of his previous irritation still lingered.

'So I see. Can you cross the road without assistance?'

The woman bridled a little and Joseph had to fight back a dark smile.

'Of course. I believe I can at least manage *that*.'

'I'm glad to hear it. In that case, I bid you goodnight.'

He tipped his hat and turned abruptly away, determined not to spend another moment in such unprofitable company. A wealthy married woman with a pretty face was still a wealthy married woman, and unless she employed him there was no reason for two such incompatible species to mix.

This time, however, it was he who walked into an ambush after barely twelve steps.

'Mr Carter? Please wait.'

He sensed a black-swathed figure behind him and suppressed a groan. After the trouble he'd already had that evening he was hardly in the mood for more—and yet for some reason he found himself turning back.

She was looking down at the ground, nothing visible beneath her hood but the very tip of her well-shaped nose. 'I was too hasty before. I think… I think perhaps you might be able to help me after all. Would you call on me tomorrow? If you have the time?'

A remark balanced on his tongue but Joseph just managed to restrain it, taking from her the little white card she drew out of her reticule. She still didn't sound entirely sure that she was doing the right thing and he wondered drily how long it would take her to regret it, their acquaintance already built on a firm bedrock of mutual disapproval.

'As you wish. About ten o'clock?'

'Ten. Yes. Thank you. Goodnight.'

The woman lowered her head and walked away, her cloak camouflaging her against the darkness as she melted into the gloom, and Joseph made a point of not watching her go. If she were to turn suddenly she wouldn't see him looking after her with anything approaching curiosity, and he waited until she was securely in the carriage before looking down at her card.

It was difficult to make out the words at first, printed very small in a curling font the dim light did nothing to make any clearer, but when he deciphered the letters Joseph let out a low whistle.

Well, well, Miss Mystery. No wonder you didn't want to tell me your name.

Chapter Two

Isabelle made sure she was sitting up perfectly straight as she waited for her guest to arrive. Another glance at the gilded clock on the parlour's mantel showed three minutes to ten. Their first meeting had been on his territory but now that Mr Carter was stepping into hers she meant to seize the upper hand, remaining calm no matter how aggravating he might be— or how much uncertainty still fluttered, the events of the previous night still fresh in her mind alongside the bruises to her throat that even her largest necklace couldn't quite hide.

If her reticule had merely contained money she would have let it go without a struggle, but the miniature of Mama and Papa she always carried in it could not have been replaced. It was the only copy, and she would have done anything to keep it safe—apparently including trying to fight off a man almost twice her size. He would have won eventually, of course, no doubt injuring far more than just her neck in the process, and the thought of what might have happened if Mr Carter hadn't arrived so abruptly on the scene sent a shiver down her spine.

If I thought he was dangerous before, I know for certain now.

In the tavern she'd been positive they could never reach an accord…but perhaps they didn't have to. He was rude, and clearly enjoyed being so, although that could be overlooked if he brought the same forcefulness to rescuing Marina as he'd shown the previous night. She'd seen what he was capable of and as Isabelle glanced towards the clock again she tried to maintain her studied calm. In less than one minute he would knock at the imposing front door of Winford House—if he was punctual—and then he'd sit across from her again, this time in daylight, which would give her a much better opportunity to assess whether she'd made another mistake.

In silence Isabelle waited, the gentle ticking of the clock the only sound in the richly decorated room. The expansive house was far too quiet now both Marina and Edwin were gone, and a sudden swell of loneliness rose to mingle with the worry and grief that never left her alone.

There was nothing she could do to bring her husband back. The lifelike painting of him above the fireplace was as close as she would ever get to seeing his kind eyes looking down at her again, and she briefly closed her own to ward off any unwelcome tears. They'd both known he would be the first to go, his poor health and the vast difference in their ages having made it a near certainty, but neither had dreamed what nightmare would begin after Isabelle had watched his coffin lowered into the ground.

If Edwin could see her now she knew he'd be appalled—devastated that his passing had left her and Marina so vulnerable to those who would exploit them; the very thing he'd hoped to avoid when he and Isabelle had wed ten years before, his devotion to her parents making him act in the best way he knew how.

The vultures had begun circling almost the moment his funeral was over, she recalled now with an unconscious grimace. The combination of Isabelle's face and fortune had been just too much for Bishop Morton's ambitious bachelors to resist. Not one of them possessed half of Edwin's goodness, however, their predatory advances based solely on greed, or lust, or some chilling combination of the two, and it had been no hardship to let their compliments fall on deaf ears.

Taking another husband so soon after the loss of her first couldn't have been further from Isabelle's mind. Her care and attention had been centred on her grieving young sister with no space for anyone else—until Marina had turned sixteen, that was, when suddenly the suitors Isabelle had dismissed abruptly changed their choice of prey, forcing her to reconsider whether remaining single might be more dangerous than she'd thought...

From somewhere beyond the parlour came the muffled thud of the heavy door knocker and Isabelle jumped, jolted back into the present by that distinctive sound.

He's here.

Hurriedly she straightened her skirts, settling back onto the sofa with all the dignity she could muster as the parlour door opened and her butler appeared apprehensively on the threshold.

'Beg pardon for the intrusion. There's a Mr Carter to see you. He says he's expected, but—'

The butler stopped short as a form appeared behind him and Isabelle rose to her feet, determined to appear unmoved by the man-shaped mountain about to enter. While he was out in the shadowy corridor it was hard to see his expression, but Isabelle made sure to arrange hers into a gracious smile, extending a hand to wave him inside.

'Thank you, Collins. I did indeed invite Mr Carter to Winford, but I appreciate your concern.'

She turned her smile on the butler, glad when he accepted her judgement without a murmur. It was hardly surprising he had been unsure about her visitor. Of all people Mr Carter probably looked the least likely to be a friend, and Isabelle felt her lips grow stiff as Collins withdrew and the mercenary stepped into the room.

Her first thought was that he was better dressed than she'd expected. In the gloom of the tavern and then moonless night she hadn't been able to make out much of what he wore, but his shirt today was clean and his coat and slim trousers were cut in the latest fashion. A shadow of stubble still remained, and his close-cropped hair hadn't grown any longer in twelve hours, but he looked tidy enough not to draw much attention—or at least not because of his clothing.

Now the February sun flooded the parlour the details of his face were fully revealed, subtleties hidden by darkness now brought out by the light, and Isabelle felt an unwelcome stirring in her stomach. What she'd been forced to recognise as 'handsome' the night before now seemed a poor description. The word did nothing to capture the sharpness of his gaze, greener than she'd realised previously, nor the naturally ironic quirk of his mouth as he looked around the room. He was more *alive*-looking, somehow, than anyone else she'd ever met…restless and dangerous and so unlike everything she was used to that Isabelle had to take a second to collect her thoughts.

Remember what we agreed. Calm at all times.

She curtsied, pleased when none of her natural elegance deserted her. 'Good morning, Mr Carter. Thank you for coming so promptly. I apologise if my butler was dubious—I've not socialised much in quite some time.'

With great determination she kept the smile in place as he inclined his head in what she imagined was supposed to pass as a bow. He moved to the chair opposite her sofa and they both sat, his presence in the room immediately changing the atmosphere of only moments before.

Isabelle had meant to speak again, but Mr Carter got there first, proving once again—as if there was any need—that gentlemanly conduct wasn't something on which he wasted much time.

'You didn't mention you were a duchess. I'll admit that took me by surprise.'

He studied her, his greenish eyes resting on her face, and she felt an odd prickle as he produced a smile of his own.

'I feel I should apologise for my rough manners… *Your Grace.*'

She didn't quite like his tone, but Isabelle let it go. Her standing in society was something she'd never grown entirely used to herself. She had risen far higher than she'd dreamed of when she'd married Edwin, the Duke of Elmbridge, and as Edwin's heir was unmarried she could keep her rank as a widow—for now, at least.

'It seemed unwise to advertise my title when I didn't know who might be listening. You needn't use it in private. I don't insist upon it.'

'No? You must be one of the few who doesn't.'

There was a hint of that same wry amusement in his voice that she'd noticed during their first meeting, although Isabelle repressed her resulting gleam of irritation. Steadily she returned his cynical gaze, curbing an unwanted instinct to allow her eyes to linger on that upturned mouth.

'Before we begin, I'd like to thank you again for your service to me last night. I didn't expect your help but you gave it regardless, and for that I'm truly grateful. I want you to know that you have my heart-felt appreciation.'

Mr Carter shrugged, at last looking away. Perhaps he found it easier to accept censure than praise, the latter probably a novelty for a man who would be considered by many as little more than a brute.

It was as though he'd read her mind.

'I may be a mercenary but I'm not a monster. I won't stand by while a woman is attacked only a few yards away…even if she shouldn't have been there in the first place.'

It was a deliberate jab, and Isabelle curbed the instinct to snap back. *Why* did he insist on being so antagonistic at every turn? Since the moment they'd met she'd been nothing but polite, and yet he seemed intent on making his impatience with her plain. If she hadn't been so desperate she might have rethought the plan she'd settled on as she lay in bed, unable to sleep as both her sore neck and racing mind kept her awake.

Evidently he took her simmering silence as a cue to continue. Sitting back in his chair, he folded his arms across his chest, unconsciously drawing Isabelle's attention to the broad span his coat couldn't quite conceal.

'Last night you mentioned your current trouble was the only thing worth risking yourself for.'

'That's correct.'

'If it's so important, why not ask your husband to help? A duke has far-reaching influence. It might be embarrassing to go to him—especially if your situation is delicate—but surely you'd prefer that to coming to someone like me?'

Isabelle's pulse sped up. Until this moment she'd been able to keep her composure—more or less—but now it was time to start telling the uncomfortable truth.

'My husband is dead,' she answered shortly. 'If he hadn't been I never would have found myself in this situation.'

Instinctively she glanced towards the portrait hanging above the fire. Edwin peered down at her encouragingly, his familiar face raising a lump in her throat, and she looked away again, just quickly enough to catch Mr Carter doing the same.

'That is—was—your husband?'

'Yes.' She heard his note of surprise but didn't acknowledge it. 'He was past sixty when we wed, and I had recently turned eighteen. We knew our marriage might not be a long one, but...'

She tailed off. There was no point elaborating any further. Mr Carter clearly didn't like her, and probably had no interest whatsoever in the circumstances that had led Edwin to offer his hand after her parents had passed away.

From the outside, of course they'd looked ill matched—she a girl without fortune and he so much older and in constant poor health—but he had helped her cope with each hideous day until at last the sun had once again begun to shine. It had never been romantic, the love both had held so dear. As Papa's oldest friend, and with no children of his own, Edwin had simply stepped into the role of guardian and their marriage had been restricted to a piece of paper in his old rolltop desk, the only physical contact between them a fatherly kiss on top of her head each night before they went to their separate bedrooms. His aim had been to provide a safe haven for her and Marina, and he'd managed it for a decade, taking Isabelle as his wife in an attempt to ensure both sisters' future even after his passing.

But the mercenary didn't need to know any of that. By the look on his face she could tell at once what he was thinking. He was leaping to the same conclusion most of society had at the announcement of the widower Duke's engagement to a woman young enough to be his daughter. Clearly she'd been after his money and he'd been an old lecher, and both had done very well out of selling themselves so cheap. Only Isabelle knew the marriage hadn't been consummated, and she would never tell, determined to keep Edwin's name out of the gossips' mouths now he could no longer defend himself.

Mr Carter appeared to be waiting for whatever was running through her mind to make its way out of her mouth. With his arms still crossed he seemed larger than ever, and yet Isabelle felt he'd moved further away, perhaps the grief building in her chest pulling her back inside herself.

'Let's make this simple. Why did you call me here?'

Isabelle looked down at her hands. At least *they* were steady, even if her heartbeat had begun to skip at the prospect of what had to come next. Taking a breath, she made herself sit up straight, meeting Mr Carter's eye with resolve she had to dig deep to find.

'On account of my younger sister. Marina. She came to live here at the same time I did…after I married the Duke.'

Her voice was far too quiet and she hesitated, clearing her throat before trying again. It was even more difficult than she'd imagined to find the right words and she groped for them, attempting to separate emotion from fact.

'My husband died almost nine months ago, leaving me this house in addition to an extremely generous jointure. I'm sure you can imagine how quickly men came crawling out of the woodwork, hoping to profit from my loss, but I had no idea of marrying again, intending instead to dedicate myself to caring for my sister. She was but fifteen when the Duke died, and we were left quite alone—financially secure, but otherwise entirely unprotected. While it was to *me* that any unwanted attention was directed I could withstand it, but when Marina lately turned sixteen… She, too, has been well provided for in my husband's will. Her dowry is several thousands of pounds and when I proved to be a fruitless endeavour some of my gentlemen callers turned their eyes on her instead.'

The lump in Isabelle's throat ached, but she didn't break away from the mercenary's unwavering stare.

'The less determined withdrew once I'd made my disapproval plain, but a couple persisted—one in particular becoming a nuisance: a relation of one of our neighbours, come to visit for a few months before the Season. He is young, and handsome, and if I hadn't known how deeply in debt he is drowning, I might have believed his addresses to Marina sincere. Once I discovered the truth, however, it seemed prudent to remove her from harm's way. In her innocence she might easily have fallen under his spell, so I sent her away to stay with an old friend of mine in Suffolk, just until the distasteful young man left the neighbourhood, when she might come home again unscathed.'

Mr Carter said nothing as she paused to draw breath. Perhaps he'd heard a similar tale many times before, or perhaps he wouldn't show any reaction until he had all the facts. Either way, he made no move to interrupt, merely listening with that unreadable set of his granite-hewn face.

'Marina had been in Suffolk for almost six weeks by the time he gave up and left, and I wrote at once to my old friend—Mrs Hart—asking when it might be convenient to fetch my sister back. My letters to Marina had begun to go unanswered and I was starting to grow concerned... And then a week ago I received this.'

A small table stood beside the sofa, and from its drawer Isabelle retrieved a piece of paper covered in an untidy scrawl. She loathed having to touch it: it felt tainted and she held it by one corner as she placed it into Mr Carter's waiting hand.

He took it without comment, running his eye over the writing with impassive speed, and only a brief flicker of one straight eyebrow signalled that he understood what it said.

'As you can see, it seems Mrs Hart had to rush to some ailing relation in Glasgow, temporarily leaving my sister in the custody of her husband and elderly mother-in-law, and in her absence her husband has contrived some match between Marina and his wastrel of a cousin about whom I know *many* unpleasant tales. My poor friend would never have *dreamed* of her husband behaving this way, and I believe his mother is too frail to understand his actions. However, the fact remains that unless I give up almost the entirety of my jointure to Mr Hart and his cousin, they will either force Marina into marriage or traduce her name so badly she will never be free of the scandal.'

Mr Carter looked up swiftly, taking a short survey of her face before turning back to the letter. It was impossible to read his blank countenance and Isabelle expected little sympathy, although that fleeting moment of scrutiny still managed to make her sit straighter in her chair.

'It's my fault for sending her away. I thought it was the answer to our problems, but in fact I simply exchanged one threat for another. I can't risk speaking of our predicament to anyone within our circle—if it were to come out Marina would be shamed and her chances of a happy future dashed. If we didn't need the money, I'd simply give it to them, but I have to pay her dowry one day and keep a roof over her head until she makes a respectable match—for *love*, Mr Carter, not out of duty or blackmail, or to be some man's pretty plaything. If my husband was still alive...'

Isabelle stopped, realising her fingers were entwined together so tightly her knuckles had paled. For the first time she'd voiced the trap she found herself in, and hearing it spoken out loud made it seem even worse—so bleak she could hardly bear to carry on. She was completely alone, relying on a man she didn't trust or even *like* to aid her, and the fact she had no other choice weighed inside her like a rock.

Marina was all she had left. Everyone else she'd ever loved had slipped through her fingers and she'd been forced to watch them go, their final hours of pain and delirium seared into her memory to add more rawness to her grief. Marina *must* be brought home, and she *must* be kept safe until the day a man worthy of her came to offer his heart—because nothing less than complete devotion would suffice after a childhood of sorrow and loss, and Isabelle would do whatever was necessary to make sure her sister's future was brighter than her past.

Even if, after all this is resolved, I have to take a new husband to help me shield her, I'll do what I must.

'There's nobody I can turn to. Mr Hart and his cousin Mr Lewis are counting on my no longer having a man to protect me or my interests, and they are assuming—correctly—that I want to avoid Marina's public disgrace. I have no experience of blackmail or blackmailers. *That* is why I came to you...and I can only pray you know of some way to help.'

Joseph skimmed the page one more time, as always thankful that he'd taken the trouble to teach himself to read. The workhouse hadn't seen the point in educating a boy destined to labour for a pittance but even as a child he'd dreamed of more, and now he was able to hold his own among the upper classes, who were probably amazed that he knew how to use a pen.

The contents of the letter merely laid out in slightly more evasive terms what the Duchess had told him, the writer apparently trying to hint at his proposition rather than state it openly. The outcome was the same, however, and as he rubbed the stubble on his jaw Joseph had to admit to a glimmer of interest.

Not some tedious argument with a lover, then, nor an errand that would inevitably turn out to be a waste of time. That doesn't happen very often among the ton.

He lifted his eyes from the page, looking up to see the Duchess watching him. In the cool sunlight slicing down from the windows her hair was every bit as golden as he'd assumed the night before, its flax contrasting with her milk-and-berries skin, and the mystery of her eye colour now revealed itself in a pretty hybrid of blue and green. Her eyes were ringed with shadows, however, suggesting she'd barely slept, and the purple tinge mirrored the bruises on her pale throat.

In all, she suddenly struck him as vulnerable—a frightened woman with nowhere to turn—and he had to steel himself against the stray spark of pity that kindled in some long-forgotten corner of his mind.

He passed the letter back to her, refusing to acknowledge that traitorous little glint. Sympathy was not something he was about to indulge. It was a soft emotion and he lived a hard life, the two so completely incompatible that even a momentary lapse was a risk he couldn't afford.

Besides...

A woman like that wouldn't *want* his sympathy, he thought as he leaned forward, resting his elbows on his knees. She wanted his knowledge of the distasteful criminal underbelly of society...wanted him to get his hands dirty so she didn't have to—just like the rest of her kind. This duchess might care for her sister, but doubtless that was as far as her selflessness went. Even her choice of husband had been made with a calculation that Joseph almost admired. She was all but a mercenary herself, in a way, prepared to sell her services if the money was right, and she must have decided that a comfortable home for herself and her sister was worth allowing an old man into her bed.

'So. What do you think?'

The Duchess leaned forward too, unconsciously drawing closer in her anticipation. There was only a small gap between them now, and Joseph caught a hint of her lavender perfume, for one unacceptable moment tempting him to come nearer still.

'You can name your price. For my sister I would gladly pay your highest rate, whatever that might be.'

She waited, hands clasped demurely in her lap, but desperate hope radiated from her just as tangibly as the scent of flowers. If he'd been a different man her face alone would have been enough to make him agree to any request, so open and admittedly beautiful that it drew even his jaded eye, but he knew better than to rush his decision.

Think it through. Don't be swayed by sentiment.

It was the code he lived by, and yet some secret part of him rebelled against the indifference he worked so hard to cultivate. Somewhere miles away there was a young girl being held against her will, and the conscience he'd never been able to silence completely murmured—just as it had in the tavern. This Marina was sure to be a copy of her older sister—prim and refined and accustomed to a life of luxury—but she was still little more than a child, and the fierce loathing of injustice that the workhouse had instilled in him wouldn't let him turn away.

Not that I'll be telling her that. As far as she's concerned it's the money that moves me and nothing else—and for the most part she'd be right.

Concealing his thoughts behind a carefully blank mask, Joseph straightened his cuffs, playing for time before delivering his verdict. If he spoke too soon she might think he'd warmed to her, her undeniable good looks probably making fools of all the men around her. Her elderly husband might have been swayed by her charms, but he would remain immune, unmoved by a woman who clearly made her choices based on her head and not her heart…a trait he recognised, in truth, in himself.

'We can discuss my rate after the job is finished. It's difficult to calculate before.'

'After? Does that mean you'll help?'

The Duchess's shoulders slackened at his curt nod, a sigh of relief escaping her lips. The shape of them was pretty, Joseph noticed before he could prevent it—something he stubbornly set aside at once.

'The question now is how you want to proceed. Are

you intending for me to retrieve your sister or negotiate with the men holding her?'

'I was hoping you could advise me.'

Joseph considered. 'In my experience it's best not to engage. If you give in to one demand they'll make another, and another, and another, until you have nothing left at all.'

He paused, allowing his thoughts to unfold. It wasn't the first time he'd dealt with blackmailers, and he tried to recall the particulars of the last case—an eldest son abducted from one of the wealthiest families in Italy. On that occasion Joseph's fee had been enough to sustain him for an entire year, the boy's father so overjoyed by his return that money had seemed to fall down like rain.

'She should be retrieved at once. The longer she's there, the bigger the risk becomes. They might grow impatient and follow through on their threat to force a marriage—Gretna, probably, given her age—and then she'll never get free.'

The Duchess's face hardened, clouding over again like the sky before a storm. 'Of course. I understand completely.'

She stood up abruptly and Joseph swiftly looked away as her bodice suddenly appeared level with his eyes.

'How soon do we leave?'

'We?'

'Yes. I am, of course, going with you.'

She lifted her chin, almost as tall standing up as he was sitting down, and Joseph couldn't help but laugh.

'Going with me? Absolutely not.'

He watched a spot of pink rise in each of her cheeks. 'I hardly think that's your decision to make. Marina doesn't know you. She might take fright if yet another man tries to claim her. And besides, I don't want to let her out of my sight again once I know she's safe.'

Joseph swallowed another laugh. She had spirit, he'd give her that, although it was built more on naivety than anything else. How could she begin to imagine the long and tedious journey, most likely broken by a stay at an inn where fleas lurked in every fold of the beds, and then the potentially violent reception that awaited his arrival? She didn't know what she was asking, and he was doing her a favour by refusing her company—even if she didn't realise it.

'That's a touching sentiment, but the answer is still no. It might very well be dangerous, and I'll not be hampered by trying to keep *you* from harm as well as your sister.'

'I can take very good care of myself—'

'As you showed last night?'

'You won't dissuade me. I'm going with you to Suffolk and that is the end of it.'

The Duchess's face was still flushed, lending a glow to her otherwise pale skin, but Joseph was almost too irritated to notice. In that moment she was far too proud, speaking as if she had the first clue of anything beyond her own gleaming front door, but he quickly pulled himself back under control.

Why should I care if she wants to tag along? I'll do the job, take the money, and then I need never see her again. If she wants to make herself even more miserable in the process, then that's up to her.

He got to his feet, darkly amused when he saw how obviously she had to check her instinct to step backwards. 'Very well, Your Grace. If that's what you've decided. Just be aware that it's your sister you've engaged me to rescue. If you find yourself in trouble along the way I trust you won't look to me for help?'

She glared upwards, no less dignified for the fact that her head barely reached his shoulder. 'You can be assured of that, Mr Carter. And I told you. I don't insist upon my title being used at every turn.'

The chill of her tone lingered as she walked away, making for the bell-pull that hung beside the fireplace. 'I'll order my carriage to be ready in an hour. I'd prefer to leave at once.'

'I agree. Time is of the essence. But we won't be travelling in *your* carriage.'

She stopped, looking back at him over her shoulder just as her fingertips brushed the velvet rope. 'I beg your pardon?'

'Think about it. Your desire is to have this incident brushed under the carpet as soon as possible, avoiding any rumours and scandal along the way?'

'That's right.'

'Then we need to avoid drawing attention to your movements. If your carriage is seen racing away from Bishops Morton, don't you think people will wonder?'

He saw her hesitate, his annoyance wavering slightly—only *very* slightly—at the sudden uncertainty that flashed across her face.

'What do you suggest instead?'

'We go by post—discreetly. You will cover your face and I'll only call you "Your Grace" when we're alone.'

'I've already said—'

'Tell your servants whatever story you like,' he continued, over the top of her, struggling to keep his lips from curling upwards at her visible annoyance. 'As long as you make it sound sufficiently uninteresting I doubt they'll care where you've gone. The important thing is to make sure nobody warns this Hart and his cousin to expect us. I much prefer the element of surprise.'

She didn't answer, her ocean-coloured eyes taking another survey of his face, and whatever amusement he'd felt at her exasperation faltered. Standing beside the fire the flames threw the ugly marks at her neck into sharp relief and for a split-second Joseph saw beneath the haughty disguise, a glimpse of the person in place of the beautiful young duchess with the world at her feet.

She'd been foolish to put herself in danger the previous evening, but concern for her sister had driven her on—just as it moved her now to accompany him into a grim world she ought never to see. It would have been far easier to send him alone, and yet she'd chosen not to; spurred on by love, he supposed, a connection so strong it apparently made warriors out of women who barely knew the meaning of the word.

Love must have the power to make people do all kinds of things, and for the briefest moment Joseph wondered what it would be like to inspire that feeling—something so outside of his experience he could hardly think how to begin.

Because not a single person has ever cared whether I live or die. I've never meant anything to anyone—and I know for a fact that will never change.

Chapter Three

The movement of the post carriage was nowhere near as smooth as her own chaise, and Isabelle was glad none of the other passengers crammed inside could see her face as they rattled down yet another pitted road. She was sure it must be green beneath her heavy veil, nausea and ever-present worry mixing horribly to make her stomach roil, and sitting so close to Mr Carter that his arm brushed hers with every jolt did nothing to make her feel better.

They'd been squeezed together all afternoon but there were still miles yet to go, the road ahead stretching out for another day before they reached Marina. That meant many, *many* more minutes pressed up against this intolerable man, with the unyielding swell of his bicep an unwanted reminder of how well he filled out a coat—a thought that insisted on coming forward at alarmingly frequent intervals, despite the far more important things on her mind.

Isabelle closed her eyes, trying to pretend she was

somewhere else as the carriage lurched round a corner, forcing her harder against the mercenary's side. He didn't move an inch, still engrossed in the newssheet he'd held in front of his face since the moment they'd set off, and if he was at all troubled by the turbulence he was certainly good at hiding it.

He didn't look up when she cleared her throat, only tearing himself away from whatever he was reading when she weakly tapped his arm.

'Mr Carter...'

He glanced down, although Isabelle knew all he would see was black lace. *His* expression was far easier to decipher, a flicker of impatience crossing his countenance as he bent his head so she could whisper—somewhat feebly—into his ear.

'Are all the carriages we take going to be like this?'

'What do you mean?'

She watched his dark eyebrows knit together, wishing the pitch of his murmured reply wasn't quite so low. Everything about him was almost *too* masculine—from the sharp jawline to the subtle scent of warm leather that hung about his towering form—and it made it more difficult than it should have been to remember his appeal was only skin-deep. His behaviour towards her was something she'd never encountered from anyone else, the vast chasm between them yawning wider with every tense exchange.

She was no nearer to learning why. He seemed to have scant interest in speaking to her unless it was unavoidable, and he'd made the arrangements for their journey with almost no input from her, his every action apparently designed to show how little he appreciated her presence.

Now he eyed the place beneath her bonnet where her face should be, his voice still dropped to a mutter that the other passengers wouldn't overhear. 'This is nothing out of the ordinary. Haven't you travelled post before?'

'No.'

'Ah. A new experience for you, then. How exciting.'

A hint of a smile passed over his lips and beneath her veil Isabelle felt her cheeks flush hot. It was irritation that caused it, she assured herself, and most definitely not that ghost of a grin, softening the otherwise severe angles of his face to make him look a little more human. Clearly if she was hoping for sympathy she wouldn't find much in Mr Carter, and she shuffled away from him as far as she was able, gritting her teeth on another wave of queasiness that made it impossible for her to say another word.

Her discomfort didn't go unnoticed by their fellow travellers, however, despite her attempts to conceal it. Something in the rigid set of her shoulders must have told the elderly woman seated opposite her everything she needed to know, and she leaned towards Isabelle, where she sat huddled in a miserable heap.

'I don't need to be able to see your face to know you're suffering. Are you feeling unwell?'

She sounded so kind that Isabelle hesitated, wondering whether to chance an answer, but a deep voice got there first.

'My wife is a reluctant traveller. She finds the motion of a carriage unsettling.'

Instantly Isabelle swung round. He must have known exactly what reaction was present behind the screen of black lace and clearly it amused him greatly, the glint in his hazel eyes both so infuriating and attractive that Isabelle looked away again at once.

Wife? For what possible reason would he call me his wife?

It was a ridiculous statement, and for a moment she was completely unable to respond. If there had ever been two people less suited to marriage she certainly couldn't think of them—not even any of the unwanted suitors she might soon have to consider as unlikely a prospect—but then she stopped herself, refusing to follow such a pointless train of thought. He must have his reasons for making such an outlandish claim and it probably wouldn't be wise to challenge him openly, although renewed aggravation surged in to mingle with the unpleasant sensations already churning through her innards.

Isabelle swallowed, grimacing at the bitter taste of bile that had risen in her throat. 'Yes. I'm afraid I can't pretend I'm enjoying myself very much at present.'

Only half of her displeasure was courtesy of the shuddering coach, but the concerned passenger didn't need to know that. Mr Carter, on the other hand, seemed to appreciate the dual meaning, and a sharply exhaled breath through his nose suggested he felt something similar as he resumed his study of his newspaper, turning the page with a pointed rustle.

The older woman was far more compassionate. Leaning forward again, she patted Isabelle's gloved hand—a liberty she never would have taken had she known she was consoling a duchess. Wearing a plain gown beneath her least expensive cloak, Isabelle might have been glad nobody suspected her rank if she hadn't been so worried that she might keel over at any moment, the twin horrors of the carriage's movement and the mercenary's proximity a combination that made it difficult for her to think of much else.

'Take heart. We'll be stopping to change horses again before long, and then you can get down to take a breath of air.'

The elderly lady turned to Mr Carter with a benevolent smile. 'You know, sir, you might try to help.'

He looked up briefly. 'I beg your pardon, madam?'

'Just a word of advice from an old woman who's been in the same position as your poor wife. I had a terrible time in anything with four wheels when I was younger, and I felt ill so much as looking at a carriage. The only thing that made any difference was my husband laying my head on his shoulder and trying to hold me steady.'

The woman smiled faintly, as if reliving a memory she still treasured.

'That certainly worked for us. You might like to think about it yourself.'

It took a moment for the well-intentioned words to penetrate Isabelle's nauseous misery, but once they had she stiffened, yet again thankful that nobody could see her face.

Lay my head on Mr Carter's shoulder? I'd sooner lay it in a bear trap!

She hardly dared look at him to see his reaction, but it seemed he'd come to the same conclusion. He didn't move, still holding his paper like a barrier between them, and if Isabelle had thought she felt awkward before now she was almost ready to burst into flames.

'Thank you for your concern, but that really won't be necessary. I'm quite comfortable as I am.'

She tried to sound composed although she couldn't prevent a hint of alarm. It would shame her if he imagined she *wanted* to get any closer than she was already, the warmth of his body warding off the growing chill as the sun began to sink. Allowing herself to rest against that invitingly broad shoulder might have been more tempting if it didn't belong to one of the most provoking men alive and even the chance of it helping her queasiness wouldn't persuade her to try...

Assuming, of course, Mr Carter had any intention of letting her. Doubtless he was as appalled by the suggestion as she was, and she might have protested more vigorously if her stomach hadn't turned over again, cold sweat suddenly rising as she pressed one hand to her chest.

Isabelle squeezed her eyes shut, distantly grateful that the older woman had turned her attention back to her knitting. If she could just hold on until they paused to change horses she might feel better, a few deep lungsful of crisp air sure to settle her writhing insides. There was still so much further to go before she reached Marina, and unless she collected herself every mile would be an ordeal, further strengthening Mr Carter's unconcealed belief that she should never have come…

With her eyes still tightly closed she started at the sound of his voice very close to her ear, lowered into a murmur only she could catch.

'You don't *look* comfortable.'

'I'm perfectly fine.'

'Is that so? You always cling to your seat so tightly your knuckles almost burst through your gloves?'

Immediately she loosened her vice-like grip on the worn leather, snatching her hand back onto her lap— and just as swiftly regretted it.

As if to taunt her the carriage barrelled over a creaking bridge, the already unsteady cabin rocking from side to side as if it might topple off its wheels. The other passengers braced themselves, but Isabelle almost slid onto the floor, only just in time managing to stop herself and unable to prevent a soft, miserable groan.

She didn't need to look up to know that Mr Carter was watching her over the top of his paper. She could almost feel his resignation as she pressed herself against the seat, the lumpy upholstery doing little to lessen her discomfort, but his rough sigh still took her by surprise.

'For pity's sake. Come here.'

He muttered the words with the air of one being forced to walk the plank, and at first Isabelle couldn't think what he meant, too dizzy to consider anything the accursed man said. It was only when he lifted his arm that she sat up straight, alarm flooding through her as he began to place it along the back of her seat.

'What—?'

'Don't rile yourself. It's for the benefit of both of us.'

Her heart leapt up into her throat. Did he intend to put that arm *around* her? She half flinched away, horribly aware that for all she intended to resist a small and shameful part of her didn't quite want to move. It was the longing to stop feeling so ill that prompted it, Isabelle thought wildly, the prospect of a well-muscled arm snaking around her something that she had absolutely no desire to experience...

Fortunately Mr Carter misread her hesitance. Bending his head, he spoke again into her ear—so close that Isabelle felt the undeniably rousing sensation of his breath through her veil against the sensitive skin of her neck.

'It wouldn't be my first choice, either, but consider the alternative. I don't imagine you want to be reacquainted with your dinner, and I certainly don't want to have to clean it off my boots. That old woman certainly seems to think this will work...unless you have a better idea?'

Mutely, Isabelle shook her head. But surely it was unthinkable to allow him such a liberty? Mr Carter was only playing a part and yet he demanded more than Edwin ever had, the idea of granting permission for the mercenary to draw her close chasing away the pallor in her cheeks. Never in her life had she been expected to fit her body against a man's but the chaos in her stomach was enough to make her think twice, the pitching and yawing of the carriage making her seasick on dry land. There seemed little alternative, and even her own good sense ventured that it might be worth a try—on the strict understanding, of course, that his muscular frame had nothing whatsoever to do with it.

He was still waiting for her answer, his already scant patience probably wearing thin, and with a deep breath—and a silent prayer for mercy—Isabelle forced herself to lean in.

His arm settled around her with the ease of one who'd practised it a hundred times, although for Isabelle nothing had ever come close to the sensation of a hand curving around her waist. It was warm and strong and held her in place like an anchor would a ship, firm yet somehow reassuring, and she felt her stomach clench with something very different from what had prompted it before. A curious kind of heat seemed to emanate from him, despite the layers of clothing that stood between his skin and hers, and every one of Isabelle's nerves focused on the patch of warmth beneath his palm, on high alert for even the most miniscule movement of his fingers.

She couldn't seem to move, holding herself far too rigidly, and it was only when Mr Carter muttered again that she came to her senses.

'You can relax. I'm not going to bite you.'

He must have assumed her stiffness was down to embarrassment, and Isabelle was only too glad to allow the misunderstanding. If he had any clue it was actually having a solid forearm cradling the small of her back that had provoked it he'd be either revolted or smug, and neither reaction was one she was eager to entertain. There was still one more ordeal to overcome before she could make any attempt at relaxing, and she had to muster all her remaining dignity as she prepared to take the leap.

It'll make you feel less sick. Just try to cling on to that.

Laying her cheek against his shoulder, she was distantly surprised at how comfortable it was, but that came as little solace as she tucked her veil firmly beneath her chin. If anybody in the coach had snatched a glimpse of her face they'd have been left in no doubt as to her mortification—a feeling that rose to fever-pitch as Mr Carter's low murmur came once again.

'Settled?'

Isabelle tried to arrange herself with a little more poise, sternly ignoring the sparks that glittered through her as his fingers fractionally tightened their grip. In truth, she felt slightly less nauseous already—although she would have done anything to avoid having to admit it.

'Yes. Thank you.'

'Good.'

She felt Mr Carter's shoulder move as he nodded, cursing herself as another thrill lit up her insides. Perhaps she'd been wrong. Perhaps he was coming to dislike her a little less…even starting to value her wellbeing rather than considering it a nuisance—

'Perhaps now I can read in peace.'

It was difficult to hold his newssheet one-handed, but Joseph persevered. It provided something for him to focus on as he tried to ignore the warm body pressed to his side—and for that he found he needed all the help he could get.

Her waist fitted perfectly against his palm in a gentle curve that invited further exploration, sweeping upwards in a subtle arc that his fingers instinctively wanted to trace, and the soft weight of her head on his shoulder was nowhere near as oppressive as it should have been. Instead it was almost calming, the lavender of her perfume even more tantalising in the confines of the carriage than it had been in her parlour, and Joseph stiffened as some feral reflex urged him to breathe her in.

Get a hold of yourself. Surely it hasn't been that long since you had your arm around a woman?

Staring down at the printed words, he tried to recall the last time he'd been in a similar position, all the while stubbornly refusing to take a deeper breath. In his profession encounters were fleeting. He was never in the same place for long enough to form any lasting attachment, and besides, he wouldn't have wanted one even if he'd had the opportunity. Sweethearts and wives were for men who understood how to open themselves up to another person—not those destined to live their lives alone.

Although he'd satisfy the physical urge when it occurred, he'd never attempted anything more. Finding a willing partner for a night had never been difficult, but as the Duchess shifted slightly, her cheekbone slotting seamlessly into place against his lapel, he had to admit his past conquests hadn't prepared him for *this*.

He turned a page, inwardly cursing at his clumsiness as he fumbled with the paper. Why had he offered her respite in the first place? It was her own fault she'd decided to come with him, after all. He'd *told* her it wouldn't be easy, and yet she'd insisted, so convinced she was right that he'd had to bite down on a grunt. Now he'd have to spend the rest of the journey pinned in place, or risk her covering the floor of the coach in something unpleasant, and the fact that the prospect of cradling her wasn't *completely* hideous didn't improve his ill humour one bit.

At least I can console myself with knowing that she's just as uncomfortable with this arrangement as I am...or even more so.

The thought almost brought a dry smile to his lips. She'd be horrified if she knew how enticing she felt against his palm, with their warmth mingling like lovers rather than two people opposite in every way. She was the highest-ranking woman he'd ever met, and the summit from which she peered down at him was lofty—the perfect vantage point for her to spot every one of his many flaws.

It was no wonder such a superior specimen had sounded so shocked when he'd had the nerve to call her his wife. Her preference for a husband was older and titled, it seemed, with money that made her overlook his age—not a mercenary living from payment to payment, and certainly not a man for whom she'd made her dislike abundantly clear. To even *consider* shuffling closer to him she must be feeling spectacularly unwell, her body still slightly limp as a bend in the road made her lean even closer to his chest.

Determined not to dwell on the sensation of her ribcage moving with each breath, Joseph scanned the page in front of him, hoping to find an escape in the smudged print. Dusk had fallen and before long it would be too dark to make out a single word, the lamps fixed to the outside of the carriage casting only a dim light that flickered with every squeak of the wheels. His unwanted travelling companion swayed with the movement likewise, in a constant undulating that made it very difficult for him even to pretend to be absorbed in the obituaries of people he had never met, and he had to admit their stop to change horses couldn't come a moment too soon.

Trying so hard to ignore her only seemed to make him more aware of every single move she made, so it was little wonder that he sensed she was about to speak before she'd even opened her mouth.

'Do you need some help?'

'With what?'

'Your paper. You seem to be struggling with just one hand.'

The Duchess's voice was still slightly unsteady, but she sounded better than she had when hunched in her seat. Obviously the improvement was enough for her to resume intruding where she wasn't wanted, because she reached for the newssheet spread out on his lap, her gloved hand making for one drooping corner.

'Here. Allow me to hold this edge...'

Her fingers accidentally brushed his leg, with the force of a butterfly landing on a flower, and yet Joseph jumped as if she'd scalded him. It was the lightest, most inadvertent contact, and no reason for his heart to crash into his ribs, but something in the intimacy of her soft hand on his thigh made him blink back sudden stars.

Hellfire, man. What ails you?

He moved quickly, turning slightly so that the paper slid from her grasp. 'That isn't necessary. I can manage well enough alone.'

To her credit she didn't try to reach out again, just folding her hands together in her lap while whatever she was thinking was hidden by that swathe of black lace, and it was a long moment before she quietly replied.

'You can "manage well enough alone"… I think that probably sums you up quite neatly, doesn't it?'

Joseph glanced sharply to the side, still slightly rattled. The veil was impassive but her tone was shrewd, and he wondered if he ought to be annoyed with her unsolicited but admittedly accurate verdict. She didn't know the smallest thing about him, and yet she was clearly perceptive, delivering a judgement he couldn't very well deny.

'I don't see that as a bad thing.'

'I wasn't criticising. Just observing.'

His lips twisted.

I think I'd prefer criticism to someone watching my every move and trying to work out the contents of my head. I very much doubt she'd like what she found, in any case.

He shook out the crumpled pages of his paper, although the gathering darkness made any further pretence at reading impossible. The warm, inescapably feminine shape beside him seemed to be growing more interesting by the minute, and he pressed his teeth together so hard they ached as the temptation to let his thumb trace her lower rib came at him like a charging bull.

It's been too long since I was in female company. That's the only reason she's having this effect.

Briefly he closed his eyes, trying to block out the niggling voice in the back of his mind that insisted on whispering things he didn't want to hear.

Her waist was sorely tempting beneath his palm, and her perfume really *did* bring to mind lavender in a field, swaying in a summer breeze…

The carriage drew to a halt so abruptly that even Joseph almost overbalanced, only saving himself by flinging down the newssheet to catch hold of one of the straps hanging from the roof. Moving on blind instinct, he wasn't aware of any other action he'd taken until he heard the Duchess gasp—a stifled breath he only caught by virtue of how closely he'd pulled her against him.

His arm had encircled her completely, one hand now splayed against her stomach to prevent her from falling, and Joseph felt a sudden pulse of heat as he realised it was a mere hair's breadth from her bodice. He must have moved to protect her without even thinking, and unease washed over him—both at *why* she'd been his priority and at the dawning reluctance with which he knew he had to loosen his grip. Cradling her against him so tightly allowed him to feel her every single breath…her chest rising and falling so near his fingertips that another secret thrill licked through him…

But he let go, and wasn't sure how to feel when she immediately wriggled away.

'My apologies. I didn't want you to fall.'

'I realise that. Thank you.'

It was probably fortunate that he couldn't see her face, Joseph thought as he stood up, having to bend almost double to avoid hitting his head. She might be spared trying to conceal her look of disgust and he wouldn't have to see her do it—something that wouldn't normally move him and yet for some reason he found he'd rather avoid.

Not that I care what she thinks of me. It's just been a long day.

Thankfully the presence of the other passengers prevented the need to speak further, the stretching of their heavy limbs and aching backs making it too noisy for a lowered voice to be heard, and as he stepped outside a slap of cold air helped Joseph order his thoughts.

The carriage had stopped to change horses at a pleasant-looking inn, and something in the welcoming glow spilling from the windows made him think twice about his plan to get back on board at once. A homely establishment like this one would have flea-free beds and good food and Joseph had spent enough years on the road to know the value of both, even if he was equally prepared to sleep in a ditch if there was nowhere else. The journey to Suffolk was long, however, and they ought to take advantage of respite where they could find it—or at least that was how he reconciled the decision to himself as he turned to offer the Duchess his hand. In truth, it was the prospect of returning to his seat that made him pause. The warmth of her soft shape beside him still lingered, despite the chill, and he didn't know if he liked the sensation in his fingers as she cautiously took his hand and allowed him to guide her to the ground.

'We'll stay here for the night. We could cover more ground today, but if we rest now we'll make better progress tomorrow.'

Without waiting for her reply, he lifted down their bags—hers far heavier than his own small one, and more suited to a trip to Bath than a rescue mission—and began to walk towards where the inn reared up out of the gloom. He knew she'd have something to say, however, and it wasn't long before he found out what it was.

'Wait. Wait!'

Reluctantly he turned, finding her barely two steps behind. Judging by the fluttering of her veil she was slightly out of breath, no doubt more used to gliding in front of men than scurrying after them.

'Mr Carter. We haven't discussed this. I want to get to my sister as soon as possible—what if I'd rather carry on today?'

'You'd be disappointed. *You* were the one who decided to come with me. I'm stopping here for the night and there's nothing else to say about it.'

The black lace fluttered harder still with her frustrated sigh. 'Is that it? You've decided, so that's what will happen?'

'Exactly so.'

Turning resolutely back in the direction of the inn, Joseph was about to walk away when a hand on his arm made him pause.

The Duchess looked around, making sure nobody was within earshot before lowering her voice. 'On the subject of unilateral decisions…why did you call me your wife? That wasn't something we discussed, either.'

Joseph shrugged, refusing to acknowledge the feeling of her delicate fingers on his coat sleeve. 'We're concealing your identity for the duration of this journey and it seemed the best explanation for a man and woman travelling together without inviting curiosity. We can hardly pass for brother and sister.'

'You could have said you were my servant. Husband and wife seems a far bigger leap.'

Looking down at the indignant figure in front of

him he couldn't help a dry laugh, too familiar with her type to be offended.

Of course she'd jump straight to servant rather than partner. Why wouldn't she?

'Perhaps you're right. Apologies, *Your Grace*, for having ideas above my station.'

Even though it was hidden, Joseph could tell her expression just by her tone. 'How many times need I tell you, Mr Carter—?'

'Joseph.'

He cut her off, in no mood to suffer another exasperated lecture. 'If you're to pass as my wife you can't keep calling me "Mr Carter", as if I was a valet. Your using my first name is what people will expect. What am I to call you?'

She hesitated. Drawing her cloak more tightly around her, she wavered, an indecisive shape in the deepening darkness, and Joseph tried to cling on to the last of his patience as the night's chill soaked into his bones.

At last she relented. 'Isabelle. If you must.'

'Good. And you'll remember to call me…?'

'Joseph.'

His name sounded different in her mouth. The shape of it was novel, and fascinating, and for a moment he was struck by how good it sounded coming from her lips. She managed to make it graceful—an elegant word in place of the throwaway label the workhouse's cruel governor had assigned him without a second thought. The Duchess's sweet voice seemed to erase all the ugliness of its origin, and Joseph found he couldn't quite manage to reply as he renewed his firm grip on their bags, hardly even noticing the weight of them as without another word he once more made for the welcoming warmth of the inn.

Chapter Four

Despite her protests Isabelle had to admit some relief as she followed Joseph through the inn's heavy front door. As much as she wanted to carry on towards Marina, she was glad to be spared another immediate stretch on that hideous coach—and not just because of the effect it had on her stomach. The feeling of the mercenary's hand pressing flat against her ribs lingered…his fingertips almost but not *quite* touching where her heart had leapt like a startled deer…and she was in no hurry to find herself in another such situation before she'd had time to recover from the first.

Watching now, as he unceremoniously dumped their bags on the flagged floor beside the landlord's counter, Isabelle had to wonder if he'd felt the same crackle of heat she had—that feeling of lightning trapped beneath her skin as his hand strayed dangerously close to places no lady should allow. The fact he'd clearly acted without thinking saved him from any suspicion of ulterior motives—he had only been clenching his arm around her to stop her from falling—although her own reaction to being pinned so close to his unyielding chest was far harder to explain.

Perhaps it had been the suddenness of it that had disturbed her, or perhaps the discomfort of having all the breath squeezed from her body by a vice-like grip? Whatever the reason, Isabelle was grateful that Joseph's attention was turned on the man coming towards them, giving her much-needed time to pull herself together before he could suspect the tumult going on behind her veil.

'Yes, sir? Were you wanting a room?'

The landlord stepped behind his counter, hefting down a ledger from a shelf at Joseph's nod. After leafing through it, he ran a finger down a column, frowning until he came to a halt at the very bottom of the page.

'We only have one room left—our smallest. I'm afraid you'll find it a tight fit.'

Joseph's dark smile stoked the embers already smouldering in Isabelle's gut.

'I can crouch. Besides, nobody is tall while lying down.'

The landlord laughed and said something in reply, but Isabelle was no longer listening. Reality was beginning to dawn and she wasn't at all sure she liked what was being implied—something no man of her acquaintance would dare suggest.

Can I have heard correctly?

She looked quickly up at that handsome, hard-featured face, praying she'd misunderstood, but as always it was almost impossible to read.

Lying down? One room? And just how small was *smallest*?

Taking advantage of the landlord turning away to hunt through a drawer of keys, Isabelle crept a step closer.

'Joseph.'

What was meant as a whisper came out more as a panicked hiss, but he glanced round at her anyway, dipping his head slightly so she could crane up to his ear.

'What are you doing? You know we can't share a room!'

'Says who?'

'Me!'

She saw the corners of his mouth turn down, more in thought than disapproval, and felt a gleam of surprise when he nodded.

'Fair enough. If you've made your mind up I won't argue.'

He sounded so reasonable that Isabelle realised afterwards that she should have been suspicious. She was about to feel relieved when he continued, his voice lowered into the gravelly murmur she was rapidly coming to realise did strange things to her insides.

'Where do you intend to sleep, then, while I go up

to my room? There's only one left, after all, so your options are somewhat limited.'

Wrong-footed, she faltered. 'I thought… I imagined that you…'

'That I would go and sleep elsewhere? Perhaps even outside?'

Joseph's face was deadpan, but she could have sworn she saw a glitter of amusement flit through his hazel eyes.

'I'm afraid I must regretfully decline. It's freezing—and besides, I need to be fit and refreshed before I rescue your sister. Of the two of us, who needs a restful night the most?'

Isabelle blinked, glad he couldn't see the wordless parting of her lips as she groped for a reply.

Surely it went without saying that a gentleman would give up his lodgings for a lady if the only alternative was for them to share? Being in such close quarters with a man who wasn't her husband was unthinkable—the risk to her reputation one that made her blood run cold. If anyone back in Bishops Morton was to catch wind of it she'd never live it down. The scandal of a duchess sleeping in the same room as a mercenary was something the town wouldn't forget, and she felt worry rising as she wondered how to explain the unwritten rules of propriety he evidently didn't understand…

The landlord was having difficulty locating the key. With an apologetic smile over his shoulder he delved into a second drawer, too absorbed to notice his customers' exchange, although Isabelle couldn't focus on anything but Joseph as he gave a quiet sigh.

'Stop wringing your hands, Isabelle. I wasn't in earnest.'

His voice was still low, the pitch of it rough as ever, but to her amazement she caught just a hint of gruff reassurance. It was well concealed, and probably anyone eavesdropping would have missed it, but for Isabelle it was loud enough to stop her in her tracks.

'I understand your kind places a lot of value on reputation, but consider this… You'll be registered here under my name, not yours, and your veil makes it unlikely you'll be recognised. I wouldn't deliberately expose you to disgrace, no matter how unfeeling you think me. As I said before, I'm not a monster.'

Joseph raised a cynical brow, the glint of bleak humour briefly returning to his eyes.

'You needn't worry about me trying to touch you, either—you can have the bed and I'll be more than comfortable on the floor. I have many failings, but forcing myself on women is not one of them. As difficult as it might be to imagine, you're safe with me.'

He turned away again, transferring his attention to the now triumphant landlord, but Isabelle was too distracted by a sharp twinge to watch him sign the ledger.

That might not actually be quite as difficult to imagine as he thinks.

He was brusque as ever, and still clearly annoyed

she'd insisted on accompanying him, but that couldn't cover the truth: she *was* starting to feel safe in his company, she realised with a start. Not comfortable, perhaps—the touch of his hand stirred feelings in her she didn't want to acknowledge—but secure at least in the knowledge that he wouldn't harm her and nor, she suspected, would he allow anyone else to try.

The unthinking speed with which his arm had tightened around her in the carriage spoke of a protective instinct she hadn't allowed for, and when combined with the hint of curt reassurance he'd given a few moments before...

Every kind thing he did seemed to be reluctantly, but perhaps there might still be more to him than met the eye. It was a doubtful prospect, and yet Isabelle couldn't quite ignore it as he gestured for her to take the key, his own hands busy with the bags he hadn't once complained about carrying. It seemed a stretch to imagine there might be a sweet, gentle man beneath the forbidding exterior, but she wondered if she ought to try harder to see the good—something easier said than done, however, as they followed the landlord towards a rickety staircase that led upwards, her chest tightening at the thought that they would soon be very much alone together in a room with a bed, even if she was thankfully to sleep in it alone.

Nobody knows me here. Nobody knows me here.

Isabelle repeated her mantra as she trailed behind Joseph, the steps creaking beneath her feet. The staircase was narrow, and she heard him mutter something as his shoulders brushed the walls on either side, his impressively broad frame no advantage in such a tight space. Their room was in the attic, it appeared, and Isabelle's unease grew as she thought that *smallest* must mean very small indeed, the intimacy of sharing with Joseph made even greater by the snug fit.

She could only hope there was room enough for her to maintain her dignity—already more compromised in one day than in the entirety of her married life. Edwin had barely ever seen the inside of her bedchamber, and her visits to his had only been towards the very end, when she had sat all night beside him so his last sensation on earth might be the touch of a loving hand...

'Will this do for you?'

The memory of that last terrible night fled at the landlord's question. A door stood open before her and she peered around the jamb, unable to see anything over Joseph's expansive shoulder.

'You weren't joking when you said it was small.'

That did little to reassure Isabelle as she stood out on the landing. Only when the landlord retreated and Joseph stepped out after him could she see inside, and the sight that greeted her made her snatch a breath.

Heaven help me. I think there are cupboards at Winford House that are bigger than this.

Almost the whole space was taken up by a bed, only a thin sliver of floor on three sides allowing for a fireplace, a washstand and a tiny table with two stools pushed right up against one wall. There would be no hope of passing each other without touching, and Isabelle felt her heart tick faster at the prospect of being forced close to Joseph once more—something that somehow didn't seem quite as terrible as she knew it should, the ghost of his hand against her ribs coming again to make her cheeks flare hot.

Never in her life had a man managed to affect her in quite the same way the mercenary did, apparently able to disturb her with no effort at all.

While Edwin had been alive the occasional young gentleman had tried to tempt her into a flirtation, believing his own charms outweighed her loyalty to her much older husband, but Isabelle had never allowed her head to be turned. Her marriage might only have been a formality, but she'd had far too much respect for the Duke to dishonour him, and had never given another man so much as a second glance. Even now she was a widow the men who came sniffing around Winford House barely registered to her as being male...which was why her helpless admiration of Joseph's powerful frame was so troubling, coming from a part of her she'd kept locked away for her whole adult life. Whoever she was forced to wed for Marina's sake couldn't hope to have half such an effect— although she imagined her fortune would be enough to console him for any lack of passion.

She heard the landlord speaking somewhere behind her. 'I'll send someone with water and to make up the fire.'

'Thank you.' Joseph's voice came alongside the clink of coins. 'And perhaps some food for my wife?'

It was another surprise display of consideration—only small, but coming so soon after the first that she was caught off balance all over again. It seemed she had been right to wonder if a kinder man might lurk beneath the rough, refusing to be revealed for reasons best known to himself, and the fact that the possibility piqued her curiosity was met with no small alarm.

Whatever the mercenary might be hiding behind that stony mask shouldn't matter to her—their situation would change not at all even if Joseph turned out to be a secret saint—and yet as Isabelle reached up to remove her bonnet she realised she couldn't *completely* ignore a little voice inside that wanted to find out.

There wasn't much room to stretch his legs, but Joseph tried regardless, leaning against the wall behind his stool and feeling the release in his tight muscles. He was well used to travelling, but being confined in small spaces never got easier, his build not one especially compatible with long periods bent almost double in coaches and berths.

It wasn't only his aching back that was causing him discomfort, however. Isabelle had at last taken off her veil, and her face was illuminated a shade too prettily by the fire as she sat on the other side of the narrow table, working her way through a hearty bowl of stew. It had to be a far rougher meal than she was used to but she hadn't grumbled, instead falling upon it with an enthusiasm Joseph had to admire.

When she wasn't preoccupied with her airs and graces she was infinitely more likeable—and that was enough to put him on his guard.

I don't need to like her. In fact, it's best I don't.

It was necessity that had brought them together and nothing else, he reminded himself as he stretched his arms above his head. He needed money and she needed brawn: both played to the strengths fate had given them and bargained for the thing they lacked. If she seemed slightly less haughty while face-down in a plate of stew it meant only that she was too hungry to cast judgement on its quality. A duchess was still a duchess even when she was scraping the bottom of her bowl, and he warned himself not to forget that as he looked once again around the tiny room.

'So. Will you manage in here, Your Grace? You're still sure you wouldn't rather sleep outside in a hedge-row?'

Isabelle glanced up at him. '*Your Grace* again now, is it? I'm not sure why you bother. For all your use of my title, it's clear you have very little respect for rank.'

She spoke with such weary patience it was clear she'd made up her mind to weather his jokes rather than take offence, and for that Joseph reasoned she deserved an honest answer.

'I'll admit that to be true. Why would I? An individual's position in the world is an accident of birth, not something they've earned through merit or hard work. Being born into money and privilege isn't something I feel makes a person worthy of blind reverence, no matter what society says.'

He looked away again, ready to let the matter lie; however, he heard a gentle clink as Isabelle laid down her spoon.

'Ah. At last I think I understand.'

Joseph turned back. 'Understand what?'

'The reason you so clearly dislike me. You think I've had good fortune handed to me without having done anything to deserve it. *That's* why you've been so determined to disapprove of me since the moment we met—isn't that right?'

She sat up straight, fixing him with a direct gaze, but she didn't appear affronted. Instead she seemed curious, and Joseph couldn't help an uncharacteristic twinge of discomfiture at how accurately she made her point.

'It's nothing personal,' he muttered roughly. 'I find it difficult to warm to anyone who's never known anything other than plain sailing and expects admiration because of it.'

'When have I given the impression I expect admiration? From you or anybody else?'

Joseph shrugged. 'It's implied in every move you make. Each time you look at me it's with the same air of superiority all your kind feels over mine. After a lifetime a man gets tired of it.'

'But I don't do that. I don't *feel* that.'

'Of course you do. You can't help it.'

He exhaled mirthlessly through his nose. There was no guile in those pretty blue-green eyes, it was true, but that didn't mean he was wrong—even if a sudden temptation to consider whether her denial might carry any weight *had* come from nowhere to take him by surprise.

Ridiculous.

Joseph knocked the thought aside as soon as it arose.

As if a woman like that could ever think more highly of a gutter-born brute like you. Perhaps all those hours in the carriage shook out all your good sense.

With studied casualness he raised one shoulder, resolved to block out his subconscious mind's trickery. 'If you hadn't needed my help you never would have spoken to somebody like me—and even now I can tell you're still uncertain. I'm hardly the sort of person who ought to feature in your charmed life.'

A jug of ale had been sent up with the stew and Joseph poured himself a measure, then with a wordless gesture offered to fill Isabelle's glass too. He expected her to refuse, something as low as common ale doubtless never having passed her serene lips, but instead she pushed her glass towards him, a hint of defiance suggested by that single move.

'You don't know anything about me. You've no idea if my life has been easy or not.'

Aha. So she's offended at last.

He watched her over the rim of his glass, looking away quickly when she set hers back down on the table. She was frowning now, although beautiful even when displeased, and he frowned himself to realise he wished he hadn't spoken quite so bluntly.

Why, though? When everything you said was the truth?

Setting the unwelcome question aside, Joseph propped his forearms on the tabletop. 'I know you live in an expensive house you didn't have to pay for, with servants to cater to your every whim. If that isn't the definition of an easy life, what is?'

He folded his arms, resting them on the table as Isabelle studied her hands now folded neatly in her lap. When she looked up she was composed, any flicker of displeasure concealed once more behind her well-bred façade, and Joseph wasn't sure he liked the fleeting flare of disappointment he felt that she had retreated somewhere he couldn't follow.

'You overlook the circumstances that led me to that house. The road there was no comfortable ride, I can assure you.'

'No?'

'No.'

She let her eyes slide away from his to focus instead on the fire curling in the hearth, its light casting shadows over her set face. Her gaze rested on the flames and yet she didn't seem to see them, a faraway look chasing out what had been sharp scrutiny. He saw her throat move as she swallowed, the bruises there vivid against the alabaster of her skin, and when she spoke he knew she was keeping herself under tight control.

'I might live in luxury now, but if I could turn back time and regain what I've lost I'd do it. Even if it meant I had to beg on the street, I would still turn back the clock.'

Joseph opened his mouth to reply—then thought better of it, reaching instead for the jug of ale. It seemed an easier prospect than trying to decide how to respond, the haunting unhappiness in her face coming dangerously close to touching something in him he didn't want to own.

Is it her husband she's speaking of? Is it his loss she'd undo?

Surely that couldn't be what she meant. There seemed little chance of Isabelle genuinely grieving for a man she must have wed purely for his money. It could never have been a marriage based on love—although for that Joseph could hardly blame her. His own opinion of such a sentiment was so low it trailed in the dust. She'd needed to provide for her sister and so she'd done what she'd had to do; but that didn't explain why she now looked so sad, her hands still twined together in her lap and her back so straight it was as though she was carved out of stone.

I suppose I could ask her. If, of course, I was interested enough...

The table shook slightly as he placed his glass down—a little too forcefully, perhaps, but Joseph knew he had to stop his worrying train of thought before it could get out of hand.

Whatever mysteries were concealed behind the Duchess's lovely face were none of his business. Already he felt more interest than he liked, and there could be no benefit in allowing such aberrant feelings to take root. For all she insisted she wasn't like the rest of her kind, he knew better—just as he knew better than she did about what she thought she could endure.

'You only talk of begging because you've never had to. If you'd ever experienced the true despair of poverty, Isabelle, you might not be in such a hurry to volunteer for it.'

The firelight turned her hair to molten gold as she turned to him, her face now so expressive that he realised at once he'd made a mistake.

'What was that?'

Joseph waved a dismissive hand but it was too late. Isabelle had leaned towards him, the table between them suddenly seeming far too small, and he had to steel himself yet again against the power of her perfume that even a day of travelling couldn't dim.

'Are *you* speaking from experience, Joseph? Have you...have you ever had to beg?'

It was the look of compassion that did it, shining from her and making it impossible to drag his gaze away. So unfamiliar and unexpected, Joseph felt something inside him shift at the kindness in her eyes: not as insulting as pity, but just as gentle, and something he'd never seen before in anyone who had looked at him in the whole of his hard and violent life.

The novelty of it made him careless. He should be guarding his tongue, but confusion prompted him to speak more candidly than he meant to, allowing Isabelle just two words—and yet more than he'd ever revealed to anyone.

'Only once.'

Her eyes widened, the dark lashes surrounding them fluttering further apart, but he was already pulling the hatches back down again and busily fastening them tight.

What's wrong with you? Why did you even say that much?

He felt his brow contract, knowing it must have lent his face an edge when Isabelle drew back, but he couldn't seem to help it. The memory he'd just come perilously close to sharing had come forward without invitation, and Joseph's frown grew more severe as events from decades ago burst upon him as though only weeks had passed instead of more than twenty years.

It had been early the morning he'd squeezed under the workhouse gate and run, aged just nine and nursing yet another blackened eye courtesy of the boys he wasn't yet big enough to fight. That winter had been fierce and every one of his bones had ached from the icy wind, his fingers blue and his threadbare clothes doing next to nothing to ward off the murderous cold, but he'd thought in his childish ignorance that something better waited on the other side of that gate.

He had soon seen his error.

Without a penny, or anywhere to go, he'd had no choice but to hold out his cap to the wealthy ladies and gentlemen gliding past him on the street, his humiliation growing with every well-bred nose turned up at the sight of him. Life in the workhouse had never come close to shaming him as much as being forced to beg from those who laughed at his dirty face, and it had been at that very moment he'd made the vow that he'd honoured ever since.

I'll never grovel to them. When I'm a man, if there's something they want from me, they can pay.

Another hiding was his reward for returning to the workhouse the next day, but the lesson he'd learned was worth the pain. He'd seen the people he had been taught were his betters and they didn't seem better at all—only richer, more expensively dressed, but just as callous as anyone within the four crumbling walls he called home. The upper classes were no kinder nor gentler than his own... something Isabelle made difficult to remember now, however, as her pale face glowed in the firelight and compassion danced in the deep pools of her eyes.

Joseph stood, resolutely turning away from her sympathy. There was no way Isabelle could really care, but her pretence was enough to throw him. It looked so close to being genuine that in truth he didn't know what to do.

'It's getting late. We've an early start in the morning and a full day of travel if we're to arrive in Suffolk by nightfall.'

He spoke more to the fireplace than to Isabelle. Concentrating on the next day helped to calm him a little, he was relieved to find, and focusing on the grim task at hand was far preferable to whatever had just passed between him and the Duchess, who still watched his every move.

'I'll want to catch your Mr Hart and his cousin when they can't see me coming. Cowardly men are even easier to frighten in the dark.'

Perhaps something in his equally dark words made her uneasy. Immediately Isabelle rose to her feet, smoothing down her skirts instead of meeting his eye.

'Yes. I think I'll retire now. As you say, we have much further to travel tomorrow.'

She hesitated, a pretty blush rising as she flicked him a shy glance that for some reason made him catch a sharp breath.

'Would you step outside for a moment, please? While I make my...preparations?'

Joseph nodded quickly, hoping she hadn't noticed his reaction. 'Of course. If you'd allow me to take a couple of blankets from the bed first...?'

He stepped round the table, hunching slightly as the angled pitch of the low ceiling touched the top of his head. To reach the bed he'd have to brush past where Isabelle had already drawn back against the wall, and only just in time he managed to stop himself from mumbling a few choice words.

He tried to breathe in as he moved past her, but all that accomplished was a lungful of the floral sweetness that hung around her like an intoxicating cloak. It made his head swim, momentarily making him clumsier than usual—which was probably how he came to bring his foot down on the hem of her dress at the very same moment she helpfully attempted to back away.

She stumbled at once, reaching out instinctively to steady herself on the first thing that came to hand, and Joseph's heart turned over as her fingers fastened around his upper arm. Pulling herself upright she leaned against him for one short breath, the pile of golden curls at the crown of her head pressing beneath his chin, and only by quick thinking did he stop himself from bringing a hand up to brace around her waist.

It would have helped her regain her balance, but he knew he couldn't risk it. That inviting curve was far too tempting when all his rational thinking seemed to hang by a thread at the feel of her body pressed closely against his own, and sudden heat blazed inside him as he realised how easy it would be to pull her into his arms.

Fortunately Isabelle acted before he could betray himself. She drew back, pressing herself against the wall, and he saw her face flame just as hot as the sparks smouldering in his gut. She didn't look at him, clearly embarrassed, but thankfully she seemed oblivious to the desire that had engulfed him, and Joseph tried to sound casual as he edged the rest of the way past her to reach the safety of the doorway.

'Sorry. I'm not built for such small spaces.'

Isabelle allowed him a weak smile, although Joseph didn't wait around to see much of it. Snatching a couple of spare blankets from the foot of the bed, he made for the door, making sure it was closed firmly behind him before he let out a quiet grunt.

Leaning against the wall of the dark and narrow landing, he briefly screwed his eyes shut, trying to make sense of what seemed to be happening to him without his consent.

A woman looks at you with something other than scorn or passing interest and you start losing your wits? Pull yourself together, man.

He glowered at nothing as he attempted to block out the image of Isabelle's face after his unwitting confession. It must be purely because he was so unused to kindness that it had affected him so strangely—although why that meant their accidental contact had left him so shaken he couldn't say. It had been nowhere near as intimate as some of the previous encounters he'd had in rented lodgings, and yet the thrill of feeling her chest against his…

A series of quiet creaks and shufflings came from the other side of the door, and Joseph tried his hardest not to imagine what they signified. If she had such a startling effect on him while fully dressed, then the thought of her in her nightgown might be a step too far—something he made sure not to dwell on as he heard her call out.

'Thank you. You can come back in now.'

With a shadow of reluctance he turned the handle. Pushing the door open, he saw the candles had been extinguished. The only light now came from the dying fire, for which he was vaguely grateful. If he kept his eyes straight ahead and made sure not to glance towards the bed he might be able to pretend she wasn't there, and he did just that as he cautiously crossed the darkened room and laid the blankets he carried in front of the hearth.

Sleeping on the floor was no hardship to him after so many years on the road, and Joseph made a nest almost without thinking, his concentration trained on the silent bed at his back. Isabelle hadn't made a sound since his return and he wondered if she was already asleep, the rigours of the day surely exhausting for one so unused to travel.

Even his own body was tired. Old injuries to various parts of it flared up on cold nights when he needed to rest, and he sighed as he pulled off his boots and began to unbutton his shirt.

A faint noise made him turn, his shirt hanging open across his chest.

Isabelle's face was a pale moon in the semi-darkness, only partly visible above the counterpane but her expression rendered words unnecessary. Even in the gloom he saw her wide eyes linger on his bare chest, transfixed for a moment before making their journey to his face, and he couldn't help an involuntary sense of satisfaction that she obviously appreciated what she saw.

Their eyes met and Joseph felt his heart give a particularly hard thump. Their locking gazes in a bedroom was *not* something he'd meant to happen—and Isabelle clearly agreed, abruptly burying her face beneath the bedclothes so her voice came as a muffled squeak.

'Goodnight!'

For a moment Joseph stood still. She didn't speak again, however, the lump in the bed resolutely not moving an inch, and turning back to his pile of blankets he slowly pulled his shirt off over his head.

He'd known his fair share of women, his countenance and chiselled form meaning he was never short of company when he wanted it, and he knew well enough how to read attraction in a woman's face. There was usually something in the eyes—some echo of a primal reaction only thinly disguised—so it was shocking that he could have sworn he'd just seen something unnervingly similar in the well-bred eyes of a duchess…

Chapter Five

The latest carriage was hardly less shaky than the previous one, but this time Isabelle was too distracted to feel much as she gazed out of the grimy window at the gathering darkness. Another day of travelling had brought her and Joseph within a few miles of where Marina was being held, and not even the sickening motion of the coach could eclipse the anxiety now turning in her stomach.

In only a few more hours she would have her sister back safe at her side—or so she prayed, terrified their intervention would prove to be too late.

If they've manufactured an engagement, or done anything to compromise her...

Isabelle took a deep breath. A litany of everything that could go wrong had plagued her since the moment she'd woken that morning, momentarily confused to find herself in an unfamiliar bed before she'd remembered why. Joseph had already gone outside, leaving his blankets neatly folded beside the hearth, but any relief had turned swiftly to shame as she recalled that final glimpse she'd caught of him before burying her head under the bedclothes.

She shouldn't have glanced over when she heard him come back into the room, but something had made her do it, and now she knew what lay beneath the cover of his shirt—and, even worse, *he* knew that *she* knew—Isabelle could hardly bring herself to meet his eye. The image of his sculpted chest had burned itself into the very forefront of her mind, hard muscle scattered with dark hair that led down to the waistband of his trousers, and no matter how desperately she tried Isabelle just couldn't seem to stop it from lingering despite the far more important things that consumed her thoughts. The fact he'd caught her staring made it a hundred times more mortifying, and it was enough to make her toes curl with embarrassment to imagine what he must think of her now.

Hidden beneath her cloak, she pressed a hand to her bodice. Her heart was leaping far too quickly and she had to wonder if it was only down to her apprehension, or if Joseph's arm around her had anything to do with it, placed there by some wordless agreement neither had questioned.

They'd hardly spoken all day, doubtless in part due to the previous night—as well as the uncomfortable conversation after dinner, when both had said more than they'd intended. His opinions on people of her class made sense now she'd had time to think them over, but she doubted he would want her to dwell on the unhappiness of his past.

The fact her interest had been stirred was neither welcome nor timely, Isabelle thought—although as she recalled the look on his face as he'd sat across the table, so closed off that he might have been a brick wall, compassion bloomed again in her already too-full chest.

No wonder he doesn't think kindly of the ton. A lifetime of being looked down upon like vermin would surely turn any man to stone...

The carriage rounded a bend and Isabelle was distracted by a sudden commotion at her waist as Joseph increased his grip, the wide span of his hand easily keeping her in her seat. His fingers pressed with surprising gentleness into the dip just below her bottom rib and for a moment she couldn't think of anything else, almost relieved when his low murmur stirred the lace of her veil.

'We're almost there. One more corner and we'll have reached the inn.'

Isabelle nodded shortly, the lurch of her innards making it impossible to speak. The Harts' home was in a village hardly more than a few minutes' walk, and she'd readily agreed to his plan of bringing Marina back to the inn before setting out for Bishops Morton again at first light.

Joseph was still resolved to act under cover of darkness and the setting of the sun had put Isabelle on edge, now counting down the minutes until her sister was safely back where she belonged. The hand at her side didn't help to soothe her nerves either, attached as it was to that solid arm fixed in turn to the granite-hewn torso that had made such an impression the night before, although she tried yet again to put *that* to the back of her mind as the coach at last began to slow.

The sound of the horses' hooves became more leisurely as they turned into a cobbled yard flanked on three sides by buildings lit with lamps that guttered in the chill February wind. The White Pheasant looked far bigger than the previous inn and Isabelle briefly wondered if their rooms would be more generous likewise before the carriage swayed to a halt, the bustle of the other passengers getting to their feet covering another deep breath.

Not long now. Very soon Marina will be out of danger. Or at least for the time being.

Joseph disembarked first and then helped Isabelle down the steps. Her legs seemed to have fallen asleep during the final stretch of the journey and she stumbled as she reached the ground, only his firm grip on her arm stopping her from falling headlong onto the cobbles.

'Careful. Take a moment to steady yourself.'

Isabelle pulled herself upright, reaching up to make sure her veil was still covering her now glowing face.

'I don't want to wait even that long. We've come this far—I won't waste time now we're so close to the end.'

She risked a glance up at Joseph, surprised to catch the tail end of what might have been a faintly approving look.

'Very good. This way, then.'

Carrying their bags, he led the way to the inn, weaving between the travellers, luggage and horses that littered the moonlit yard and moving so briskly Isabelle had to hurry to keep up. Evidently she wasn't the only one who wanted to settle matters quickly now they had arrived: Joseph didn't slow down until they were inside, where the warmth and clamour of the inn's tavern welcomed them almost as much as the landlady's smile as they approached her desk.

Isabelle watched the woman's eyes flicker over them, taking in Joseph's expansive form in one quick glance.

'Is it lodgings you're wanting?'

'Please. Two rooms, if you have them.'

The sharp eyes darted over them again. 'Two?'

'Yes. One for my wife and I, and one to spare. We will be joined by an addition to our party later tonight.'

Mercifully it seemed they were to be spared another attic room. Instead Joseph stopped on a narrow walkway one floor up, the numbered doors overlooking the courtyard below and the sounds of the carriages drifting through the cold night air to creep beneath ill-fitting windows.

'Here. Numbers eight and nine.'

With his usual lack of grace he pitched the bags onto the floor and held out his hand for a key, raising one eyebrow when Isabelle hesitated before passing it to him.

'When you said a room for you and your wife...'

'I was keeping up the pretence.'

He fitted the key into the lock and turned it, pushing the door open to reveal a somewhat dingy but at least spacious room.

'Of course, you'll really be sharing with your sister this time, rather than me. I'm sure even once was one time too many.'

The little flutter in Isabelle's stomach was difficult to decipher, although as she stepped inside the darkened room and peered around she was stubbornly determined it wasn't disappointment. Surely it was relief at being spared another night of being almost within touching distance of Joseph's bare chest, something no woman of her standing should accept and certainly not enjoy. Her standards seemed to be in serious danger of slipping beneath the assault Joseph didn't even realise he was placing them under, and she felt her stomach stir again as she thought how little he would *want* her to be intrigued, his disapproval of her and everything she stood for already spelled out so clearly even a simpleton would understand.

He doesn't particularly like you, Isabelle, as he has made quite plain. If you insist on allowing this ridiculous interest to develop then it will be to your det-

riment—because there's certainly nothing good that can come from it.

The only man she *ought* to concern herself with was the one she'd be forced to marry to prevent Marina from falling into the wrong hands again—whoever he might be. It was a decision she would have to attend to soon, Joseph's intervention buying time rather than providing a permanent solution, and Isabelle braced herself against the wave of dread that rose at the thought.

None of Bishops Morton's bachelors filled her with much enthusiasm, and yet she would have to seize the lesser of the evils eventually, with her only solace being the knowledge that her sacrifice would be Marina's gain. Time spent focused on the mercenary rather than her dilemma was time wasted, and she knew there was already precious little of it to spare before the vultures began to close in once again.

The voice of reason should have been helpful, but instead Isabelle's unease increased as Joseph placed her bag down just inside her door.

'Will you be comfortable in here?'

'Yes. At least there's space to breathe this time.'

'Agreed. Less chance of me concussing myself on the ceiling, too.'

He stood in the doorway as he surveyed her room. The lamplight from the landing spilled in, but aside from that there was no illumination, only grey ash in the grate in place of a fire, and Isabelle felt another mysterious flutter as she saw something close to concern cross his face.

'No fire in here. I'll ask them to send someone up on my way out. There's no need for you to freeze in the dark while you're waiting for me to return.'

'Waiting for you to return? From where?'

The ghost of concern turned into the kind of look one might give a child asking a particularly silly question.

'From fetching your sister. The sole reason we've been crammed into a carriage for two full days.'

Isabelle frowned, pausing in the act of removing her veil. 'Why would I be waiting? I'm coming with you.'

She waited for him to realise his mistake, probably acknowledging it with a short nod of his close-cropped head, and her frown deepened when he shook it instead, emphasising his point with one single, decisive word.

'No.'

Without further comment he turned away, leaving her to stare at the empty doorway as he abruptly left the room. For a half-second she faltered, caught off balance by the shortness of his reply, but then she collected herself, striding after him without stopping to think.

The door to his room was ajar and she burst through it, only dimly aware of the scandalous impropriety of marching into a man's quarters uninvited and unannounced. Ordinarily she wouldn't have dreamed of such a thing, but his directness seemed to be rubbing off on her—something she didn't know whether to be grateful for or not, although it gave her the courage to glare up into his impassive face.

'What do you mean, "no"? This isn't the time for another of your one-sided decisions. I was always going to help you get her back.'

'No, Isabelle. You weren't.'

Joseph's tone was flat, any feelings he might have carefully hidden behind the maddening composure he could summon when he chose.

'I allowed you to come with me to escort your sister home, as you insisted, but there's not a chance in hell I'll let you be present when I retrieve her. I don't know what kind of reception I'll have, and I don't need you there getting in the way.'

He picked up his bag, placing it on the end of the bed and unbuckling the leather flap to reach inside. In the semi-darkness Isabelle saw him pull out a coat and then something else, a gleam of metal suddenly winking at his knuckles, and she felt her chest tighten.

What is that? Some kind of weapon?

For the first time she hesitated, the reality of the situation beginning to dawn. With his attention fixed on his bag of mercenary's tools only his profile was visible, and Isabelle studied it uncertainly, unease starting to stir.

It was as if a card had been turned over to show the picture on its reverse. While they had been travelling together Joseph had slowly begun to defrost, even coming close to showing concern for her on a couple of occasions, but now the hardness in him had returned abruptly to the fore. On the night he had saved her from the thief he'd seemed like a dangerous animal, and the same air emanated from him now—a distant coldness that made Isabelle shiver as she took a pace towards the bed.

'Joseph—'

He looked up, and she only just managed to stop herself from stepping back again. It wasn't that she was afraid—more that the eyes that gazed back at her were a pair she almost didn't recognise, so devoid of warmth it was like peering down into an empty well.

'Reconcile yourself to this, Your Grace. I said no, and that *no* is final.'

His reverting back to her title stung far more than she might have expected. It had been more pleasant than she'd realised to have someone use her first name, something only Edwin and Marina did, and both had been missing from her life for so long that loneliness must have crept up on her while she'd been otherwise engaged. Somehow Joseph had gone some way to filling the gap they'd left and she hadn't even noticed—too distracted by her worries and her alarming reaction to him to see what was unfolding in front of her.

But now he was reinforcing the barriers between them, and for that she should be grateful. She shouldn't have strayed so far in the first place, determined as she was that nothing would distract her from where her attention ought to lie: firmly fixed on her sister, without anyone or anything standing in her way. Any other feelings were pointless and not to be encouraged... although she couldn't help a pang of something suspiciously close to disappointment at his coolness now.

Apparently unmoved by her silence, Joseph shrugged off his green coat, not looking at her as he exchanged it for the black one he had taken from the bag. From one pocket he produced a rough labourer's cap, pulling it low over his eyes so his already dimly lit face was reduced to a shadow, and when he turned back to her Isabelle gave a dry swallow.

Heaven help Mr Hart and his foul cousin when Joseph finds them. I'd almost feel sorry for them if they didn't have Marina in their grasp.

He was like a brooding giant, dressed all in black from the shabby cap to the toes of his boots, even his scarred hands covered by black gloves that couldn't hide the sheer size of his fists. It was a fearsome sight and yet his untamed masculinity was strangely mesmerising, power radiating from him so effortlessly it was difficult to look away, and as he brushed past her to reach the doorway the accidental touch of his hand sent a static shock through every one of her nerves.

Some measure of her feelings must have shown in her expression—a tangled mess of confusion and foreboding that she couldn't have put into words. Apparently she didn't have to, however, as to her surprise he paused, one hand on the doorframe as if to prevent her from following him outside.

'I can see your frustration, but believe me... If you knew the nasty turn these things can take you'd be grateful to be staying here.'

Isabelle blinked, unsure how to answer. For all his blank face and monotone voice there was *something*... something lurking just out of sight, just below the surface of the offhand words that anyone else might have mistaken for a warning. There was no threat there, however, only the roughest, least sentimental kind of concern he'd shown so many times over the past few days, and it was enough to prompt her own fears to come spilling from her lips.

'Please be careful. I wouldn't want you to get hurt.'

Joseph didn't reply. With his back to the feeble light coming in from the landing his face was now completely hidden, the peak of his cap and the gloom fully concealing his chiselled features, and Isabelle had no way of telling what he might be thinking. Perhaps he was touched by her concern, springing up from nowhere to surprise her as much as him, or perhaps he wanted none of it; the latter more likely, Isabelle thought vaguely, too flustered by the unexpected emergence of her subconscious feelings to protest as he turned to walk through the door.

'I'll be back as soon as I can. *With* your sister. On that you can depend.'

* * *

Joseph strode grimly through the darkness, his head lowered against the cold wind that tugged at the upturned collar of his coat. The streets were deserted, every window covered and only the moon lighting his way to the house Isabelle had described, and he tried again to banish the rogue thoughts that kept attempting to distract him. It was time to be clear-headed, not diverted by anything, and yet that was exactly what seemed to be happening as he walked quietly through the night.

The picture of Isabelle's anxious face flitted past him again, her lips moving on the first words of worry for his safety anyone had ever spoken, and Joseph felt his own lips thin in response. There was an odd sensation in his chest and he didn't know what it was, only that it was strangely warm, but not uncomfortable, and sat squarely where his heart seemed to be beating a little too fast. If he was forced to describe the novel feeling he might even have used the word 'pleasant'—which was enough to make him very uneasy indeed.

All this nonsense just because she wants you to come back in one piece? Probably she only wishes that so you will deliver her sister with no further trouble.

He grunted, but the unfamiliar feeling didn't flee from his cynicism. Instead it kept him company as he walked, insistently warming his chest despite the wind, and its presence made it difficult to avoid the other unwanted thoughts that crept in behind it.

You said you didn't want her to come with you because she'd get under your feet. That's true—but wasn't there another reason? One you didn't want to say out loud?

His answering scowl was fierce, but that didn't mean it wasn't the truth. For all he might want to deny it there *had* been an ulterior motive for so harshly leaving her behind, although Joseph would rather have spent another year in the workhouse than admit it.

If he'd allowed Isabelle to come with him she might have been hurt—and the thought of that deepened his already carved frown. She was stubborn, and proud, and her naive bravery was almost as maddening as it was admirable, but for some reason that mattered less and less the more time he spent with her. He didn't want to feel that way, and heaven knew he'd fight it, frustrated beyond measure that of all the women in the world it was a spoiled gentlewoman who was the first to threaten the boundaries he'd been so careful to build.

He shook his head, wishing that would help to clear it of the things he neither wanted nor understood. That description of Isabelle didn't ring completely true. *Spoiled* was perhaps not quite the right label to place on her, despite the privilege of her birth. She'd travelled without complaining, not uttering a word at the state of the inns they'd stayed in and even accepting him in her room without much resistance, and his pulse increased a fraction as he recalled how she'd looked at him as he'd begun to undress. There had been definite interest—if of the shy and maidenly variety—and he wondered briefly how a widow could be so clearly unused to the sight of a half-dressed man. Surely her husband must have insisted on his marital rights?

Joseph felt his jaw tighten involuntarily at the idea of any man imposing upon her, another gleam of concern for her wellbeing that matched the kind she apparently—unbelievably, miraculously—felt for him in turn.

Enough of this.

He clenched his teeth together even more firmly. He was running away with himself, letting uncharacteristic fancy get in the way of good sense, and he had to rein himself in before he let it go too far.

He shouldn't get used to her kindness, nor allow it to make him soft, even if her openness invited him to return it. As soon as he'd rescued her sister and escorted them back to Bishops Morton his association with the Duchess would come to an end, and if in the meantime he allowed himself to thaw he'd be placing himself at a disadvantage he refused to entertain. If he let himself weaken he wouldn't be able to do his job, his strength the only thing he had worth selling, and he'd be a fool to jeopardise it for the sake of a few pretty words.

A particularly strong gust snatched at his cap and Joseph pulled it down tighter onto his head. The house he was aiming for should be just ahead of him now, and with a monumental effort he set aside everything other than the task at hand, resolutely turning his back on thoughts of sentiment he didn't want to encourage.

He needed his wits about him, and he took a slow, measured breath, collecting himself as he drew to a halt beside a gently stirring tree.

Leaning casually against the trunk, he threw what a passer-by might have thought was an uninterested glance at the house on the other side of the street— although they would have been wrong. With that one practised look he took in the number of doors and windows, the height of the fence that surrounded the front garden, as well as the gate that would open with very little persuasion. There was nothing to stop him from walking straight up the path and pushing himself away from the tree, he swiftly crossed the road, his quiet footsteps the only sound in the otherwise unbroken serenity of the night.

He felt perfectly calm as he lifted the brass knocker, its sharp crack echoing in the empty street. All the curtains were closed, but he caught one twitch as he moved back a pace to look up at the front of the house, stepping forward again when he heard a key turn in a lock.

'Yes?'

A maid peered at him around the door, not opening it enough for him to see past her. Her wary gaze swept over him and Joseph saw her hand tighten on the handle, clearly the combination of his size and indistinct face making her question the decision to answer the door.

'Forgive the lateness of the hour. I come with an urgent message for Miss Marina.'

He spoke lightly, trying to put her at ease. The last thing he needed was for her to slam the door shut before he'd managed to wedge his foot in it, only resorting to breaking a window for entry if left with no other choice.

'It's very important. Please bring her to speak to me at once.'

The gap didn't open any wider. 'I can take a message to her if you'll give it to me.'

'Unfortunately I'm to deliver it in person.'

The maid hesitated, seeming to waver. 'I'll have to check with the master...'

At once Joseph shook his head. He'd have no problem whatsoever with knocking this Hart and his cousin into the middle of next week—their actions proof of the cowardly nature he despised—but he'd still avoid it if he could. A quick and clean extraction was preferable and if he could get away without involving them he would, Isabelle surely wanting her sister to witness as little bloodshed as possible.

And what Isabelle wants seems more important than anything else of late—doesn't it?

Joseph leaned down, subtly placing his boot in the very corner of the doorframe. 'There's no time. If you bring Miss Marina down now your help won't go unrewarded.'

The maid opened her mouth to reply, although whether to agree or tell him to leave he would never get to find out. Another voice issued from behind her and she drew back, the look she threw him too quick to read as a different face appeared at the door.

'I heard my name. Is someone asking for me?'

A young girl stood before him, her head tilted inquisitively, and even if Joseph hadn't already known she was Isabelle's sister one glance would have told him. The shape of the eyes was the same and the chin tapered in an exact copy of the Duchess's own, although the strained air of worry was missing from Marina's youthful face.

It was like seeing a vision of what a less world-weary Isabelle must have looked like as a child—because a child this most definitely was, appearing even younger than her sixteen years with her slight stature and golden hair, and he felt a wave of revulsion for the men who had schemed to use her as a pawn in their grubby little plans.

'Miss Marina.'

He nodded a swift bow, aware that time was rapidly slipping away. The maid had gone—to inform Mr Hart of his presence, he had no doubt—and if he wanted to free the girl without causing a scene he hadn't a moment to spare.

'Your sister sent me. I've come to take you home.'

Marina's smooth forehead furrowed. 'You've come to—? I beg your pardon? When?'

'This very moment. If you have any valuables with you, collect them now. Otherwise leave your belongings and come with me at once.'

The furrow grew more pronounced. 'I don't understand. Why so urgently? And at this time of night?'

She paused, running a doubtful eye over him that made her look more like Isabelle than ever.

'Who are you, sir? I'm afraid I don't recognise you as one of Issy's acquaintance...'

She seemed to be wondering whether to shut the door, and Joseph made sure his foot was still in place even as he tried to find a smile more reassuring than grim. It was a task easier said than done, but he persisted, uncomfortably aware as he loomed over her that he was almost twice her size.

'Your sister will explain everything. If you come with me, you can see her in a matter of minutes.'

Her obvious naivety worked in his favour. A more cynical individual would still have been cautious, but Marina's face lit up at once.

'Issy's here? Now?'

'Staying in the village. She's very close by.'

Marina's eyes widened. 'At last! I've longed to see

her! But why didn't she write to tell me she was coming? Why send you instead?'

Joseph's forced smile hardened. 'You haven't had word from her?'

'Not for weeks. I was beginning to worry...although Mr Hart said there must have just been a delay...'

She looked up at him, so innocent and ready to trust, and Joseph had to stop himself from cursing out loud.

They've been intercepting Isabelle's letters. They were blackmailing her, holding her sister hostage, and Marina knew nothing about it.

A slow beat of anger began to thump in his chest. It was a reaction he shouldn't entertain, underlining the fact that he was becoming far too involved in things that shouldn't concern him, but the knowledge of how their duplicity had caused Isabelle to suffer made it very difficult to remain unmoved.

'Never mind that now. It doesn't matter any more.'

He spoke as gently as he could, which translated into only a slightly less gruff version of his usual tone, but it was the best he could do.

'Fetch your cloak and we'll go to Isabelle at once. There's no need to discuss anything with Mr Hart—'

'Who are you talking to, Marina?'

It was as though the mention of his name had summoned the man himself. Marina hesitated on the threshold, looking from Joseph to the figure coming up behind her, and then a slim, dark-haired man ushered her aside, stepping in front of her as if he had a chance of standing in Joseph's way.

'Who are you?'

Mr Hart tried to glare at him, but his eyes didn't quite meet the ice in Joseph's, and he took half a step backwards when Joseph squared his shoulders.

'I'm a friend of Her Grace, the Duchess of Elmbridge. I'll be escorting Miss Marina home tonight— in fact at this very moment.'

He stared down at the other man, unflustered by the prospect of a confrontation even if he'd hoped to avoid it. Hart deserved to lose a few teeth for his wickedness. Joseph flexed one hand, feeling the underside of the brass knuckles he'd slipped on at the inn heavy against his palm. Marina still hovered in the hallway and Joseph gave her what he hoped was a reassuring smile, although he couldn't guarantee that the warmth of it extended to his eyes. If Hart didn't let her go soon there would be unpleasantness, and he would much rather spare her a sight he knew Isabelle wouldn't wish her to see.

Mr Hart wavered, apparently thinking fast. Looking from side to side, he scanned the street as if hoping for someone to help him, making it painfully obvious what he was about to do.

'If you'd wait here...'

Moving quickly, he tried to swing the door swiftly shut; found it blocked by the toe of a sizable boot, and then the colour drained from his face as Joseph came forward, striding into the house as if he was an invited guest.

'No, thank you. I think I'll come inside. It's a freezing night and I've no desire for frostbite.'

The other man fell back against one wall of the hall, stark fear in every line of his pallid face, but Joseph paid him no mind. Glancing around, he saw the maid standing a little further away, apparently rooted to the spot by either surprise or dread.

'Miss Marina's cloak, please. As quickly as you can.'

The maid dithered, only the raising of one stern eyebrow prompting her into useful action. A cloak was drawn from an armoire in one corner of the hall and Marina took it, bewildered but at least sharp enough to sense that the atmosphere wasn't one to question as she swung the cloak around her shoulders and fastened it at her neck.

She moved as if to approach him, uncertain until he held out his arm. Mr Hart made a strangled sound as she took it but Joseph's cold stare silenced him at once, only able to watch in mute despair as Joseph led Marina towards the door.

On the threshold Joseph stopped, turning to look behind him at the scene laid out in the hall. The maid had disappeared and Mr Hart was alone, slumped against the wall as if he'd had the worst shock of his life, and Joseph made sure Marina's hand was firmly in the crook of his arm as he grimly savoured his victory.

'Do you have anything to say? Any message you'd like me to pass on to Her Grace?'

Mr Hart peered up at him with watery eyes, revoltingly close to tears. Whether they were from anger or disappointment Joseph didn't know, but he felt his lip curl as Hart shook his head, not uttering so much as a word of apology for the pointless suffering he had caused with his greed.

'As I thought.'

Joseph turned away, coolly determined to remove Marina from the presence of the pathetic creature behind them as soon as possible, and she followed willingly, casting only one doubtful glance behind her before they stepped into the night. He didn't bother to close the door behind them before he led her down the front steps, her hand on his arm even lighter than Isabelle's but the gleam of her hair in the moonlight so similar that Joseph couldn't help his thoughts turning back to the Duchess, a fight he always seemed to lose.

She'll be delighted to have her sister back. She might even be delighted with you...

The prospect made his insides execute a strange flip, although he had no time to consider it. The little hand on his arm was tapping him tentatively, and he glanced down, almost having to bend double to catch her bemused voice.

'What's happening, sir? I don't understand. One

minute I was about to ready myself for bed and the next you appeared, telling me I have to come with you at once. And your clear displeasure with Mr Hart... Can't you tell me why?'

He made a noncommittal noise. 'I think the best explanation will come from your sister. She'll know how to—'

A shout cut him off, coming so unexpectedly from the other side of the street that it carved through the quiet like a knife.

'Behind you! Watch out!'

Instinctively he twisted round, throwing out his arm just in time to avert the club being borne down towards his head. Instead it glanced off his forearm, pain blossoming where wood connected with bone, but he managed to catch hold of the weapon before it was raised again and with a powerful wrench tore it from his attacker's grip.

Without thinking he pushed Marina behind him, allowing the club to fall from his hand as he seized hold of his assailant's lapels and hauled him off his feet. The man dangled helplessly, squirming towards the ground just skimmed by his toes, but Joseph showed no mercy, too focused on his prey to heed Marina's gasp.

'So. The cousin, I assume?'

The man tried to speak but nothing came out, only a choking gulp as he twisted to free himself. Glaring downwards, Joseph watched him writhe, his own heart leaping but feeling none of the fear written so vividly on the other man's face. If he felt any emotion at all it was anger—anger of a cold and calm nature, however, nothing threatening his self-control, although something else was beginning to bleed into his awareness that almost managed to distract him.

I know that voice. The person who called out to warn me...

Marina was still behind him but he sensed another presence approaching through the gloom, rapid footsteps pattering in the darkness, and he had to shake his head as he realised he knew exactly who they belonged to.

Of course. Of course she wouldn't do as I asked and stay away. Why did I ever think otherwise?

His already quickened heart beat faster as Isabelle appeared on the very edge of his vision, wrapped in her heavy cloak but without the veil he'd come to expect, immediately followed by a flurry of skirts as Marina ran to her, the sisters clinging together so fiercely it seemed they might never part. He heard Isabelle murmur something low and urgent that only Marina would hear—and then his heart pounded harder still as the Duchess came slowly towards him, an unreadable expression on her pale face, and with careful gentleness laid her bare hand on his arm.

'Joseph. Thank you so much for everything you've done. I think it's safe to put Mr Lewis down now.'

He looked down at her, his stomach tightening as

his eyes met hers, and whatever he'd planned to say in reply died in his mouth. There was something unspoken in her expression and it lit a spark inside him, fanned by the unwavering connection of hazel and blue-green until it burst into flame.

He should be annoyed that she'd ignored his instruction to wait at the inn, angry that she'd placed herself in what might have been danger, but instead he couldn't quite manage to think of anything but how beautiful she was as the moonlight made a pastel masterpiece of her face and her little hand lay on the broad expanse of his arm, and she gazed up at him with a strange emotion he knew she couldn't fake. There was gratitude there, certainly, but also something else— something confusing and so unfamiliar it took Joseph a moment to remember that he still held a squirming stranger in his grasp, so completely absorbed by Isabelle's presence that everything else melted away.

'As you wish.'

Abruptly he opened his fist, allowing Mr Lewis to fall heavily to the ground. The man groaned and Joseph leaned over him, too rattled by whatever had just passed between himself and Isabelle to risk another glance at her.

'You're fortunate there are ladies present. Otherwise I would have left you with a far more permanent souvenir of my visit than just bruised pride.'

Out of the corner of his eye he saw Isabelle turn back to her sister and take her in her arms, holding the

girl against her as if there was nothing more important in the entire world. It was a scene surely any person made of flesh and blood would find touching, and
for a single fleeting moment Joseph realised he was
one of them, for the briefest of beats letting himself
be a man rather than a statue carved from ice. Something in Isabelle's relief pierced through the armour of
his indifference to find the closely guarded softness
beneath—a weakness he would never admit to but was
equally powerless to deny. He had no idea what it felt
like to care about another person as much as Isabelle
cared for her sister, or what it was to have someone
care that much for him in return, but for the first time
he had to wonder if it was something to strive for…
something even an unwanted foundling might one day
find if he was willing to try…

It was a dangerous thought, attempting to under-
mine the rules he'd lived by since he was a child, and
he could sense the peril of believing it like smoke rising from a fire. He knew he ought to turn away, before it could threaten the walls he'd been so careful
to build, and so he did, crouching next to the figure
curled on the ground so he could mutter directly into
its ear.

'It would be in your best interests to forget everything that happened here tonight. If I hear so much as
a whisper about either the Duchess or her sister—and,
believe me, I *would* hear—I'll have to come and see
you again. Would you like me to do that?'

Mr Lewis shook his head vigorously and Joseph nodded as he got to his feet. With any luck neither he nor Hart would want to risk any further visits, too cowardly to pursue the matter now they knew Isabelle wasn't as defenceless as they'd thought. They had only targeted her because they'd imagined she had nobody to protect her interests, the absence of her husband having made her an ideal target in their eyes, and a sudden desire to be the one she knew she could rely on roared up from nowhere to make him freeze where he stood.

What on earth...? What are you thinking now?

He almost reeled beneath the unexpected thought. It was an unacceptable idea and he attempted to brush it aside like a troublesome fly, swatting at it as it buzzed around his head, although the ridiculousness of it didn't make it any less alarming.

You're getting soft. It's about time you put an end to this job if it's beginning to make you lose your wits.

Slightly unsteadily he straightened his cap, pulling it lower to conceal his face. He'd done what he had been engaged to do and that meant his involvement with Isabelle had almost reached its end—a natural conclusion to a decidedly *un*natural acquaintance he shouldn't wish to prolong. She would go back to her world and he would go back to his, and nothing as baseless as some fleeting mutual attraction would threaten the order of things too deeply entrenched for him to fight.

'I think we should take our leave.'

He saw Isabelle glance at him over the top of Marina's head, still holding her sister as if daring anyone to try parting them. Once again their eyes met, and neither the darkness nor the span of a few paces was nearly enough to disguise the unnamed emotion in that one long look that sent a shiver down Joseph's reluctant spine.

But then she nodded, her hair flashing silver beneath the moon, and without a word she took her sister's hand and fell into step behind him as he walked through the garden gate and out into the street beyond.

Chapter Six

Isabelle pretended she couldn't feel Joseph watching her as she drew a blanket over Marina's sleeping form, the girl still fully dressed but curled up on the bed like a little cat. It was past one in the morning and Isabelle preferred to let her exhausted sister sleep where she'd dropped, although her own nerves were far too jangled to allow any rest as she finally gathered the courage to look over her shoulder.

'Are you going to your room now?'

Standing just inside the door, Joseph nodded. 'Yes. I'll sit for a while, though, before I go to bed.'

Isabelle carefully tucked in a corner of the blanket that didn't really need any adjustment. Now Marina was asleep there was nobody to act as a distraction from the strange feeling that had engulfed her as she'd watched him emerge from Mr Hart's house, guiding her sister so protectively it had made her throat suddenly tight.

Marina had looked so small at his side, and yet

he'd been more guardian than threat—a realisation that had set Isabelle's heart skipping even faster when combined with the crackling look that had passed between them when she'd laid her hand on his arm… The atmosphere had felt charged, with a brittle tension stretching out that she knew he must have sensed too, and it was difficult to meet his eye now as she finally took a step back from the bed.

'I don't think I'll be able to sleep just yet. I'm tired, but I still feel on edge.'

'Understandable. It's been quite a day.'

He lifted his cap, rubbing the short hair at the back of his neck. It looked spiky, but perhaps it was softer than it appeared… a thought she had to silence quickly when he cast her a glance.

'I had some ale sent up to my room at the same time I ordered the fire. It isn't your favourite, but a glass might help you relax enough to get some rest.'

Isabelle paused in smoothing down her skirts, seizing on anything to busy her hands. 'A glass of ale? In your room?'

'Obviously. I think we're past the point of obeying social etiquette by now, don't you?'

Joseph turned away, speaking quietly over his shoulder so as not to disturb the slumbering figure on the bed. 'It's up to you. The offer's there if you want it.'

He left the room, half closing the door behind him, and Isabelle listened to his heavy footsteps retreat the short distance down the landing. A faint scratching noise signalled him unlocking his door and then there was nothing—only the sound of Marina's soft breathing as Isabelle hesitated, not sure whether to follow.

It was probably best not to. No matter what Joseph said, it was still inappropriate to be alone with him in a bedroom—and besides, the alarming feelings that were trying to grow made it risky for her to spend too much time in his company. If she had any sense she'd crawl into bed beside Marina and hope sleep came to claim her without having to resort to Joseph's jug of ale, and with a decisive nod Isabelle made up her mind to do just that.

For approximately two minutes.

She silently cursed her weakness when he opened his door to her soft knock, but she found herself slipping inside the room anyway, hoping her face didn't look as hot as it felt. There was something oddly thrilling about being somewhere so off-limits, and she wondered briefly what her unwanted suitors would say if they could see her now, alone at night with a handsome man who gestured for her to sit in a chair beside the fire as he poured her a drink.

'Here.'

He passed her a slightly chipped glass and Isabelle had to stop herself from flinching as his fingertips accidentally brushed hers—a tiny touch that nonetheless sent shock waves the length of her arm. She kept her eyes on her drink as he pulled up a low stool from against the wall, preferring to look anywhere other than into his sculpted face while she got herself back under control.

Joseph sat gazing into the fire, cradling his own drink between both hands. Out of the corner of her eye Isabelle watched him take a sip, following the movement of his throat as he swallowed, and hurriedly she groped for some way to fill the quiet that left her far too much time to stare.

'I want to thank you again for taking such good care of my sister tonight. You would have got her out without any fuss if Mr Lewis hadn't come after you. I was so frightened when I saw him behind you, but you stepped in front of Marina as if it was nothing.'

He exhaled roughly. 'You wouldn't have been frightened if you hadn't been there. I told you to stay here.'

It wasn't the most gracious of replies. Isabelle opened her mouth to answer, but a brief sidelong look silenced her at once. He didn't seem annoyed, as she would have expected: there was something else in his tone that was much harder to identify…still brusque, but not as irritable as before.

'I told you that for a reason. You could have been hurt.'

Isabelle struggled to keep her voice steady as she risked a fraudulently casual shrug. If she hadn't known better she might have thought it sounded as if he *cared* that something might have happened to her…a prospect so intriguing she didn't dare let it take hold.

'So could you, if I hadn't been there to warn you. If I hadn't shouted you might have been knocked unconscious—or even killed outright.'

Joseph snorted again, although this time with a ghost of amusement. 'I suppose you expect me to be grateful for that? How the tables turn.'

The glance he flicked her didn't help to slow her pulse. His hazel eyes were darker in the firelight and impossible to read, his swift study posing a test Isabelle didn't know if she'd passed.

'You have the most reckless amount of mettle I've ever seen in a woman of your kind. It borders on foolishness at times. But I'll not deny you have some nerve.'

It was the closest thing to a compliment he'd ever given her, and Isabelle felt the surprise already circling within her step up another notch.

'Thank you. That almost sounds like a commendation.'

'It may well have been. Perhaps you should accept it as such.'

He took another swift mouthful of ale—possibly to excuse himself from having to say anything further, although for Isabelle the words he'd already spoken were enough. It was more approval than she'd ever thought he would bestow upon her, and she sat still as a curious warmth spread inside the confines of her chest, lighting up dark corners she hadn't known were in shadow.

'You still don't like *"my kind"*, though. I can see it's difficult for you to say anything that might come close to being flattering.'

'No. I'll never be an admirer of the *ton*. But after tonight… I'm willing to admit you might not be *quite* as bad as the rest of them—even if your refusal to do as you're asked is irritating in the extreme.'

The faintest hint of a smile disappeared behind the rim of Joseph's glass, but Isabelle was too amazed to take much notice. If anyone else had uttered something so gruffly unsentimental she might have suspected them of damning her with faint praise, but from Joseph…

Even the most lavish compliment from the Regent himself couldn't have been more pleasing to her than knowing she'd won Joseph's grudging respect, and Isabelle had to clamp her lips together to stop a sudden smile of her own. That unexplained warmth still sat in her chest and she felt it burn brighter at his words, knowing she was ridiculous to set such store by a mercenary's opinion, yet unable to prevent the secret pleasure from nesting inside her like a wild bird.

For all his sternness apparently Joseph wasn't such a completely impenetrable fortress, and the hint of something beneath his armour only made him more attractive—if such a thing was possible, the image of his tantalisingly bare chest already called to mind by once again finding herself alone with him behind a closed bedroom door. If she wasn't careful she might find even more things to admire, his face and complex nature drawing her further and further in.

She tried her hardest to seem unruffled as she picked up her glass. 'Well. Thank you very much. If we're sharing confidences, I suppose I should say you're not *quite* as objectionable as I originally thought either—even if your regard for decorum is sorely lacking.'

To her relief Joseph inclined his head, accepting her equally barbed praise without suspecting how much it concealed.

'Such kind words—and from a duchess, no less. I might even believe you if I didn't suspect you're merely delirious with joy at having your sister back. Now you'll be able to keep a close eye on her twenty-four hours a day—to prevent anything like this from ever happening again.'

Isabelle stilled, her glass halfway to her lips. It was a throwaway comment but it sent a stab right through her that she was sure Joseph hadn't intended, and she set her glass down again without taking a sip.

'What is it?'

Joseph's sharp gaze swept her face but suddenly Isabelle felt too cold to blush at his scrutiny. The warmth beneath her breastbone faltered and she felt it drain from her, a chill rising where once there had been heat.

'Just as you say... It would be far too easy for something like this to happen again.'

She saw him sit forward on his stool, apparently

about to argue, but she fended him off with a raised hand. He'd only voiced what she already knew— although somehow hearing someone else speak her worst fear out loud made it seem altogether too real.

Slowly Isabelle shook her head, hardly aware of anything but the worry that had begun to tie her stomach into a knot. 'You're right—even if you didn't mean to be. And it's something I know myself. There's nothing to stop another man from coming along, trying to exploit our apparent defencelessness for his own gain. You may have prevented our disgrace this time, but news of Edwin's death will only spread wider the more time goes on, and my sister doesn't know how to be on her guard—'

She broke off as uncertainty began to rise, casting its unhappy shadow over her racing mind. All the relief of having Marina out of Mr Hart's clutches had receded, leaving in its wake fresh apprehension that squeezed her in a merciless fist.

How soon after their return to Bishops Morton would the cycle begin again? Their neighbour's handsome young relation who had tried so hard to catch Marina's attention might have been defeated this year, but what was to stop him returning the next? If it wasn't him, it would only be another, Isabelle thought despairingly. There would never be a lack of calculating rakes with half an eye on Marina's lithe figure and the other half on her dowry, and Isabelle knew she couldn't combat them all alone. She needed an ally—

someone to support her in her arduous task—and she needed him before it was too late.

'My sister is too naïve to see the danger. You must have seen she didn't have the first clue about Hart and Lewis's scheme. Marina is too trusting by half—and that's entirely my fault.'

Mechanically Isabelle reached again for her untouched glass, barely tasting the ale when it finally hit her tongue. It didn't improve with a second sip, but at least drinking meant she didn't have to pretend composure, the tangle inside her growing painfully tight.

Distantly she heard Joseph's stool creak as he changed position. Probably he was fidgeting from boredom, having no reason to care what might happen after he'd been paid—so it was unexpected when he folded his arms on the tabletop, looking right at her instead of letting his gaze stray around the room.

'Why do you say that? What happened to make you so pivotal to her development or lack of it?'

It was Isabelle's turn to regard him over the rim of her glass. Was he genuinely interested in the inner workings of her upper-class existence, for which he'd never bothered to hide his disdain? It seemed unlikely—and yet if she'd learned anything about the mercenary during their unlikely acquaintance it was that he never shied away from the truth. If he hadn't wanted an answer he wouldn't have asked, too blunt to pretend curiosity in the absence of it, and even the dismay circling inside her couldn't completely stop a flicker of gratitude that he hadn't simply left her talking into thin air.

First admitting I'm not so heinous after all, and now showing an interest in my worries? If I didn't know better I might think we were on the way to becoming friends.

The thought was strange, but not displeasing, and as she forced herself to swallow the bitter ale Isabelle marvelled at how far they'd come. A grudging connection now existed between them where once there had been only animosity—although she couldn't deny that on her side at least that growing regard wasn't *strictly* platonic.

Even the worry now nagging at her didn't make her blind to the sharp line of his profile, or the way his eyes creased when he smiled, and the fact that he was so far below her in rank didn't seem to matter when she recalled the readiness with which he put himself in danger. He was brave and capable and she'd never known anyone like him, so frank and straightforward that she couldn't help an equally honest reply.

'I was barely eighteen and Marina only six when I took over her care. In many ways I've been more of a mother to her than our real one had a chance to be.'

She thought she caught a subtle change in Joseph's expression, although he didn't speak. Instead he watched her closely, his unwavering focus sending a prickle beneath her skin.

'Our parents were taken by the same wave of influenza. I made sure Marina didn't see their suffering—kept her distanced from the worst of it so her childhood might not be tainted by witnessing their pain. After they died we had nobody but each other: no aunts or uncles to turn to, and Papa's estate was entailed away to some distant relation we had never met. We were saved from destitution by my marriage to the Duke and I dedicated myself to Marina's happiness, hoping to make up for the loss of our parents by making sure she grew up knowing nothing but love. As a result, she has no idea that there are people in the world who would seek to use her badly, and in all honesty the idea of shattering her innocence is more than I can bear.'

Isabelle stopped, vaguely bewildered at having shared so much. She hadn't meant to lay her soul quite so bare—the only other person she had ever spoken to about such private sorrows was Edwin, but she scarcely had time to wonder how Joseph had managed to draw her out before his face made her mind stutter to a halt.

He studied her with such unreadable intensity that she felt her cheeks begin to burn—although from the swiftness with which he looked away it seemed he hadn't meant her to see it. Switching his attention to his scarred hands, he inspected a healed welt on one thumb, unwilling to meet her eye when only seconds before he had pinned her to the spot with that powerful hazel stare.

'Your devotion is a credit to you. I hope she realises how fortunate she is to have it.'

Isabelle stared down at the table, hoping the firelight hid her confusion. What he'd meant by that intense look she didn't know—although the force of it had made her heartbeat scurry like a rabbit through a field.

'I'm not sure it's worth admiring. It's my duty as her sister to keep her safe, and even more so now I have no husband to help me.'

Joseph dipped his head, as if acknowledging a valid point. 'You could remarry. That would keep the wolves from your door like nothing else.'

'I know. I don't want to…but I think it's the only way.'

A renewed heaviness descended on her chest and Isabelle hunched slightly in her chair, unconsciously wrapping her arms around herself as if she might ward off grim reality. He was right again. Another man in her house would act as the ultimate deterrent for anyone thinking of abusing Marina's position, the prospect of a protective male sure to make any unscrupulous individual hesitate. Her own reluctance mattered little when weighed against the alternative: her sister left exposed to those seeking only profit, too credulous to realise what danger a fortune heaped on a woman's shoulders.

'It's something I must reconcile myself to. I've only been widowed these past nine months, however, and the idea of allowing one of those men who have come prowling around me to take Edwin's place...'

The heaviness beneath her bodice was getting more oppressive by the minute, like an invisible rock on her chest weighing her down, and she hated the fact that she was beginning to feel afraid.

'The Duke was a good man, but so many are not. You only need look around to see how many women are trapped in unhappy marriages, their money squandered and unable to trust their own husbands. For Marina I would do anything, but I confess I'm afraid to make a mistake that would bring us more sorrow than safety.'

She gazed unseeingly down at a stain on the table-cloth. Out of the corner of her eye she could just make out Joseph, still examining his hands. His handsome face was set as he listened in silence, and it was the oddest kind of comfort that he didn't try to dismiss her worries as she began to wade through the mire of her jumbled thoughts.

What she needed was a man she could rely on—a man who would understand that her first duty was to her sister, and not try to impose any kind of masculine rule upon her house. Even when Edwin was alive Isabelle had been her own mistress and she wouldn't stand for anything less now, the notion of a man trying to exert control over her laughable if not for the danger. A husband who would largely leave her to her own devices was the ideal—never seeking to interfere unless his assistance was required—but the tallness of the order made Isabelle huddle even deeper into her chair.

Where am I supposed to find a man like that? And quickly enough to head off all those other useless young men with designs on my sister?

Her despair didn't lift even the smallest fraction as she thought of her insistent suitors—a parade of entirely unsuitable prospects marching one after the other to be rejected at once. Each was too greedy, too scheming, too covetous of her money and her self, and the fact she hadn't felt able to approach any of them for help when Marina was in trouble told Isabelle all she needed to know.

If she hadn't trusted them *then* there was no way she could do so *now*, her sister's future too precious to entrust to anyone but the most dependable. A strong man was what she needed, with principles and the courage to defend those in his care, and when the answer came to her it was in a burst of inspiration so bright it might have eclipsed the sun.

There was only one man of her acquaintance who might fulfil every criteria…and his brow creased when her head snapped up, his frown growing deeper when she fixed him with a wide-eyed stare.

Of course. Who else?

Her heart crashed into her ribs as she let the startling idea sink in. It had come so suddenly, shocking her to the core, although the moment it seared itself into her consciousness she knew it made perfect sense.

Who else but Joseph Carter would be the answer to my prayers?

She swallowed hard, aware of a new unsteadiness in her hands. Her pulse flickered at lightning speed and she took a breath, trying not to choke on it as Joseph's confusion turned swiftly to suspicion.

'What? Why are you looking at me like that?'

It was a ridiculous, outlandish, nonsensical idea—yet it was the best she had, the possibility of escaping from being forced to choose among her undesirable suitors shimmering before her. If *Joseph* was the man, wouldn't it solve all her problems in one fell swoop? He was neither grasping, nor lecherous, and best of all he wouldn't balk at a challenge. She needed a husband quickly, and Joseph was used to jumping in without hesitation. His courage was the very thing she required to match her own, and the irony that a mercenary, of all people, would be the perfect pairing for a duchess flitted through her whirling mind.

It shouldn't work. Certainly on paper, it doesn't. But in practice...?

Her stomach turned over as the full magnitude of what she was contemplating hit her like a physical blow. It was true Joseph had warmed to her—by his own admission he held her in higher esteem than before, although her building spirits dimmed slightly when her own feelings forced themselves to the fore.

Her regard for the mercenary had improved likewise, but not quite so innocently. His physicality affected her in ways she hadn't known were possible, stirring things inside her that had lain dormant for her entire adult life, and it would take all her nerve to wade into waters already muddied by desires she couldn't seem to fight. They might complicate matters, adding another dimension she would have to conceal, but for Marina's sake she had to try.

There was nobody else and as Isabelle tried to suppress the tremor in her fingers she hoped she was right to place such faith in a man she was still getting to know. It was a risk but the rewards might be great indeed, of benefit to both parties if she could only persuade him to consider...

Which he just might—if I can make it sound worth his while.

Joseph waited for Isabelle to break the tense silence, hoping she'd hurry up and share whatever it was that had struck her dumb so he could draw their conversation to an end. It had taken an unexpected turn, and to his alarm he realised he didn't like where it was heading, a strange ache growing inside him at the thought of her wedding again. It was the most unwelcome reaction imaginable and he tried at once to ward it off, but he couldn't seem to help a sensation so close to jealousy it almost made him wince.

You're being an absolute fool. Why on earth should

you have an opinion on whether or not a duchess chooses to marry?

It was a question he didn't want to answer, and he shifted slightly on his too-small stool, wishing Isabelle would look away. She seemed transfixed, however, and instead it was Joseph who broke the connection of their eyes, uncomfortably aware his feelings must echo Isabelle's on catching *him* staring only minutes before.

He hadn't meant to allow his reaction to the sad tale of her past to be so obvious, but he'd been unable to stop his usually impassive face from betraying his thoughts, unexpectedly moved at finding a parallel between them he never would have suspected.

Isabelle had to fend for herself just like I did. Not in the workhouse, perhaps, but she was still orphaned and alone—or almost—having to care for her sister even though her own heart must have broken when her parents died. I suppose her life hasn't been quite as charmed as I thought.

The notion was uncomfortably striking and Joseph glanced at the clock on the mantel, his desire to escape growing with every second when she still didn't speak. It read two in the morning—long past the hour he would have expected her to retire—although she certainly didn't *look* tired as she continued whatever discussion was taking place inside her head.

Finally he could stand it no more.

'Please stop staring at me like that. If I was a more delicate man I might start to feel self-conscious.'

She started, the rosy glow already enhancing the lines of her cheekbones deepening to crimson. 'I'm sorry. I was lost in thought.'

'About anything you want to share? It's already late, and I'm sure you'll want to get all the sleep you can before our return journey. Don't forget we leave at dawn.'

Isabelle was far too well bred not to pick up on such a stark hint, but he drove it home regardless, standing so quickly it was fortunate the ceiling was high enough not to collide with his head.

'If there's nothing else you need, I think I'll say goodnight. We could both do with the rest.'

To his unending relief Isabelle rose to her feet— although it still seemed she was held prisoner by her own thoughts. She moved towards the door with an unsteadiness he would have noticed immediately if he hadn't been so distracted, and he cursed inwardly when at the very last moment she turned back.

'Joseph…'

She tailed off, his name hanging in the air between them. Not for the first time it occurred to him how much more pleasing it sounded coming from her mouth than anyone else's…spoken so quietly, and yet the only thing he could focus on in the whole room.

'I wonder… Would you ever consider…?'

Again she left the rest of her sentence to falter, and

Joseph felt his desperation rise once more as he looked down at her, so flushed now that she resembled a poppy more than anything else. If she didn't stop hesitating with such sweet uncertainty he might lose his wits, already threatening to scatter as they stood so close together near the door. One more step and she could be in his arms—something he immediately regretted realising when his breathing grew faster.

'Would I consider…?'

Isabelle's lips parted but nothing came out. Whatever she wanted to say was clearly difficult, and a hundred possibilities chased each other through Joseph's mind—although when she finally managed to finish what she'd started it wasn't anything he'd dared to imagine.

'Would you ever consider marrying me?'

It came in a breathless rush and Joseph didn't move, standing perfectly still as he stared down at that scarlet face.

What? What did she just say?

That he was astounded must have been obvious. Isabelle wavered, steadying herself by leaning back slightly against the wall, but to her credit she found the courage to carry on.

'I know it's sudden. I know it's something you never would have thought about. But will you let me explain?'

He felt his jaw loosen and distantly hoped his mouth hadn't gaped open—although there was little he could

have done about it. All he seemed capable of was staring, at a complete loss for words, as Isabelle laced her
fingers together and began to speak quickly, her words
tripping over each other in her haste to force them out.

'I need a husband to help me shield Marina from
fortune-hunters until she finds her true match. It has
to be a man I can trust, who understands that for me
she comes above anything else, and who would be
willing to protect her from any further harm. I can't
think of anyone more able to do all that than you.'

Joseph's stomach lurched as he stood immobile, one
hand still on the door. Was this some kind of cruel
joke? He searched her face, unable to believe what he
was hearing. There was no trace of a smile, however,
no barely contained laugh, and when he didn't answer
Isabelle hurried on.

'In return you'd live at Winford House and wouldn't
have to sell your strength to people you despise any
longer. You could stop being a mercenary at the beck
and call of others and be your own man—financially
secure and of such standing that nobody would look
down on you ever again.'

She exhaled, clearly relieved to have delivered her
little speech. Although she was still leaning against the
wall she seemed to have collected herself slightly—
but the same could not be said for Joseph.

'Isabelle… Surely you can't be serious…?'

He placed both hands behind his head in an instinctive gesture born of pure bewilderment. Finally

he had regained the ability to speak, but there was nothing to say, the whole thing so ludicrous it barely warranted a response.

Should I start listing why this is a bad idea?

It was the wildest bargain he'd ever been offered—and yet with a dawning sense of amazement he felt his initial shock begin to give way to consideration. The terms she'd laid out were so life-changingly generous surely only a mad man would decline, but still he held back, refusing to give way to the clamour starting to build. He had to think clearly, but it was impossible while his head felt so full, too many questions shouting to be heard although one in particular came louder than the rest.

Are you tempted to accept because of what Isabelle is offering—or for Isabelle herself?

His gut gave another unpleasant tweak and he was only just able to hide a grimace. There was more truth to that suggestion than he wanted to admit, but he swept it aside, stubbornly shunting it to the very back of his racing mind. She was offering him an alliance—a business proposition above anything else—and the unfamiliar feelings she inspired in him were entirely surplus to requirements.

'You can't truly want to wed *me*. What of all those other men who came crowding round when the Duke died? Surely one of them is a better match? Both in position and everything else.'

'They are little better than scavengers, looking to

pick over my husband's bones. Not one of them is trustworthy enough to be my sister's guardian, for all their rank and family name. You may be below them in society's eyes, but I would wager your sense of decency is far superior in every way.'

Joseph unlaced his hands from behind his head, bringing them forward to pass over his face.

'Think about what you're saying. Aren't you afraid of making yourself even more vulnerable than you are already? If I was your husband, everything that's yours would pass to me. I could sell your Winford House out from under you and there would be nothing you could do to prevent it.'

He watched her lips press into a straight line, their pink fullness as always never failing to catch his eye and in their unsmiling seriousness more striking than ever.

'Any husband is a gamble, but with you I think I already know the stakes. You pretend to be made of stone, but I suspect that somewhere deep down you might not be quite as hard as you'd have the world believe. You are a far better man than you give yourself credit for. You already said you no longer dislike me as you once did—and I feel very much the same about you.'

She looked up at him with such straightforward frankness that for a moment he couldn't think of a reply. Her cheeks were still flushed, and her chest seemed to be rising and falling a touch more quickly than usual, but it was her words that held him still, fixed in place by a sensation he had no idea how to name.

For someone to have such faith in him was a complete unknown, and it sliced directly between the gaps in his defences. Never in his life had anyone suggested there might be more to him than met the eye or, even further, that the nature he concealed could be worth uncovering—the hidden humanity inside him something of value rather than a weakness he should try to stamp out. The idea flew directly in the face of everything he'd ever known, every vow he'd ever taken to hold himself so coolly apart, and yet the thought of Isabelle's acceptance lit a fire in his chest he was powerless to douse.

'I never thought to marry anyone...much less a woman of your rank. What would your peers say?'

He heard himself speaking although he seemed to have very little control over his mouth. All his attention was fixed on Isabelle's ocean-blue eyes as they glittered in the firelight, any trace of fatigue wiped away by the earnestness of her gaze.

'And what of the risk of scandal, attaching yourself to a man like me? For myself, I wouldn't care in the slightest, but your reputation—and that of Marina— would never recover.'

Isabelle's face clouded. 'I'd have to surrender my title if we wed, it's true, but I've never been very much attached to it. For the rest... As nobody of my acquaintance will have the first clue who you are, we have a blank slate and can make you acceptable with a few well-chosen rumours as to your eligibility. The circles we move in are so different none of them will ever have met you—unless, of course, they've previously engaged your services. In which case they would take great pains to make sure no hint of your former occupation became known, so people might not begin asking why they should have needed a mercenary in the first place. We can safely rely on the hypocrisy of the *ton* to keep our business private.'

She tried a smile, the corners of her lips twitching briefly, but he knew she was too honest to force one where it didn't belong. The situation was too serious for anything but the stark truth, and both were all too aware of how their futures hung in the balance.

Isabelle let the smile slip away. 'I'm not asking you to love me. I know how the world works, and to marry for love is my ambition for my sister, not myself. All I want is to build on the respect I believe is already growing between us and make an alliance of benefit to us both.'

Joseph felt the tendons in his neck flex sharply. That one little word—*love*—rang in his ears and he swallowed reflexively, his mouth so dry even that small movement was painful.

Again she intends to marry for what she needs rather than what she wants. In that regard she's as much a mercenary as I am—perhaps we're the perfect match after all.

Of course Isabelle would make it clear there were no feelings involved—he shouldn't expect anything else. Any agreement between them would be based solely on mutual convenience and nothing more. It wasn't as though *he* loved *her*, naturally... But for some reason hearing her spell out the terms of the bargain with such clarity made a heaviness settle upon him, the final death of something he'd barely realised was alive.

'I need to think about this. As flattered as I am... it's a huge decision to make.' Joseph shook his head slowly, steeling himself against the desire to rub his knuckles against his aching eyes. 'I think you need time to consider, too. Come morning, you might regret it.'

'Of course you can have time. As much as you need.'

Isabelle nodded, peering down at her slender hands. For the first time Joseph noticed they were twining together in a repetitive movement that betrayed the nerves she was trying so hard to hide, although when she looked up at him it was with such renewed courage he felt his already too-strong admiration for her swell all the more.

'You must come to your own conclusion. For myself, though, I've no doubt whatsoever that I've made the right choice. If it helps you to believe my resolve... I'm willing to prove my certainty right this moment.'

Joseph frowned. What did she mean? There was no need for her to prove anything. The determination in her eyes was so clear nobody could have mistaken it for anything else—but then she took a step towards him and his mind grew blank as the space between them was abruptly reduced to nothing at all.

She had to stretch up on tiptoe to reach his mouth, and for one agonising heartbeat Joseph froze, the soft brush of her lips over his robbing him of all thought. It was the most gentle, uncertain of kisses and she dropped down again almost at once, her face flaming with all the heat and colour of wildfire, but as he regained control of his limbs Joseph couldn't help reaching out to stop her.

Without thinking he bent to recapture her mouth, acting on a yearning he hadn't known until that moment had been building inside him like water against a dam. Isabelle had finally torn down the barrier and now he was helpless to resist, drawing her back towards him with a grip weak enough for her to break any time she wished; but she made no attempt to escape. Instead his chest constricted as she arched against him, his palm fitting around her waist to pull her nearer still, and he could scarcely breathe when he felt her run a tentative hand over the broad landscape of his back. His own hand tightened its hold on the supple sweep just below her ribs as the other dived through her golden hair, her eyes closed now and her face turned up like a flower seeking the sun's light.

His pulse thrummed with frightening speed at feeling the warmth of her body held so close to his own. It soaked through the layers of silk and linen that stood between them as if there was nothing there at all, bringing to mind a far more intimate act than a fully clothed kiss, but Joseph held back, hazily aware that Isabelle was no pretty tavern girl in search of a good time. She was a lady, and a lady who saw something in him that he hardly saw himself, and he owed her more than to give in to the desire that coursed through him as powerful and unstoppable as the tide. For all a fierce longing to carry her to the bed tried to consume him he refused to give in, certain she would regret allowing such a liberty even if at present her instincts drove her on.

With painful regret Joseph pulled back, moving his hands to cradle her face between his callused palms. Her breathing was as ragged as his and her cheeks a brilliant scarlet, although as she met his eye the half-defiant gleam in hers tempted him to throw caution to the wind and pull her to him once more.

'That wasn't quite what I was expecting.'

'No. No doubt you thought me far too proper to do something so bold.'

Isabelle's voice was slightly hoarse and Joseph knew his own was no steadier, roughened by the desire he was still struggling to fight. A distinctly ungentlemanly ache had begun somewhere low down, and despite Isabelle's defiance he imagined she'd be mortified to realise it, a world of difference between a kiss and the activity he was trying to be careful not to let cross his mind. There might not be any love in her shocking proposal, but apparently physical attraction was another matter, her gaze straying back down to linger on his lips even as she carefully moved out of his reach.

'I would never behave like that with a man I wasn't entirely committed to. I hope that was enough to convince you how serious I am about the idea of a match.'

She took another step away, sideways this time, to bring her closer to the door, and Joseph moved aside to let her pass. Her shoulder brushed his chest with a feather-light touch but he felt it all the way down to his boots, so attuned to her presence that even the accidental graze of fabric against fabric stirred him.

'I'll be waiting for your answer. Whatever you decide, I hope you know that you'll always have my thanks for everything you've done—and my friendship, should you want it, even if after we've returned home we never see each other again.'

She dipped her head, her flaxen hair much darker in the gloom, and with quiet footsteps she was gone, leaving Joseph to close his door and sink wordlessly into the chair she had so recently vacated.

Chapter Seven

The return journey was uneventful—or at least so it would have appeared to anybody watching the mismatched trio making its way back down south. By some wordless agreement neither the mercenary nor the Duchess mentioned the unfinished business between them, and by the time the post carriage reached Bishops Morton Joseph might have thought he'd imagined the whole thing had the memory of Isabelle's kiss not lingered so vividly on his lips.

Her attention had remained fixed on her sister for the duration, save for a couple of snatched sideways glances when she'd thought he wasn't looking, and as the carriage began to slow he wondered if she would speak before they went their separate ways.

Not that there's much else for her to say. She painted a very clear picture and now it's down to me to think how to reply.

The cold air came as a relief after the unpleasant warmth of the crowded carriage, and Joseph took a

deep breath as he stepped out onto the cobbles. Soon
he would be back in his rooms at the Drake, at last putting some distance between himself and Isabelle, and
frankly their separation couldn't come soon enough.
It was impossible to think clearly when she was in
front of him, her full lips inviting him to recall how
he'd traced their softness with his own, and he took a
moment to gather his resolve before turning to hand
her down the steps.

She accepted his help with a minuscule hesitation
nobody else would have noticed, although Joseph saw
her cheeks flush with sudden colour when she slipped
her fingers into his palm.

'Thank you.'

He nodded, refusing to acknowledge how the feel
of her slender fingers scattered sparks in his gut. She
withdrew her hand almost at once, perhaps just as
affected by the deceptively chaste touch as he was,
and he swiftly reached up for Marina, thankful that
the girl's presence saved him from having to find a
response.

'Will you need escorting home?'

To his relief, Isabelle shook her head. 'No, thank
you. I sent ahead for a couple of my manservants to
meet us here.'

She gestured towards a pair of men emerging from
the shadows. 'They'll take care of our luggage and
anything else we need.'

'Very well.' Pulling his coat around himself, Joseph gave her a curt nod, followed by a matching one for Marina. 'If there's nothing more you require of me, I'll bid you ladies goodnight.'

Marina dipped him a graceful curtsey, although he barely noticed. It seemed everything else came a poor second when Isabelle was near, and she was all he could focus on as she came a half-step closer, one hand reaching out as if to touch his arm before she changed her mind and let it fall back to her side.

'You'll come to call on us soon, I hope. We need to discuss your payment…if nothing else.'

She looked up at him, the angles of her face suddenly brilliantly illuminated by the moon bursting from behind a cloud. It made her eyes shine like precious jewels, uncertainty clear in them but holding his gaze nonetheless, and Joseph had to bite the inside of his cheek in a warning to himself not to try to pull her into his arms. The burning kiss that had set his heart leaping had been bestowed as proof of her *intentions*, not her *feelings*, and any attempt to repeat it—in public or in private—would surely be pushing her a step too far.

Joseph cleared his throat, belatedly realising he was frowning. It must look like impatience, but in reality it was the effort of controlling the desire to bend and capture her mouth.

With some difficulty he relaxed his brow. 'I'll be there, Your Grace. As soon as I can.'

* * *

It seemed half of Bishop Morton's hidden under-class was in the Drake when Joseph ducked through the low door and into the dimly lit tavern. The room was thronged with people, and he had to nudge a few aside with his bag to push his way towards the bar.

The landlord looked up at Joseph's approach, al-though he didn't pause in wiping a tankard with an increasingly grubby cloth. 'Back again, then?'

'As you see. Any messages?'

'Over there.'

He jerked his head towards a small pile of envelopes stacked on a shelf behind the bar and Joseph reached for them, shuffling through them like a deck of cards as with one foot he hooked out a stool and dropped heavily onto its worn leather seat. The choice he had to make wouldn't leave him alone, and he stared un-seeing down at the various unfamiliar handwritings, only aware of a presence at his elbow when he heard the landlord speak.

'I've already told you: we only do credit for cus-tomers who pay their bills. Come in with money and *then* I'll serve you—not before.'

'No need to get excited. It's no crime to ask.'

Joseph glanced briefly at the man standing beside him, more out of instinct than interest. His hair was greying beneath a shabby cap and he leaned on a cane, but his face wasn't as old as one might have imagined and something about it struck Joseph as vaguely familiar. For a moment he couldn't place it and he was about to shrug the thought off when the man turned to leave, a spark of recognition kindling alongside his ill temper as he looked at Joseph for the first time.

'Carter? I'll be damned. I hadn't thought you'd still be alive.'

He smiled—not a particularly pleasant smile, but it helped Joseph identify him nonetheless. A trio of missing teeth was the clincher, and Joseph felt recognition dawn as the name of his fellow mercenary at last swam up from the depths.

'McAvoy. I didn't know you worked in these parts.'

'I don't. The only work I can get now is on the street and there's precious little of it. Got this to thank for that.'

The other man tapped his right leg with his cane and, peering downwards, Joseph saw why. It was twisted, as if from a badly healed break, and he was surprised to feel a faint gleam of pity where once he would have remained unmoved. He hadn't particularly liked McAvoy when they'd known each other years before, but for some reason he found it difficult to retreat behind his usual indifference.

Perhaps Isabelle was to blame, suggesting there might be a better man inside him just waiting to get out, or perhaps it was the fact that her face loomed so large in his mind it made all sensible thought nearly impossible. Whatever the reason, he heard himself speaking before he'd fully decided to, acting on some impulse he had rarely felt before.

'If you're out of money I don't mind buying you a drink. And some food, I suppose, if you want it. Seems a shame to leave with an empty belly on a night as cold as this.'

He kept his voice rough, but all the same unease circled as McAvoy's eyebrows rose. 'You've changed your tune. Used to be you never did anything for anyone—unless you were paid to.'

The other mercenary eyed him closely, with the slight mistrust all men of their profession soon learned.

'What happened? Have you gone soft?'

Joseph stiffened. The comment was closer to the bone than he liked. 'Are you taking the offer or not? Don't do me any favours.'

As he'd hoped, McAvoy let the matter drop. He pulled out the stool beside Joseph's, hardly letting his trousers touch the seat before he was giving the landlord his order. The lure of a free pie and ale was far more interesting to him than whatever might be happening in Joseph Carter's head and Joseph was glad of it, unwilling to explain his motives to another person when he could barely manage to explain them to himself.

Is it Isabelle's influence wearing me down? Making me softer, just as I feared?

He set his jaw, unwilling to look the unwelcome thought in the eye. Before he'd met Isabelle he'd been just as McAvoy claimed: cool and unapproachable, and looking to his wallet before anything else. Now, however, the Duchess seemed to be getting under his skin, her unfamiliar concern for him just as enticing as the deer-like set of her eyes.

The idea of having somebody in his life who genuinely cared for him was something he hadn't realised he wanted, and for all his determined cynicism the goodness in her seemed to call to something buried deep down inside him to respond in kind—whether he wanted to or not. His entire life he'd coached himself to be tough and unyielding—his very livelihood depended on his ability to shut himself off—and it suddenly occurred to him that unless he tried harder to reject the humanity she'd encouraged him to show he might find himself with nothing left to sell.

Unless, of course, I accept her offer. Then I wouldn't need to...

'What are those? More cries for help from people with more money than sense?'

McAvoy poked at the pile of envelopes with a gravy-covered knife and at Joseph's affirmative grunt sagely shook his head.

'Take my advice. Find something else.'

'Something else?'

'Something other than fighting. While you still can.'

The other man took a gulp of ale, wiping his mouth with the back of a scar-knotted hand. He could only be a couple of years Joseph's senior but he looked at least a decade more, hard living and poor circumstances having aged him far too fast, and an echo of the pity Joseph had felt before came again as he studied the ravages a violent life had left on McAvoy's face.

'Nobody is invincible—you never know which job will be your last. As I say, get out before it's too late.'

The ex-mercenary shook his head again, perhaps misinterpreting Joseph's silence as disregard.

'Don't believe me? *This* was supposed to be an easy one.' He patted his misshapen leg with an air of bitterness. 'No risk at all. Just escorting some young lady to meet her sweetheart after dark—until her husband showed up, waving a pistol around. Shot clean through the bone. The mend went wrong, leaving me with this accursed limp... I was the best, but now who wants to hire a mercenary who can barely walk?'

He gave Joseph a significant look before returning to his pie, evidently feeling he'd dispensed enough wisdom for one day, and Joseph didn't try to stop him. The bleak words had hit their target and he considered them now, picking them apart as he pretended to read the notes spread out on the bar.

McAvoy was right. Their chosen field was a dangerous one, as he had always known, but he'd never been confronted with such tangible proof as the man sitting beside him. McAvoy was the walking—now limping—embodiment of a mercenary's worst fear: losing the vigour that was all he had to trade, and even the thought made Joseph's blood run cold. He'd built his whole life around the belief that his only asset was his strength, and if he lost that he would have nothing, just an empty husk reduced to scrabbling for whatever scraps he could find.

I said I'd never beg again. That's one thing I swore I'd never do.

He gripped the letter he was holding, coming close to crumpling it in his fist. He'd never forgotten the shame of those upper-class faces turning away from his desperation, his contempt for the *ton* stemming from that one day when he was just a child. Ever since that moment he'd known he would never give them anything for free and the idea of being maimed in their service was more than he could stand, sick of risking his life for people who didn't care whether he lived or died so long as they got their money's worth first.

But Isabelle was different.

He was coming to believe that she didn't see him merely as a beast of burden. For some reason she thought there was more to him than that, and he was no longer able to deny he liked the way it felt. If he accepted her offer it would mean having to walk among the people he'd made up his mind to despise, but her argument had been so persuasive that resistance seemed almost futile, McAvoy's disfigurement and Isabelle's blistering kiss working in tandem to help him make up his mind. Having a wife and a young sister-in-law depending on him was something he never would have imagined, but suddenly it seemed a fair price to pay for his independence, for no longer being bound to look to others for the means to survive.

It would mean living with Isabelle, though. Seeing her every day, knowing you'll risk coming to feel things for her she would never think to return...

His growing respect for the unorthodox Duchess was a problem, and not one he had any idea how to solve. If it had been just her face and figure he appreciated he imagined he could have overcome it easily enough, but it was the way she made him *feel* that was far harder to understand.

From the moment his mother abandoned him he hadn't known kindness from anyone, and it was hard to think how to react to Isabelle's bewildering concern, his only certainty that she hadn't intended to make him so confused. She'd asked him to marry her because she *needed* a husband, not *wanted* one, and just because she trusted him enough to choose him as her business partner didn't mean her regard went any deeper than that.

All the same...

The feel of her body pressing against him, rousing him in ways—and places—it would be vulgar to admit came back to him as he sat on the threadbare stool, oblivious to the smoke and noise that surrounded him. Her kiss had lit a taper and it still smouldered now, stubbornly resisting any attempt to douse its heat with reason, and the fact he realised he *wanted* to help her only added fuel to the fire. He could try to tell himself it was out of calculation—just a mercenary's willingness to act if the price was right—but he'd be lying to himself. Somehow Isabelle had begun to pry beneath the mask he'd worn for over twenty years and as Joseph stood up, gathering the letters in a suddenly decisive fist, he could only pray he wouldn't regret letting her try.

There was a fine fire blazing in the tavern's wide hearth and it took Joseph only a few strides to reach it. Without pausing to think he bent down, thrusting the handful of letters into the flames, and then he watched them burn, their edges blackening as they curled in on themselves and whatever was written was reduced to ash.

The sun was bright and the morning air bracingly cold as Isabelle walked back to Winford House. Marina had been too tired to join her at church and Isabelle hated that she'd hesitated for a moment at the idea of leaving her sister at home, fleetingly worried that something might happen before she'd pulled herself together. Clearly it would be some time until she could put their unwanted adventure behind her, although until she received Joseph's answer there was no hope of getting much sleep.

She'd lain awake for the past two nights and not even being back in her own bed had helped her drift off, the memory of Joseph's lips bearing down on hers jolting her awake every time she'd closed her eyes. Her breathing quickened again now just thinking about it, and she deliberately tried to slow it down, finding a polite smile for a couple of passers-by who respectfully tipped their hats. There were quite a few people out for a stroll, wrapped up warm to take advantage of the sunshine, although one particular individual coming towards her from the opposite end of the street caught her eye at once.

There could be no mistaking Joseph's towering form, and yet Isabelle found herself needing a second look to make doubly sure it was him.

If not for the distinctive breadth of shoulder beneath his elegant new coat she might have thought it was a gentleman bearing down on her rather than a gruff mercenary, so bewilderingly smart that he seemed another person entirely from the one she knew. In a tall black hat that gleamed in the sun and with his boots polished to a mirror shine there was no chance any well-bred onlooker would guess his true station, and Isabelle couldn't help but stare as she saw him notice her, feeling her stomach flip as a lightning-fast expression crossed his face too quickly for him to hide. To her surprise the firm set of his features seemed to soften for an instant before his usual sternness returned, the whole thing over so swiftly she couldn't be sure of what she'd seen.

She could be more certain of her *own* reaction, however. Heat had flared in her cheeks the second she'd recognised him, and it didn't recede as he stopped in front of her, folding into the most genuine bow she'd ever seen him make.

'Isa— *Your Grace*, I was just on my way to call on you.'

Isabelle gazed at him, her brain trailing a couple of beats behind. For a moment all she could focus on was the movement of his lips as he spoke and she hurriedly dropped a curtsey, hoping none of the upper-class passers-by—or indeed Joseph—had noticed how her face glowed like the setting sun.

'How kind of you, Mr Carter. I was taking a walk after church.'

She hesitated, painfully aware her mouth had run dry at seeing him so unexpectedly well-dressed, so stylish he would now only turn heads among the *ton* for the right reasons. He must be coming to give her his answer, and her heart began to thump even harder than it was already. Her future was in the palm of his hand and the time had come for her to learn which way he had jumped, all the fretting of the past two days about to reach its conclusion.

It was impossible to tell by his face what his decision was and, forcing herself to think quickly, Isabelle made a bold choice.

'Perhaps you'd care to accompany me? I thought a turn about the park would be pleasant in this sun.'

To her relief she'd managed to sound almost normal, her feeling of reprieve increasing at Joseph's nod. It would be infinitely easier to talk to him side by side rather than face-on, the thought of sitting opposite him across a tea table more than she could currently bear. While her heart raced and she flushed poppy-red she would rather he saw as little of her as possible, and she surreptitiously tweaked her bonnet a shade lower to hide the colour in her cheeks.

'It would be my pleasure, Your Grace.'

He stepped aside to let her pass and then walked beside her, shortening his stride—with some difficulty—to match hers. From that angle she could only catch glimpses of him as he outpaced her bonnet, but nothing could make her completely immune to his presence as she tried to find something to say.

At last there was a lull in the number of people walking past them and she seized the opportunity to break what she feared might become an uncomfortable silence.

'Two *Your Graces* in the space of two sentences? I never know which manner of address you'll use from one moment to the next.'

She heard his short laugh. 'I didn't think you'd appreciate me calling you Isabelle in public. Onlookers might think I was being overly familiar.'

'How thoughtful of you.'

'I manage not to be a complete oaf on occasion. At least once or twice a year.'

'You certainly don't look like one, at least. I've never seen you so smart.'

There was a brief hesitation before Joseph answered. 'I thought I'd better dress respectably if I was to call on you at home. I wouldn't want anyone to suspect you of mixing with undesirables.'

His reasoning caught her sharply beneath the ribs. That he had gone to the effort of wearing what, for him, amounted to a disguise had to mean something—didn't it? If he had come to call on her wearing his usual clothing he would have stuck out a mile among the stylish *ton*—something that wouldn't have bothered him unless he had cause to want to blend in. Perhaps he merely didn't want to expose her to ridicule, or perhaps it was a clue to whatever decision he was about to impart; it was so damnably hard to tell, and the quiet between them returned as they approached the wrought-iron gates gleaming at them from the end of the street.

The park was Bishop Morton's crowning glory, its evergreen hedges and wide lawns shining emerald in the sunshine. It was a place to see and be seen—although Isabelle had already made up her mind to find as private a spot as possible. The conversation they were about to have wasn't one she wanted overheard, her anxiety building as she wondered once again what the outcome would be. The potentials flitted through her mind like a procession of swooping birds, chasing each other in ever decreasing spirals, and they distracted her enough not to remember to push her bonnet back before stepping into the road.

'Careful!'

Joseph's hand closed around hers and jerked her onto the pavement just as a young man on horseback cantered past, riding far more quickly than he should have been. The horse's glossy flanks flashed mere inches from Isabelle's nose and she reeled backwards, the firm grip on her hand not relaxing for a second as she found herself leaning against a broad, firm chest.

For one frenzied heartbeat she couldn't move. Flustered by the near-miss, she felt her chest rising and falling quickly, but it was the warmth of Joseph's body that refused to let her stand up straight. It was the same heat that had passed between them when she'd kissed him and her mind leaped to revisit that scene, something they could so easily recreate now if she turned to look up into his face...

'Damn it, Isabelle. On the night we met you assured me you could cross a street unassisted. Am I to assume that was a lie?'

She straightened up at once, hurriedly pushing herself away from him to shake out her crumpled skirt.

'*You* try wearing a bonnet,' she muttered, praying her desires hadn't shown on her face. 'They can make it difficult to see sometimes.'

He was still holding her left hand and she tried to withdraw it, but Joseph didn't loosen his grip. Instead Isabelle had to bite down on a sharp breath as he carefully placed it in the crook of his elbow, her fingers held in position by the swell of a bicep too large to ignore.

'I think it might be safer for both of us if you take my arm. Between fast-galloping horses and the frost on the ground there's a chance you might get yourself killed before we've had our *discussion*.'

There was an undercurrent of dry amusement in his tone, but it couldn't completely conceal the unconscious emphasis he'd placed on the final word. For all he might pretend nonchalance, it was clear he was just as preoccupied with their imminent conversation as she was, although the broad forearm under Isabelle's fingertips managed to draw a little of her attention away from what was to come.

She was so close to him that her shoulder brushed the sleeve of his coat as he began to lead her away and she felt the solid muscle beneath, faintly glad her face couldn't burn any hotter at the reminder of the sculpted form she knew lay hidden under his shirt. If he accepted her bargain she might be expected to get to know that chiselled body even better, she realised, and she stumbled as a fleeting image flashed through her mind.

Joseph stretched out against her pillows, his shirt hanging open just as it had that night at the inn, and then rising up on one elbow to reach for her as she approached the bed, his eyes dark as a hungry smile curved his lips...

'Careful on this frost. Apparently I was right to think you might lose your footing.'

Joseph's voice pulled her back from the brink, and

with instinctive horror Isabelle snatched a glance up at his face. She'd be mortified if any hint of what she was thinking betrayed her, but he didn't seem to have noticed anything was amiss, his sharp profile composed as they moved through the park gates and she looked quickly away again before he could see her agitation. The image lingered, however, the picture of his burning eyes searing itself into her mind, and beneath the cover of her cloak she pressed her free hand against the rapidly moving bodice of her gown.

Control yourself. You're on the cusp of a conversation that could very well shape the rest of your life and all you can think of is bedrooms? As if there aren't more important things!

The green majesty of the park surrounded them now and a couple strolled past—a captain and his equally stylish wife—and Isabelle was forced to find a strained smile to answer their greeting. She saw them cast a curious but not suspicious look at Joseph before the Captain tipped his hat—a gesture that, to her surprise, Joseph returned with only the barest hesitation. Evidently he was able to hide his contempt for the upper classes when he chose, although she was still too shaken by her own wanton thoughts to focus on much else.

Would he expect her to grant him such liberties if they married? Edwin never would have dreamed of touching her, but Joseph… The way he had drawn her closer after she'd kissed him did *not* speak of a man with innocent intentions. His hands had closed in her hair and around her waist and he had pressed her against the hard planes of his body as if they might merge into one, his clever mouth so skilled it had made her head spin.

While she had spent the last decade going to bed alone it was clear he had not, his touch too expert not to have been honed by considerable practice. If he wanted their marriage to be physical, rather than a formality, it would be something she had never experienced before… but as he drew her towards a secluded bench, surrounded by a discreet semi-circle of trees, she realised she would be all too willing to learn.

That's if he agrees, however. There's no point getting carried away before he's even given his answer.

Her hand still lay on Joseph's arm, and Isabelle prayed it wouldn't tremble when he released it, quickly sinking down onto the bench before her legs could give way. He sat beside her, the wooden seat not big enough to afford either of them much room, and her breath caught at the friction of his shoulder brushing against her own. It felt as though each was waiting for the other to speak, a tense quiet descending broken only by the sound of the trees stirring in a cold breeze.

It was Isabelle who gave in to the strain first.

'So… I imagine you were intending to call on me to give me your answer?'

'That's correct. I've given your proposal a lot of consideration. At first I thought it was madness, but having had some time to think…'

Joseph paused with uncharacteristic uncertainty. He didn't turn his head, but Isabelle thought she caught his eyes flick in her direction. Her own were fixed forward, while her heart beat so hard she could hear the blood rushing in her ears. Once he'd finished speaking she would know her fate, and her chest tightened to admit how much she hoped he would accept.

Do you wish it for Marina's sake alone, though? Or for yours as well?

A shiver seized her that the cold wind played no part in. This was hardly the time to confront something as pointless as feelings and she immediately slammed the brakes on that train of thought, bringing it to a screeching halt.

If for some reason she allowed herself to be distracted it could only end badly. Their whole acquaintance was a transaction, after all: even if Joseph *was* coming to like her more, he was still a mercenary, with money his motive, and she would be foolish indeed to entertain hopes of anything more.

He was speaking again, and with an effort Isabelle concentrated on what he was saying, trying to ignore the iron fist that had taken hold of her stomach and begun to squeeze.

'As I said… Now I've had time to think, I can see its advantages. If the offer still stands…and with the same terms… I accept.'

All the breath left Isabelle's body. 'You accept? Truly?'

At last forcing herself to look at him, she caught his brief nod. His face was set, as if to be purposely difficult to decipher, but she thought she saw something flit through his eyes, vanishing in the next moment to leave behind nothing but his usual steady gaze. Clearly he had no intention of sharing whatever he was thinking, and she wished her own face could be more opaque, the jumble of her spinning feelings probably written large for him to see.

'You don't know what a relief it is to hear you say that.'

It wasn't *only* relief that coursed through her, however, although she would never admit what else his verdict had set whirling through her head. A tangled web of secret pleasure, apprehension and alarm was weaving itself inside her, each thread pulling her in a different direction while she tried to maintain some outward semblance of composure. She was going to *marry* Joseph, actually *live* with him as man and wife, and the reality of what that meant was so overwhelming she could hardly bring herself to speak.

There were too many aspects to consider—*Where will he sleep? What will having him under my roof truly be like?*—but it was her new fiancé who asked the most important question.

His mouth was moving, the roaring in her ears louder than ever but his words managing to fight through.

'I said, have you told your sister?'

Isabelle shook her head, distantly worried that it might fall off her shoulders. 'Not yet. I didn't know what your answer would be, and now… I'd like her to get to know you a little before I suddenly announce you're to be her new brother. As far as she's concerned, you appeared out of nowhere in the middle of the night.'

Joseph exhaled wryly. 'Understandable. Any announcement will be made only when you're ready. But will she mind? Her sister wedding a mercenary, I mean?'

'She doesn't know your profession. All I've told her so far is that you're a friend. But…'

Isabelle paused, risking another glance up at Joseph's face. His gaze was as even as ever, as if they'd just agreed to go and see a play together rather than enter into marriage, and only the rapid tick of the pulse visible just above his collar betrayed he wasn't quite as unruffled as he seemed.

'I think she'll be pleased. She feels the house is too big just for the two of us, and besides…she misses my husband. In the absence of him and our father, she'd like to feel there's a man around whom she can trust.'

Joseph's expression sharpened. 'And you think that can be me?'

At her faint nod he leaned back, the bench shifting slightly as he moved. Tracing the line of his lower lip with his thumb he looked deep in thought, a slight frown making him almost fierce although still so handsome that Isabelle couldn't tear herself away.

'I've never met someone with as much confidence in my merit as you. It makes me wonder...'

'Wonder what?'

He slowly shook his head and Isabelle felt her heart turn over as he sat upright again, never breaking the suddenly taut contact of their eyes. They were already close enough to touch, but now Joseph seemed to draw nearer still, as gradually and carefully as one might approach a wild bird, and the commotion in Isabelle's mind petered out into silence as she watched his gaze flicker down to her mouth.

Evidently her unthinking words had spoken to him far more deeply than she'd intended, but she had no idea what they had said, too entranced by the gleam in his eyes to waste thought on anything else.

'Many things. It makes me wonder many things I've never thought about before.'

He was so close she could have reached out and traced his hard jawline and the desire to do so flared like a lit match, making the embers his nearness had already kindled burst into flame. He wanted to kiss her, of that she was sure—and she was equally certain she would let him if he tried. His movements were deliberate, slow and measured to give her time to flee if she chose, but as he bent his head to find her mouth she knew she would not. Against all odds it seemed something was growing between them—

a powerful physical attraction, if nothing else, and a tiny voice at the very back of Isabelle's mind ventured that it was better than nothing as she allowed her eyes to drift closed…

The sound of footsteps far too close by sent her flying to her feet, only just in time managing to straighten her bonnet before a veritable parade of wealthy ladies came gliding past the secluded bench.

Joseph leapt up likewise, following her lead, and she felt a pulse of wild panic as the ladies dropped into a flurry of curtseys, coming up smiling but every curious eye trained on the handsome stranger none had seen before.

'Good morning, Your Grace. A beautiful day, is it not?'

The leader of the group—a matriarchal type well known for her interest in other people's business—was the first to speak. Her question was aimed at Isabelle but her gaze hardly wavered from Joseph's face, clearly wondering who such an attractive young man could be, and Isabelle groped hurriedly for a reply.

'Indeed it is. The perfect weather for a walk.'

She smiled—probably rigidly, but her face felt far too hot to co-operate fully. If she'd been caught kissing Joseph it would mean her immediate disgrace and an abrupt end to her plans, and only the older woman's waiting expression made her realise she'd allowed the expectant pause to go on for a fraction too long.

Hastily she gestured at Joseph, hoping the colour in her cheeks wouldn't give her away.

'I don't think you will have met my friend. May I introduce Mr Carter? He's… He is…'

'Very recently arrived in Bishops Morton. Good morning, ladies.'

Joseph's bow was so accomplished Isabelle could barely believe him capable of it, but it hit its mark. His audience fluttered delightedly and Isabelle was hardly unmoved herself, feeling the flush beneath her skin burning hotter at this suavity she hadn't known he possessed.

When she didn't speak, Joseph went on, only the barest flicker of a glance in her direction betraying his unease at the unblinking attention of some of the *ton*'s finest.

'This is my first week in town. I'd been living abroad, and when on my return to England I learned the Duke of Elmbridge had passed away I came at once to give my condolences to Her Grace.'

Another glance was Isabelle's cue to nod vigorously. How Joseph had managed to think of a suitable cover so quickly was beyond her, but a sympathetic murmur from the group confirmed its acceptance.

'Yes. A very sad loss.'

The self-elected spokeswoman's sigh would have been more convincing if her eyes weren't so alight with interest. 'Were you well acquainted with the Duke, sir? To come so quickly after hearing the news?'

'We met many years ago on some business I've long forgotten, although I'm afraid I neglected the connection while I was abroad. I hope to make amends for that neglect now by offering my service to Her Grace.'

Isabelle's eyes widened at such a bare-faced lie, delivered without a half-second's hesitation. He spoke so smoothly, so convincingly, that for a moment she almost believed the outrageous falsehood herself. He was far more skilled at thinking on his feet than she was, although her amazement didn't stop her from noticing the smiles from a couple of the ladies that suggested they would be all too happy to accept his service if she declined the offer.

One of them piped up now, her head tilted in a co-quettish manner Isabelle found she didn't quite like.

'What was it that had taken you overseas, Mr Carter? Anything exciting?'

'Adventuring, madam. Exploring foreign lands and learning more about the world around us.'

Once again Joseph's answer was more creative than accurate but stated with a perfectly straight face, and once again it was accepted with coy eagerness.

'How *fascinating.*'

The speaker gazed up at him—perhaps somewhat *too* intently—and Isabelle sensed his manfully concealed discomfort. Clearly his forced confidence only stretched so far, and it felt like a reprieve when the matriarch sank into another curtsey.

'It was a pleasure to see you, Your Grace, and to

meet you, Mr Carter, but we must continue. We're expected at Lady Albright's, and it wouldn't do to keep her waiting.'

'Of course.' Isabelle nodded graciously, sweeping a curtsey of her own to conceal her obvious relief. 'Good morning.'

The older woman walked on, her followers falling into place behind her. When the last skirt had flicked away around the corner Isabelle let out a deep breath.

'That was very well done. You've sown exactly the right kind of seeds—your tall tales will be all over town in a matter of hours.'

Joseph frowned doubtfully, tugging the knot of his cravat away from his neck. 'That's a good thing?'

'Of course. You managed to charm some of the most fashionable ladies in Bishops Morton—and if they're impressed by you others are sure to follow. I hadn't thought you could be so agreeable, but I'm glad to be proved wrong.'

'As I told you… I'm not a complete oaf *all* the time.'

He sounded unsure whether to be insulted or proud, and Isabelle turned away to hide the twitch of her lips. A swarm of bees still resided in her stomach from their almost-kiss, but she had regained control of herself. The interruption of Joseph's new admirers had given her time to recover her wits—even if her legs *did* still feel slightly weak when he came to stand beside her, looking down at her with an expression she couldn't possibly read.

'I ought to return home. Marina will be waiting, and I need to start work as soon as possible now we've broken cover.'

'Work?'

At Joseph's narrowed eyes Isabelle clarified. 'Gradually introducing you as my new suitor. You started well today, but there's still much more to do. Will you come again tomorrow? Marina and I will be walking, and it'll be a good opportunity for you to be seen with us, as well as for her to know you better. As I said before, I don't want her to be taken by surprise when the announcement is made.'

'Very well.'

Joseph's hand had returned to his cravat and Isabelle tried not to watch as he loosened it, revealing a tantalising glimpse of tanned throat.

'I don't wish to go to the *ton*'s haunts—no dances or theatres or any other place where I'll be trapped in a corner with some braying admiral—but a park I will grant you.'

'Thank you. I appreciate your co-operation. There's just one more thing…'

His dry huff of a laugh suggested that she'd already asked quite enough of him for one day, but he didn't try to stop her as she hurried on.

'You'll need to take some respectable lodgings. I'm afraid no acknowledged friend of a duchess can reside at the Drake, and now your name is connected with mine you can't be seen frequenting that kind of establishment. If you take rooms in a respectable hotel I'll settle the bill.'

'You will not.'

Joseph folded his arms, suddenly as solid and immovable as a mountain. 'I have my own money. Perhaps once we are wed I'll spend yours, but not before—and that's final, *Your Grace.*'

Isabelle opened her mouth, but closed it again almost at once. There was no point in arguing. If he had made up his mind then it was indeed final, the provocative use of her title now a strange joke between them where once it had been annoying in the extreme.

'Well... I suppose if you've made your decision...'

'I have, and I'll thank you to accept it.'

Joseph's dark smile sent a current of something through her. There was nothing more to say now that their business was concluded, and it struck Isabelle that it would be dangerous to linger, her self-control already woefully undermined by a single glance of those hazel eyes down towards her lips.

'Until tomorrow, then. Around the same time as today?'

Under normal circumstances she might have offered him her hand, but that, too, seemed ill advised. His touch made her do things she knew she shouldn't and the park was too full of people to risk another slip. If she let him kiss her hand she might lose her head and pull him down for a real one; and so with a short nod she turned and walked away, hoping despite all good sense that he was watching her go.

Chapter Eight

One or two voices in the packed church muttered that the former Duchess's remarriage had come about somewhat quickly—almost a year to the day since the expiry of her first husband—but for the most part it was curiosity rather than disapproval that drew so many onlookers that bright spring morning.

She'd spent her youth tied to a man old enough to be her father, nursing him devotedly throughout his various illnesses, and most of the congregation judged that it seemed churlish to condemn her for turning to such a handsome replacement now she was finally free. There was little reason to expect her to wait, after all. She'd been sufficiently devastated by the old Duke's death as to garner the sympathy of the *ton*, their blessing not required but nevertheless it made Isabelle's mind slightly easier as she took Joseph's arm and allowed him to lead her back down the aisle and towards the church's open doors.

Emerging out into the sunshine, she found a smile

for the well-wishers clustered around the steps, accepting their compliments with a curtsey as pretty as the small bouquet she clutched to her chest. That they had decided to look upon the match with a friendly eye was a victory: she'd wed solely to minimise the risk of scandal, not court it, although it was difficult to remember that fact as she looked up at her new husband.

Joseph's back was straight and his shoulders squared, a faint crease between his brows the only sign that he still wasn't entirely comfortable with being surrounded by the best and brightest of Bishop Morton society, and Isabelle felt another flutter ripple through her. It mirrored the one that had taken hold when she'd stood at the top of the aisle, looking towards the altar where he'd waited for her to approach, so tall and handsome in his smartest coat that she'd hardly been able to move. Only knowing that so many pairs of eyes were upon her had forced her legs into action, each step taking an effort nobody watching would have suspected, and when she'd finally reached him it had come as the strangest relief to stand at his side.

Their marriage might be nothing more than a convenient arrangement designed for the benefit of both, but somehow it had felt like something else as he'd slipped the ring onto her finger and vowed to be hers until death, the unwavering seriousness in his hazel eyes coming back to her now to make Isabelle almost lose her footing on the worn stone steps.

Joseph's bicep tightened under her lace-gloved fingers, just hard enough for her to regain her balance. It was the smallest of movements but it cast sparks into her already knotted stomach, caught between her helpless reaction to his closeness and the enormity of the leap they had just taken together.

And so now I am Mrs Carter. From duchess to mercenary's wife in a matter of minutes—and I can only hope we don't come to regret it.

The thought made her catch a breath, but she couldn't risk letting her uncertainty show. Their inquisitive onlookers were still watching, avid gazes moving from Isabelle's blushing face to Joseph's set one, and if she hadn't been keeping herself under such tight control she might have been amused by their oblivious acceptance. A few very public walks and the rapid chatter of the ladies they had encountered in the park had been enough to set the wheels of Joseph's respectability in motion, and once ensconced in the plush surroundings of the Mayland Hotel his good standing had seemed set in stone.

Every time she'd gone out to take tea Isabelle had been careful to mention her new friend, embellishing his story until his name and exotic travels were known all over town, and the day she'd overheard him described in the haberdasher's shop as a 'gentleman explorer' was the day she'd known they had done the impossible: turned a mercenary into a man eligible enough to court a duchess, and nobody had the first clue they had been duped.

'Shall we return to Winford House?'

The intrepid adventurer himself glanced down at her question, his eyes shining almost green in the cold sunshine.

'Please. I'm not sure how much more I can take of being stared at.'

Fortunately he'd bothered to lower his voice, and Isabelle's nape prickled at its gravelly cadence. He didn't like *'her kind'* and probably never would—although she appreciated the attempts he had made over the past six weeks to make it marginally less obvious. If their arrangement was to have the desired result he would have to be a significant figure in Marina's life—enough of a presence to deter any man with evil designs—and if he looked to despise everything about their situation it would invite scrutiny they didn't wish to encourage.

Glancing over her shoulder, Isabelle picked her sister out of the crowd and beckoned her closer. 'Marina. We're going back to Winford now.'

Marina nodded, her face still alight with the same excitement she'd shown since the moment she had woken that morning. Being a bridesmaid was the most wonderful thing in the world to a girl of barely sixteen, as Isabelle well remembered, her sister's enthusiasm helping her to feel she'd made the right choice. Marina had been in full favour of the match, perhaps her grief at losing Edwin's steady presence making her readily accept another man taking up his mantle, and now, without even the slightest hesitation, she came forward to take hold of Joseph's other arm.

'Let's all go home.' She beamed up at him with absolutely no trace of the reserve most people might show to a giant they were still getting to know, her determined cheerfulness as always at the fore. 'You must be given a full tour before dinner, Joseph, now that Winford is your home, and then you'll tell me all about your time in the Mediterranean. I heard Mrs Crait in the milliner's talking about you last week, and the things she was saying about your time in Italy were thrilling!'

At once Isabelle looked to see his reaction. In her innocence Marina was as easy with him as she was with everybody else, and it crossed Isabelle's mind that he might object to the overfamiliarity of his new sister-in-law hanging off his arm as if they'd known each other for years rather than a few short weeks. He wasn't the most open of men, as she well knew, unlikely to appreciate Marina prying into his past, and she was about to intervene when he took her by surprise.

His dark eyebrows rose, but he didn't look annoyed, instead the merest suggestion of a smile playing about his lips. 'I'm not sure how this Mrs Crait knows any-thing about my visits to Italy, but I don't mind filling in the gaps...or at least some of them. Not every story is suitable for a young lady's ears, and I don't think your sister would thank me for sharing them with you.'

He didn't say anything more as they moved through the churchyard gate, a cold breeze chasing them with each step. Frost glittered on every roof of the houses and shops that lined the street beyond, and as they waited to cross the road Isabelle caught a glimpse of three shadowy reflections captured in an icy window—two small shapes flanking a much larger one that towered between them like a mighty oak. For a split-second she didn't make the connection, the fleeting image so unfamiliar it didn't immediately register who the figures might be, but a second look was enough to make her heart miss a beat.

With Marina on one arm and herself on the other Joseph looked for all the world like a devoted family man, and the transparent reflection of his face betrayed no impatience at having an upper-class lady pinned to each elbow.

We do look like a family. An unlikely one, it's true, but all the same...

Her heart thumped harder to make up for the skipped beat but it couldn't distract from a warm sensation building in her chest, managing to chase away the spring chill. With Joseph in her life she could at last begin again, knowing that Marina was safe from anyone who might try to use her for their own ends, and she could finally find a space to breathe after the months of unhappiness that had made her feel she'd aged ten years.

'Are you excited, Issy?'

Marina's voice broke into her wonderings and, peering past Joseph's broad shoulder, Isabelle found herself fixed by a pair of sparkling blue eyes. For one horrible moment she feared her face had given something away, but then her sister went on.

'To show Joseph around Winford and the grounds? There's so much he won't have seen!'

'Oh…yes. Of course.'

She could feel Joseph looking down at her but she didn't turn her head, pretending to concentrate on keeping her hem out of the mud as they turned into Bishop Morton's largest street. There was still a risk her countenance might give him a clue as to what she was really thinking and that was something she couldn't allow, the firm bicep beneath her fingertips already chipping away at her paper-thin self-control.

She wouldn't forget that Joseph had accepted their marriage as a true mercenary, trading his daunting presence for the chance of a better life. Doubtless he harboured none of the feelings that writhed like snakes beneath her bodice and she knew she ought to try harder to stamp them out before they escaped, her new husband entering into their agreement purely out of sense rather than sentiment. If she was coming to feel anything for him other than a respectful regard then she must keep it to herself: anything to achieve her objective of keeping Marina from harm, even if it meant turning her back on her own happiness in the process, and Isabelle tried to ignore a twinge in her chest as they approached Winford House's pristine front gate.

Marina's grand tour of the house and gardens took up much of the afternoon, and it wasn't until after supper that Joseph was allowed to retreat to what was now *his* study.

Isabelle watched him go with a mixture of vague amusement and relief. The poor man was clearly hoping for some respite from the relentless questions Marina had harried him with, ranging from his least favourite food to how he had collected each of the many scars on his hands. Not that the answers had been particularly enlightening... It seemed he was still determined to keep anything personal to himself, and other than a dislike of green olives she'd learned nothing of note about her new husband in spite of Marina's best efforts to draw him out.

Now, as she and her sister sat together in front of the parlour fire, Isabelle tried to relax, her nerves wound tight as a bowstring after such a taxing day.

There was still one hurdle left to jump, however, and the thought of it made any prospect of relaxation seem like a distant dream.

It's our wedding night. Will he be expecting...?

She tried to focus on her needlework, but the neat

stitches blurred with the tremor of her hand. It was an issue they *should* have discussed, making sure there could be no confusion, but how was she supposed to have brought it up? Her face would have burst into flames if she'd alluded to anything to do with bedrooms, and her memory of his bare chest in the firelight would no doubt have rushed in to make her stumble over the words. Besides, she could hardly risk appearing keen. It was vital Joseph had no idea that the thought of him lying on her bed had crossed her mind, and if she was the first to broach the subject he might guess the mortifying direction of her thoughts, already so unladylike she hardly recognised herself.

Curled beside her on the sofa, Marina yawned. 'I think I'll go to bed. Such an exciting day has made me so tired I can barely keep my eyes open.'

From somewhere Isabelle managed to dredge up a halfway convincing smile. 'I'll come up too. I need to check everything is as it should be in Joseph's rooms before he turns in.'

It should be safe enough, she thought as she got to her feet, feeling the tension in her back as she moved. Joseph was still in his study, and if she was quick she could make her survey without being seen. The temptation to stay well away was strong, but she had to resist—he was all but a stranger to Winford and as its mistress it was up to her to make sure his rooms were satisfactory, the master's quarters having lain empty since Edwin had last occupied them almost a year before.

Isabelle's mind turned to the Duke as she followed Marina up the grand main staircase to the second floor, where the corridor leading to the bedrooms stretched out in front of her. What would he have thought of her wild scheme, born out of the desire to protect her sister but now slowly shifting into something she didn't fully understand? He wouldn't have blamed her, she knew for certain—she was only acting as he had a decade before, marrying with the intention of keeping those he cared about safe, and he might even have been pleased that she was forming a deeper connection with the man who had taken his place. All Edwin had ever wanted was her happiness and Isabelle felt a lump rise in her throat as she glanced down at her fingers, her first wedding ring now shining on her right hand to make way for Joseph's on her left. All of a sudden her heart felt too full, sorrow for her losses warring against the blossoming regard for her new husband that she didn't dare admit, and she was glad when Marina disappeared into her own bedroom to leave Isabelle outside alone.

Trying to set her sparring emotions aside, she carried on to a door set further down the corridor. The sooner she completed her inspection the better, her apprehension again beginning to rise, and she briskly pushed open the door before she could talk herself out of stepping inside.

For one long, painful moment her heart stood still.

'Forgive me—I thought you were downstairs…in the study…'

Heat roared into her face as she watched Joseph turn towards her, rising from his chair beside the fire. In one hand he held a book, and it was that Isabelle focused on, too embarrassed to meet his questioning eye.

'I was. I decided to come up and read for a while. Is something the matter?'

Quickly she shook her head. 'No, not at all. I just wanted to check your rooms before you came to use them. The bed and…and so on.'

Immediately she felt her cheeks burn even hotter. Why had she mentioned the *bed*? It was the one word she should have avoided and yet there it was, slipping out of her mouth before she could stop it and coming dangerously close to giving away her true thoughts.

One of Joseph's dark eyebrows quivered and she rushed on, hating the unsteadiness of her voice. 'Have the servants put away all of your things?'

'There weren't many to put away, but yes. Thank you.'

'Good. I hope you'll be comfortable in here.'

'I'm sure I will. It's a good sight better than the rooms at the Drake, at any rate.'

He glanced around, his hazel eyes lingering on the tasteful wallpaper and plush rug beneath his boots, and abruptly it occurred to Isabelle that she wasn't the only one who would have to adjust to the change in her life. Joseph had entered a whole new domain, and it was for her to help him get used to it—if he would accept, of course, his determination to hold himself apart making that by no means a certainty. They were married now and yet she still knew so little about him, having only a few clues as to why he felt the way he did about the world, and as she hovered in the doorway she didn't know whether to stay or leave.

Probably he wants to be on his own. It's been a long day and no doubt he came upstairs for some time to himself, not imagining you'd burst in without even knocking.

Her subconscious was right, and Isabelle felt another sting of mortification. Striding into his room at the White Pheasant Inn had been one thing, but this was something very different. This was his home now just as much as it was hers and he had every right to expect privacy behind a closed door, and she was on the very brink of turning away when Joseph's voice called her back.

The moment he spoke Joseph didn't know why he'd done it—or so he told himself. Isabelle's hesitancy was obvious as she wavered on the threshold, and he was seized by the desire for her to stay a while longer. Her company as always far more agreeable to him than he knew was strictly safe, and today of all days he would defy any man not to want her to linger a few more minutes.

'How did you find today? Was it as you imagined?'

'Oh…' Isabelle paused in her retreat. 'More or less. What about you?'

'Far less painful than I envisaged. I thought there would be a wedding breakfast, where I'd be obliged to make small talk with various people I'd rather not, but somehow we managed to get away without one.'

To his surprise, a small, faintly triumphant smile lifted her lips. 'Yes. I made it known that my widowhood is too recent for me to countenance any kind of party. I said I wanted a quiet wedding out of respect for Edwin's memory—although in truth I knew you wouldn't enjoy being around the ladies and gentlemen of the *ton* for any longer than was strictly necessary.'

Joseph frowned. 'You did that on my account?'

'Of course. I may not know the exact details of *why* you feel the way you do about people of my station, but that doesn't mean I don't respect your right to feel it. I don't expect you to change entirely just because we've wed.'

She moved one shoulder in the ghost of a shrug, her hand still resting on the door handle as if she might escape at any moment, and Joseph wasn't sure how to reply. He'd had no idea she had given so much thought to his comfort, taking his feelings into account rather than just barrelling ahead with whatever *she* wanted. Probably she was curious about his past and why he held the beliefs he did, but she hadn't pressed him for information, respecting his privacy instead of trying to pry, and he realised—with a flicker of alarm—that her discretion tempted him to reward it with the truth.

No.

He recoiled immediately. There was no way he could tell Isabelle about his early life. It would shame him to admit that even the woman who'd given birth to him hadn't been able to love him, and it was sure to make her see him differently. At the current moment she had some measure of regard for him, possibly even outside of the physical attraction he knew she felt as much as he did, and the idea she might lose any of that esteem for him was more than he could stand.

She was the first person to show him even a glimmer of concern, and he was uncomfortably aware he didn't want its light to dim—something he'd never thought he would experience and now far more valuable than he could have dreamed.

In the firelight he saw her look of triumph had turned to uncertainty, and Joseph realised he was staring, transfixed by the way the flames glanced off her golden hair. She didn't seem to know whether she wanted to leave or not, he realised, although she made an attempt at pretending otherwise as she took a step backwards into the corridor.

'I ought to leave you in peace. Unless there's anything else you need...?'

Her eyes slid away from his, only for the span of

a single blink, but the direction of that lightning-fast glance clamped Joseph's chest in a vice. If he wasn't very much mistaken it was the bed she had looked towards with such unthinking speed, and the question of why leapt up to take him by the throat.

Is she thinking...?

He let the sentence finish itself, suddenly unable to focus on anything but what might be circling through Isabelle's mind. That one instinctive glance spoke more clearly than any words and by the colour in her cheeks he could tell she felt she'd revealed too much, and the thread of tension stretching between them grew tauter still when Joseph didn't speak.

Was she thinking about spending the night with him?

His heart stepped up a pace, its steady rhythm now akin to the galloping of a horse. They hadn't talked about their wedding night—he hadn't wanted to make her uncomfortable, and no doubt she was too much the lady to bring up such a delicate subject—but Isabelle was no fool. She'd been married before, and she knew what was required to set the final seal on any union. He might be mortifying her by requiring it to be spelled out so clearly, and he could kick himself for being so slow off the mark.

The very last thing he intended was to do the wrong thing, to frighten or pressure her into something she had no wish for, although a blazing memory of the intense look in her eyes when she'd kissed him flashed into his mind and suddenly all he wanted was to hold her close once again.

He tried to smile, although in the breathless atmosphere of the room Joseph knew it must look forced. 'I think I have everything. You obviously run a very efficient house.'

'Thank you. I hope you'll manage to get some sleep.'

Isabelle made what might have been an attempt at a smile of her own. Clearly she was still uncertain, the tension between them holding her hostage just as much as it was him. It struck Joseph that she might well be waiting for him to make the first move—a thought that sent a pulse of heat straight through him to settle somewhere too low down to mention.

Be careful. Even if she is waiting for you, that doesn't mean you ought to rush. Take your time.

With deliberate slowness he took a step forward, carefully laying aside the book he hadn't had a chance to read. Isabelle watched him closely, her eyes reflecting the light of the dancing fire, but she didn't move back as he came towards her, and the movement of her bodice betrayed how her breathing quickened as he closed the space between them.

He stopped a pace away, looking down into her rosy upturned face. Her lips were slightly parted and he saw her swallow, the movement emphasising the delicate shape of her neck. She was more tempting than any woman he had ever known, and he had to force his voice to remain even, holding himself in check despite the assault on his restraint.

'Perhaps I might be permitted to kiss my bride goodnight?'

Isabelle's eyes widened. There was a touch of brown in her left iris, Joseph noticed for the first time, like an island in a green-blue sea, but any such thought evaporated at her single tentative nod and he felt his heart turn over as he heard her take a breath, that one soft gasp among the prettiest sounds he'd ever known.

Two loose ringlets lay over her shoulder and he reached up to twine one around his fingers, distantly realising it was just as silky as it looked as with the other hand he skimmed the smooth line of her cheekbone—and then tilted her chin so he could bend down and finally, *blessedly*, take possession of her mouth.

The sense of relief was so strong it almost floored him as he traced the contours of her lips, savouring the sweet warmth he'd wanted so badly to revisit. They tasted like wine, and promise, and he couldn't get enough, feeling as though his every prayer had been granted when Isabelle moved against him and yielded willingly to the deeper questing of his tongue. A burning palm came up to fit against the nape of his neck and hold him in place, her grip so much weaker than his but Joseph more than happy to do as he was bid, obediently continuing his blistering exploration of Isabelle's perfect mouth as the blood pounded in his ears and he revelled in having her in his arms once more.

They were half in the corridor and half in his room, and without thinking Joseph drew her inside, closing the door with a blind kick. Isabelle didn't release him for so much as a moment, one hand still at his neck while the other skimmed over the muscular planes of his back, and he was gladder than he could articulate that he had already removed his jacket. He could feel the heat of her fingers through his shirt, scalding him through the linen as though she had set his skin ablaze, and he dropped his own hand from her hair to her waist, finding the secret curve he hadn't been able to put out of his mind and seizing it like a man possessed to make her arch in his hold.

With her mouth on his and the lines of her body so clear beneath the scant cover of her gown Joseph feared he might run mad, his heart beating far too fast and his breath coming in snatches that matched Isabelle's own, and he could have sworn he saw stars when he felt her gently graze his bottom lip.

There was only so much a man could stand, and Joseph knew he was rapidly reaching his limit. While Isabelle swayed in his arms he was powerless to think of anything else, the luxurious room around them fading into nothingness when pitted against the deft movement of her tongue. The only thing that registered at all in his new quarters was the bed, standing tantalisingly close and inviting him to duck beneath an embroidered canopy probably worth more than everything he owned, but he couldn't go too fast. An ache might be growing in a particular part of his anatomy, and desire welling up inside him like an overflowing sea, but somewhere deep down he knew he wanted this to last.

She let out a tiny sound as he bent lower, to trail his lips from her mouth to the corner of her jaw, a sigh escaping when he softly nipped the sensitive place just below her ear. Her fingers tightened, tangling in his shirt, and a ripple of satisfaction washed over him as she tipped her head back, allowing him greater freedom to traverse the slender length of her neck. His mouth lingered where the bruises had been, kissing each spot with a gentleness he hadn't known he possessed. They had long since disappeared, but Joseph could remember each one perfectly, each purple blotch imprinted on his mind from days spent watching her without intending to, his feelings growing hour by hour in spite of his reluctance. There seemed little point in trying to fight them now, he supposed distantly, too intoxicated by her lavender perfume to concentrate on forming a cohesive thought: Isabelle might only have married him for her sister's sake but they were still bound, destined to live together until death did them part, and if he chose to secretly indulge his weakness for her it would only be himself he hurt. Isabelle need never know his true regard for her and he was man enough to bear the pain of it being unrequited, an entire life spent never knowing affection preparing him to bear more of the same without complaint.

As if of their own volition his hands drifted higher, passing over her ribs to venture closer to the fastening of her gown, although he stopped immediately when Isabelle stiffened.

'Isabelle? Is something wrong?'

With an effort he drew back to look down into her glazed eyes. Despite their haziness he was sure he caught a glimmer of hesitation and at once he released her from his hold. Dazedly she shook her head, her chest rising and falling as quickly as Joseph's own— but not convincingly enough to ease his mind.

'No. Nothing.'

'Forgive me, but I don't believe you.'

She gave a shuddering sigh, reaching up a quaking hand to push back her hair. It had come loose, and it lay around her shoulders in a thick cloak so shiny Joseph wanted to run his fingers through it and admire each silken strand.

'It's nothing to worry about. It's just that I've… It's just that I've never…'

'You've never what?'

Isabelle wavered. Her voice was unsteady, as if coming from a throat made dry with longing, and Joseph had to bunch his hands into fists to stop himself from reaching out to gather her into his arms again. She looked so unsure now whereas scant moments ago she had seemed to be acting on the same unquestioned impulse he was, taking an unconscious half-step away, as if to prevent him from coming so close again. 'I've never done this before. I—I feel a little overwhelmed.'

'You've never done what before?'

'This… What happens on a wedding night.'

She looked away. A crease appeared between her sandy brows and Joseph felt his own move likewise.

'What do you mean?'

'Just as I say.'

'But you were married for ten years. Surely you and your husband…?'

The old Duke was perhaps the last person Joseph wanted to think about at this moment, but Isabelle's face made him reconsider. She flicked him an unreadable glance from beneath her long lashes, only a swift cut of her ocean-coloured eyes, but it held some meaning he couldn't quite grasp.

'Edwin and I *were* husband and wife—but only in name. We never had a physical relationship of any description. Not on our wedding night…nor on any night after that. Not even once.'

Joseph felt his lips part but nothing came out, only able to gaze down at her as the cogs in his brain began to turn.

They had no physical relationship? None at all? How on earth could that be?

He tried to bully his brain into accepting what she'd said but it made no sense. How could it? That the old Duke had a woman like Isabelle as his wife and never wanted her in his bed was impossible to believe, her heart-shaped face and golden hair enough to stir even a man of stone. Once her determination and quick wit were added into the mix she would surely tempt a saint, so attractive both inside and out it defied comprehension that her first husband should have remained unmoved, and Joseph had no earthly idea what to say in reply.

'You're confused?'

At his wordless nod Isabelle laced her hands together, looking down at them as if they might tell her what to say.

'I can understand why. Most of Bishops Morton thought Edwin married me out of lust and I married him for his money, but that wasn't the case. He was my papa's closest friend—more like a brother, in truth—and when our parents died he wanted to ensure Marina and I were kept safe and provided for. We had no close relatives, and he had been widowed years before, so it made perfect sense for us to come together to create a new little family the best we could.'

Her frown deepened, her eyes still downturned and seeming to focus more on some invisible spot on the floor now than on her clasped hands. The atmosphere of breathless longing had dissipated completely, giving way to a solemn seriousness that dashed any hope of rekindling the flames, but Joseph was too intent on Isabelle's revelation to feel any disappointment.

'I loved him, and he loved me in turn—but as a father would love a daughter.'

Joseph watched her blink—and then his stomach dropped to see something glistening among her eyelashes, its glitter betrayed by the flames leaping in the grate. The desire to take her in his arms was so powerful it took his breath away, but he made himself stand still, determined his own emotion wouldn't take the stage from hers. She brushed the tear away at once, doubtlessly hoping he hadn't seen, and when she looked up again it was with a half-smile so sad that once seen he knew it could never be forgotten.

'I was at his bedside when he died…just as I had been at my parents'. He slipped away while I held his hand, and I can't pretend he didn't take a piece of my heart with him when he went.'

She gave a slight shrug—a tiny movement of her shoulders that she probably intended to lighten the mood. Instead, however, it drove a dagger into Joseph's heart, easing itself into the vulnerable part only she was able to inspire, and only just in time was he able to stop himself from snatching a sharp breath.

His mind reeled backwards to the night they had sat together at that first inn, Isabelle staring into the fire and wishing aloud that she could turn back the clock to regain what had been lost. At the time he hadn't imagined she meant her husband, but he had clearly been wrong, the shadow of the death of both the Duke and her parents evidently lying long across her soul.

'I'm sorry. I had no idea.'

'Don't apologise. I don't blame you for suspecting the motives of both Edwin and myself.'

There was a dark, weary amusement in her eyes that was painful to behold. 'I don't generally like people to know the intimate details of my first marriage—in fact, you're the only one, other than me, who does.'

Joseph passed a hand over his hair. It seemed every assumption he'd made about her previous marriage was wrong, and he felt a pang of guilt to think he'd judged her motives so poorly. She wasn't a mercenary after all: she'd been a broken young woman in the depths of grief and her feelings for her husband had been genuine, not based in greed or necessity or anything less than pure. She'd been looking for a safe haven, attempting to recreate the family she had lost, and a complex mix of shame and admiration flooded through him.

If anybody in the world could chip away at the ice around his heart it would be his new bride. She was warm enough to melt any frost, gentle enough to tame any beast, and that he was the man lucky enough to have married her seemed more than he could believe. He didn't deserve it, or her, or any of the new feelings he was beginning to accept, and the only thing he could do was strive to be better in turn.

She seemed to be waiting for him to say something. Her head was slightly bowed and her gaze fixed again on her hands, although her chin came up at once when she heard him start to speak.

'I'm honoured you chose to confide in me. You didn't have to take me into your confidence, but I'm glad that you did.'

A little of the apprehension left her face and Joseph felt a flood of relief that he had said the right thing.

'So am I. If we're to have a happy marriage—of sorts—I don't think there should be any secrets between us. There's nothing left now that you don't know.'

Joseph nodded, although a fist seemed to have clamped around his throat. Now would be the time to tell her the things he'd resolved to conceal, her honesty surely deserving of the same from him, but as she looked at him with those beautiful guileless eyes he couldn't quite find the nerve.

Years spent living on his wits and his courage had honed both until they were weapons in themselves, and yet they abandoned him now when he needed them most, the idea of revealing his low and loveless past a leap he couldn't bring himself to take. In telling him about her first marriage Isabelle had only made herself more faultless in his view, her virtues even greater than he had imagined, and in contrast to her light the shadows inside him seemed darker than ever before.

'No. I have nothing to tell, either.'

The lie rang hollow, but he hoped Isabelle wouldn't

notice the forced note of composure. She was far too sharp to fool for long, however, and for the first time since she'd entered his rooms Joseph wished she would withdraw so that he could collect his thoughts. What had begun as one thing had turned abruptly into something very different and he needed time to wrap his mind around it, evidently a feeling Isabelle shared as she took a flatteringly reluctant step towards the door.

'I think perhaps, given the circumstances...'

'Of course.' Joseph nodded, a contradictory sense of disappointment rising at once. She might be moving away slowly, but moving away she most certainly was, and the desire to stride after her took all his strength to check. 'Whatever you think best.'

She tried for an uncertain smile that highlighted the pretty shape of her mouth and Joseph watched as she went for the door, his eye drawn like a magnet to the subtle sway of her hips as she walked away, although on the threshold she paused.

Looking back over her shoulder, fresh colour rose in her cheeks and she seemed to be struggling to force out whatever it was she wanted to say, embarrassed but determined—as ever—to make herself heard.

'I hope... I very much hope you aren't...you know... That you don't think me...'

Joseph felt his chest tighten but he kept his voice as steady as he could. 'I have no expectations, Isabelle. Anything that might happen between us will do so only at your pace—and if it takes you a lifetime to feel ready, then I will simply wait.'

He saw her throat move as she swallowed but she didn't reply, only the swiftest of nods his reward—and then she was gone, only her lavender perfume lingering to make Joseph groan aloud into the empty room.

Chapter Nine

Isabelle's eyelids fluttered as she rose slowly from the depths of sleep, the sound of rain lashing against her bedroom window coaxing her into wakefulness. The room was still cloaked in darkness, the curtains firmly closed, although a tea tray on the bedside table suggested her maid had at some point tried—unsuccessfully—to rouse her.

After the scene in Joseph's rooms Isabelle had lain unmoving for hours, listening to the wind howl around Winford's chimneys as her mind whirred away like a mechanical toy, and when she'd finally fallen asleep it must have been well past three o'clock.

The knot that had tightened as she lay trying to sleep resurfaced again, just as uncomfortable as it had been in the silence of the night. She hadn't gone to see him with the intention of revealing all, but it had slipped out regardless, the passionate turn the evening had taken forcing her to speak the truth. The step they had been about to take together was significant, and while the spectre of her marriage to Edwin had hung between them she couldn't allow herself to take that final leap—no matter how much she had yearned to.

He looked so confused, though...and his face when I asked that there be no secrets between us now...

That he was concealing something she had no doubt. She knew barely anything about him aside from what she'd seen for herself, no idea at all where he came from or if he even had any family, and it seemed unlikely he would volunteer that information willingly.

For some reason he was resolved to remain a mystery, even in the face of her openness, and her curiosity simmered, her head aching as she tried to think how she might convince him to let her see beneath his enigmatic mask. His previously caustic demeanour towards her had mellowed considerably over the weeks and her own feelings grown to match it, perhaps enough trust existing between them now to encourage him to share whatever he felt he had to hide...

A soft knock interrupted her thoughts and she sat up a little higher against her pillows as her maid's head cautiously appeared around the door.

'Ah, ma'am. You're awake.'

Anna came into the room, bearing a fresh tray that she set down beside the untouched one, and Isabelle found a bleary smile.

'Yes. I seem to have overslept this morning. What time is it?'

'Half-past ten, ma'am. I brought your tea at the usual time, but you weren't to be disturbed.'

The maid moved to the window, drawing back the heavy velvet curtains to allow daylight into the room. There wasn't much of it. The sky was iron-grey and rain hurled itself against the glass as if trying to break in, and Isabelle pulled her coverlet a little higher as she reached out to pick up her steaming teacup.

'Have my sister and J— Mr Carter been down yet?'

'Yes, ma'am. They breakfasted together at around nine, although Mr Carter went for a walk at six o'clock this morning and didn't go back to bed afterwards. He was wet through on his return, but that didn't seem to bother him an inch.'

Isabelle nodded absently, although she felt something twist inside her. Joseph had risen early and gone for a walk despite the rain and dark, apparently too restless to remain in his bed a moment longer. Perhaps he too had been unable to stop thinking about what had passed between them in his rooms, and either her revelation or their unfinished business had prevented him from sleeping?

She sipped quietly at her tea until the uncomfortable sensation subsided.

'I see. What are they doing now?'

Anna paused in laying out a choice of linen shifts. 'Mr Carter and Miss Marina are…exercising, ma'am.'

'Exercising?' Isabelle's eyes flew at once to the murk beyond her window. 'Marina has ventured out in this storm?'

'Not outside, ma'am. In the upper gallery.'

'Oh. Walking, then?'

Her instinctive unease receded again, although a glimmer of doubt came to take its place. Joseph going for a stroll in torrential rain was far less surprising than the idea of him solemnly promenading up and down the gallery, most likely suffering Marina's endless questions as she hung off his arm. If he *had* surrendered to that fate then it would mean he was showing more patience than she might have given him credit for, and a hint of a smile tugged at Isabelle's lips to think of it.

But the shake of Anna's head brought her up short.

'No, ma'am. I don't think I'd call it that. In truth... I don't know *what* I'd call it.'

The maid turned away, moving to the armoire to riffle through the hanging gowns, and Isabelle was glad her frown went unnoticed. If Marina and Joseph weren't walking in the gallery, what could they be doing that defied description?

Her interest growing by the second, she set down her cup, pushing the covers to one side as she prepared to get up.

'You've made me curious, Anna. I think I'll go and see for myself.'

Clad in a dove-grey gown that seemed the best compromise between mourning and newly wed, Isabelle made her way towards the gallery at the top of the house. The long room was where she and Edwin had often walked when he was too ill to go out, Isabelle sometimes pushing him in the wheeled chair he'd come to rely on more and more towards the end, and it was with mixed feelings that she approached the half-open door. She'd only been inside a handful of times since he'd died, but the sound of footsteps on the creaking boards drew her on and she made sure to arrange her face into an encouraging smile as she pushed open the door.

For one sickening beat she stood completely still, unable to comprehend what she was seeing.

Joseph was standing behind Marina with one arm locked around her neck, pinning her against him as he squeezed his forearm against her throat. She wasn't trying to resist, and Isabelle felt her lungs seize as pure, heart-stopping horror flooded her like a cascade of ice. What was he *doing*, so calmly and collectedly strangling her sister before her very eyes? And how could she stop him, unable to understand what was happening but her protective instincts roaring into life to make her lunge blindly into the room—

'And now bring your elbow back into my ribs.'

'Like this?'

Isabelle stumbled to a breathless halt as she watched Marina jab backwards with one skinny elbow, bringing it smartly into contact with Joseph's chest. He nodded approvingly, and Isabelle's confusion grew tenfold as he released her sister from his grasp.

'The movement is good, but you need to strike harder. In real life you'll want to use all your strength.'

Marina narrowed her eyes, as if trying to absorb every word, but she broke into a wide smile when she caught sight of Isabelle hovering mutely by the door.

'Issy! Come and see what Joseph has been teaching me!'

Joseph turned quickly, dropping her an unusually formal bow as she came unsteadily towards them. Her heart was racing at lightning speed, but she caught the swift flicker of something that crossed her new husband's face—perhaps a memory of the previous night coming back to him now she was before him once again.

'I was showing your sister some ways a lady might defend herself.'

Joseph sounded unruffled as ever, his even voice contrasting starkly with Isabelle's bewilderment.

'It was too wet to go outdoors, and she expressed boredom at only being allowed to walk endlessly up and down this gallery. She asked a few questions about my time abroad, and the conversation brought us here.'

Isabelle looked up at him, wondering when he would begin to make sense. 'So because she was interested in your travels you thought you would teach her how to fight? Something no respectable young lady ought ever to do?'

'Not to fight, exactly. Just to use some tools that anyone—lady or otherwise—might find useful to know. The best place to hit a man to wind him, for example, and how to use the heel of the hand to strike a blow...'

It was a rough, unsentimental, and entirely inappropriate way to show his commitment to guarding his new sister-in-law. Of course Marina couldn't really go around reducing men to quivering heaps on the ground—her reputation would be sure to go up in flames if she ever attempted any of Joseph's teachings—but the fact that he had tried to step up to his new role of protector in the only way he knew how was more moving than Isabelle could have expected.

His gruff kindness to Marina was the most direct route to Isabelle's heart, and she felt herself flush to wonder if her fledgling feelings for her brusque husband might be starting to be returned.

At one time she never would have dared to hope for such a thing, but now Isabelle hesitated, gripped by the desire to know for sure. He'd listened intently when she'd told him the truth about her first marriage, showing his carefully concealed inner goodness when he had vowed to wait for her to invite him into her bed, and now his misguided attempts to safeguard Marina added to the list of qualities she was ashamed to have doubted he had.

Far from a heartless brute for hire, he was a decent man right down to his core, capable and dependable in spite of his attempts to hide it, and Isabelle was forced to bite the inside of her cheek in a reminder not to reach out for him in front of Marina's innocent eyes.

'You're not angry, Issy?'

Her sister's plaintive voice filtered through the haze of Isabelle's thoughts and she collected herself just in time to shake her head.

'No. Just a little surprised.'

She thought she heard Joseph murmur something, but she didn't turn to question him. With her heart so full it would be too dangerous to look into his face, Marina's presence the only thing stopping her from giving in to the temptation to strain up on tiptoe and find his mouth.

'Good. It isn't as though I'm planning to practise on the vicar, after all.'

The mental image her sister's words conjured almost made Isabelle smile, although her insides were stretched too tightly to allow her lips to move. Instead she must have looked accidentally disapproving, as Marina wavered for a moment before straightening her skirts.

'I think I've had enough exercise for one day. I'm quite worn out. I'll just go down to the kitchen and see if I can find something to revive me.'

She withdrew to the door and both Isabelle and Joseph watched her go, neither speaking as Marina left the gallery and her light footsteps retreated down the corridor. The atmosphere seemed to shift the moment they were left alone, but Isabelle tried to ignore it, even though the desire to claim another kiss nevertheless still circled as she cleared her dry throat.

'That was *not* what I was expecting to find when Anna told me you and Marina were exercising.'

Joseph exhaled through his nose. 'I apologise if you were alarmed. In hindsight, it probably looked somewhat sinister.'

'It did a little, I'll admit. Is it something you make a habit of? Teaching that sort of thing?'

'No. Your sister is the first.'

'I see.'

Isabelle inclined her head, hoping he hadn't noticed how she struggled to look at anything but him. For all his studied calm there was still an edge to the way Joseph gazed down at her, the barest trace of something less restrained lurking just out of sight, and it threatened to send a delicious shudder right through her.

'Something of an honour for her, then. Why did you never attempt it before?'

Joseph shrugged, a sudden shadow of something like wariness entering his eyes. 'I don't know. Perhaps I didn't feel I had reason to.'

'But you feel you do for Marina?'

Joseph's lips parted, as if to make some reply, but instead he turned away, pacing towards the window to look out at the storm beyond. The sky was still a deep gunmetal-grey and the downpour showed no signs of stopping—although he didn't seem to register any of what was before him, gazing straight ahead so his sculpted profile was all Isabelle could see.

'Yes.'

He spoke quietly, more to the heavy-bellied clouds outside than to Isabelle, and she took an unconscious step closer so she might not miss a single word.

'I feel responsibility towards your sister. You were clear when we wed what you expected of me, and I have always prided myself on keeping to any agreement.'

He spared her a swift sideways glance, the hazel force of it catching at her breath. He didn't seem to have finished, perhaps instead trying to gauge her reaction before he continued, although Isabelle was distantly sure her face must have told him everything as she willed him to carry on.

For the first time in the whole of their strange acquaintance he was sharing his thoughts, giving her some clue as to what was passing through his guarded mind, and she couldn't tear her eyes away even as he turned his own back towards the rain.

'You placed your trust in me and I intend to justify that faith. I won't pretend I've the first idea how to care for anyone other than myself—but you have my word that I shall try.'

Isabelle's gut executed a dizzying flip. Had he just admitted out loud that he wanted to foster a closer connection not only with Marina, but also herself? It came so close to her own secret desires that her heart leapt up into her mouth, only Joseph's obvious discomfort preventing her from racing ahead. Clearly he didn't enjoy acknowledging any kind of private feeling, the slightly too firm clasp of his hands behind his back a tell-tale sign that he wasn't at ease, and with immense difficulty she reined herself in.

It wouldn't do to let him see how her spirits had soared upwards at his stilted confession, and yet she couldn't completely prevent a tentative glimmer of hope, a flickering spark gleaming where once there had been only ash.

The temptation to let her mind go on running down that path tugged at her, but she set it aside as firmly as she was able. Joseph might have been speaking of their agreement in purely mercenary terms, assuring her of his intention to uphold his end of the bargain with no emotion involved, but somehow that didn't seem right. He was holding himself a shade too rigidly for a man comfortable with what had just transpired, although the idea that proved his feelings dimmed a little as belatedly Isabelle realised exactly what he'd said.

Did he imply he's never had anyone to care about before?

Slowly she came another step closer, making sure not to look directly up at his face. He hadn't turned from the window, that proud profile still all she could see as she stood beside him at the glass, and she peered out into the sodden garden as she wondered where to begin.

Her heart thumped against the bodice of her gown, both from her proximity to Joseph's broad form and apprehension at what she was about to do. The last thing she wanted was to invade his privacy, but her curiosity gleamed like a candle in a winter night, throwing its undulating light over things normally cloaked in darkness.

After what he'd just shared, wasn't there a chance he might be persuaded to go a step further, unravelling some of the mystery Isabelle longed to solve? He'd said he had no secrets, but that hardly seemed possible. The book of his life was too firmly closed for its pages to be blank.

'You say you've never cared for anyone. Have you no family? No one whose wellbeing you would want to guard?' She purposefully kept her voice light, hoping no trace of her vivid interest would betray her. 'Forgive me for asking. I know so little about you—but I would like very much for that to change...'

She tailed off uncertainly, feeling the rush of blood through her veins. He didn't move, only the minuscule tightening of his brow showing he had heard her, and she was just beginning to wish she'd never asked when he slowly shook his head.

'No. I have no family. My people were lost to me when I was very young.'

Isabelle looked quickly down at the floor to hide

the sympathy she knew had blazed into her eyes. Joseph wouldn't want to see it, was far too stoic to entertain the idea of anyone pitying him, but all the same she couldn't help but feel how a cold fist took hold of her chest.

'I'm sorry to hear that. I know what a heavy load that can be to bear.'

He half turned towards her but appeared to change his mind, one short nod his only response.

If he had never grown to care for his family he must have lost them at a very young age, but surely that didn't mean he didn't feel their absence? No words could sum up the deep, gnawing ache of loss...it was all-consuming, intruding even into happier moments to bare its sharp teeth, and that it was an experience they shared lent an unexpected edge to her sorrow on his behalf.

She wanted to comfort him, to hold him in her arms and assure him that *she* at least was still at his side, but at the same time she doubted he would want her to try. It was a private hurt that he had to deal with in his own way, and all she could do was walk beside him if he ever decided to journey into the past.

Carefully Isabelle reached out her hand. She was pleased to see her fingers were still as she laid them on Joseph's arm, feeling the strength and warmth contained within his sleeve, but it was the look in his eyes as he turned towards her that captured her attention more than anything else.

'I know it's a pain that never truly goes away, no matter how many years may pass. If you ever want to talk about it, I hope you know I'll always be here to listen.'

Joseph could have sworn he actually felt the powerful, genuine compassion radiating from Isabelle alongside the gentleness with which she touched his arm—and it made the discomfort in his stomach a hundred times worse than it had been already.

You idiot. You've made her think you're some poor orphan rather than just unwanted!

He might have winced if she hadn't been watching him, the sweet kindness in her face almost more than he could stand.

'Thank you. I shall keep that in mind.'

What he'd told her wasn't a lie, but neither was it the complete truth, and an unpleasant combination of guilt and regret tied his insides into knots. He'd been caught off balance by her earlier question regarding her sister, revealing more about his commitment to her and Marina than he'd intended, and he hadn't had time to recover before she'd asked about the family he had never known.

It was perfectly possible he had a mother still living, perhaps a father too and siblings he wouldn't recognise if he passed them on the street, but his feelings for his unlikely wife ran too deep now to tell her *why* he had no idea if he was alone in the world. Clearly

Isabelle had been cherished by both her parents and the old Duke and if she learned of her new husband's abandonment she'd surely wonder at the reason why, soon coming to realise what Joseph was so resolved to conceal: that he was impossible to love.

The four letters of that word burned into his mind and he couldn't dismiss them, knowing without a doubt that he was walking a perilous path. For the first thirty years of his life he'd had no idea what that emotion felt like, never expecting or wanting to experience what so many other men lost their wits to, but now he could feel something stirring where once there had been nothing but a barren plain. Perhaps he didn't love her quite yet, but he was well on the road to that destination, and it frightened him more than he'd ever admit to know there was no turning back.

Her slender hand still rested on his arm and he had to steel himself against the urge to cover it with his own. Her fingers would be warm beneath his palm, perhaps able to thaw some of the ice that had begun to build in his chest, but the gesture might too easily be misconstrued. Isabelle might think he was asking for more comfort, when in reality he wanted to change the subject—and quickly—before she had the chance to ask him anything else.

While he was in the midst of far too many new feelings he had to cling to something safe, pull himself back to shore before he drifted away on an unfamiliar tide, and he seized on the thing he knew best in the world to anchor him.

'Do you want me to show you what I taught Marina?'

Isabelle blinked, probably taken by surprise by the abrupt question that had no bearing on what they had been discussing. 'Show me?'

'I thought you might prefer to know what I've been filling your sister's head with. Perhaps it wasn't the *best* way to try to fulfil my duty to her...'

To his immeasurable relief she smiled. 'I can't deny it was a little unorthodox, but I appreciate your motives. When I told you I needed help protecting her against men with dark intentions that wasn't quite what I had in mind—although I suppose any man who tries to importune her now will soon wish he hadn't.'

She dropped her hand back to her side, the place on his arm where it had rested immediately missing its warmth. Thankfully his ploy to lead her away from more hazardous subjects seemed to have worked as he saw fresh curiosity cross her face, her green-blue gaze enquiring as she looked up at him.

'What was it you were doing when I first came into the room? With your arm around her neck?'

'A chokehold. One of the basics in any mercenary's toolkit.'

'I see. And you imagined that would be a good lesson for Marina?'

'Invaluable. In my experience, an attack often comes from behind.'

Isabelle's fair eyebrows rose, but her ready courage seemed to come to the fore, determination crossing her upturned face. 'In that case you'd better teach me how to parry one, too. That's if you think I'm able?'

Joseph turned away from the rain-streaked window, relieved to be on steadier ground. While Isabelle had been set on burrowing into his past he'd been teetering on the brink of disaster, but now they had returned to familiar territory he was far more at ease.

'I've no doubt you'll make a good student. On more than one occasion you've shown more nerve than many men I've known.'

She looked pleased, a tinge of pink just lighting the fine lines of her cheekbones, and she followed with endearing enthusiasm as he moved into the centre of the room. Just as with Marina, he instructed her to keep her shoulders square and then circled round to her back—although in sharp contrast to working with his sister-in-law this time he hesitated for a half-second before making his approach.

It would be the first time he'd touched her since the previous night, when she had shivered in his arms as he explored the intoxicating terrain of her body, and he felt his pulse quicken. Standing behind her afforded him an excellent view of the elegant sweep of her waist, reaching up to a narrow back and down towards the tantalising swell of her hips, and he closed his eyes briefly as he recalled his promise to let her set the pace. After what she'd revealed about the nature of her first marriage he had resolved to go as slowly as she needed him to…but that didn't stop his imagination from running away from him before he could snatch it back under control.

'I'm going to come up behind you and place my arm around your throat.' Mercifully his voice was only slightly hoarse as he stepped forward, so close behind her now that he could see her shoulders moving as she breathed. 'A real assailant would squeeze far more tightly than I'm going to, so when you strike me I want you to put all your strength behind it.'

He watched her nod, her crown of golden curls gleaming in the firelight. She half turned her head, as if to peer over her shoulder, but then faced forward again at once, the colour in her cheeks seeming to deepen as he came nearer still.

'Clench your hand into a fist. Bring your arm forward, bending it at the elbow, and then pull it back as hard as you can, forcing the point up into my ribs.'

'Are you sure? I don't want to hurt you.'

Joseph almost smiled at her unnecessary concern. 'You won't. Someone of your stature is unlikely to do me much damage. In your case it would be more about making yourself too difficult to restrain than inflicting real harm. Are you ready?'

She nodded again, and with only a momentary pause Joseph reached out, hooking his right arm around her neck. Very carefully, applying no pressure at all to her delicate throat, he drew her towards him until her back was flush against his chest...and he wondered distantly if he was going to burst into flames as the heat of her body soaked through the layers of silk and linen to set his skin on fire.

He thought he caught a tiny sound fall from her lips, so close to a gasp it stoked the blaze inside him to new heights. It was the same half-breath she'd snatched the night before, when his hands had skimmed over the entrancing swell of her hips, and he hardened his jaw, trying desperately to hold on to what he was *supposed* to be doing. With her head pressing just beneath his chin, however, he could smell the floral perfume of her hair and even the subtle scent of her skin, uniquely feminine and far too intimate to ignore.

Control yourself. Remember what you promised.

A dull ache had begun to spread through his chest, but he did his best not to acknowledge it, even when it started to move to places much lower down. It was the most painful temptation he'd ever known: simply standing with his rapidly breathing wife in the strong circle of his arms, allegedly playing the part of a predator but in truth feeling more like a guardian protecting the most important person in the world.

If she'd turned around to look at him she would have seen the helpless want in his face, but she didn't move, perhaps held in place by the same thrilling tension that had Joseph in its thrall, and the temperature of the gallery seemed to rise as they held the moment a fraction too long.

'Now...your arm...'

Joseph heard his voice crack beneath the strain. It seemed too much to hope that Isabelle hadn't noticed its pitch had dropped an octave, and he felt her throat move as she swallowed, doubtless all too aware her husband was struggling to keep his cool.

Tentatively she extended one arm, her hand balled into a fist, but when she brought her elbow back he barely felt the blow.

'I told you to put more power into it than that.'

His words were still like gravel, and Isabelle's were little better when she turned her head slightly to speak over her shoulder, her voice low and so suffused with *something* that it was like sweet music to Joseph's ears.

'And *I* said I didn't want to hurt you.'

The idea of her slender elbow doing him any kind of harm had been more amusing when she hadn't been pressed so tightly against him. If she didn't escape from him soon he would have to be the one to back away, her confession from the previous night still at the forefront of his mind, and for all his strength Joseph didn't know how much more temptation he could bear.

'One more time. I know you can do better than that.'

Again the arm was hesitantly extended, and again when it came back it was far too light. Even Marina had hit him harder than that, and Joseph bent his neck, leaning down to speak more easily into Isabelle's ear.

'I'm not sure you're trying.'

There was a pause—long enough for him to admire the perfect shell-like shape of her ear—before her reply sent his heart to flail against his ribs.

'Perhaps I'm not. Perhaps there are reasons I might want to stand here like this that have nothing to do with defending myself.'

Joseph sucked in a harsh breath, realising far too late that in turning her head to the side she had brought her lips now mere inches from his own. Her soft breath on his skin lit up his nerves like a firework display, every inch of him yearning to abandon his restraint and guide her mouth up to his, and when he saw the heavy-lidded desire in her eyes he almost forgot to breathe.

I said I'd go at her pace. I said I wouldn't rush her. But if she's the one to invite me in...

Slowly he relaxed his arm, allowing it to fall slightly looser so she could turn beneath it. Her cheeks were pink and her chest rising and falling rapidly with each snatched breath but she didn't falter, instead moulding her body to his as he brought his other hand up to cradle the span of her waist, and he felt himself burn as her eyes dipped down to linger on his suddenly parched mouth. It wasn't a drink he wanted, however—the only thing that could slake his thirst was to kiss his wife again, and as her eyes closed and her fingers gripped the material of his shirt he pulled her to him so he might finally bend and slant his lips over hers.

'Oh! Oh, I'm so sorry...'

Joseph straightened up faster than a whipcrack to see a scarlet-faced Marina in the doorway, looking as though she wished the ground would swallow her up. He didn't need to glance at Isabelle to know she would look the same. Being caught in a compromising situation by anyone would have been bad enough, but for it to be her *sister* was probably the very worst, and Jacob stepped smartly away.

'Nothing to apologise for. I was about to take my leave anyway.'

It was an obvious lie, but at least it gave everybody an escape from the awkwardness rapidly flooding the room. Isabelle was suddenly extremely interested in the gallery's ornate ceiling, and Marina fascinated by the floor, and it seemed best for everyone that he took the opportunity to get out while he could. The sisters would settle things between them as soon as he was gone and he strode towards the door a little more quickly than he'd meant to, Marina quickly skipping aside to let him pass.

Standing perfectly still with one hand at her throat Isabelle was like a statue, frozen and beautiful with her hair *just* coming undone at one side, and he guessed it was Marina's giggle rather than his wife's that he heard as he walked away.

Chapter Ten

The rain continued to fall solidly for almost a full week, and by the sixth relentlessly sodden evening Isabelle had begun to fear for her sanity. There was no question of leaving Winford House while such a determined storm raged outside, the screaming wind and unceasing downpour forcing her instead to remain confined within the same four luxurious but restrictive walls—which meant no escape from either her husband's stirring presence or the equally rousing thoughts that followed her wherever she went, nipping at her heels like a pack of hungry wolves.

It just felt as though Joseph was *everywhere*, even the vast sprawl of the house not enough to keep them apart. Every corner she turned, every room she entered; no matter where she was or what she was doing, they seemed to find each other, drawn together like a pair of opposing magnets powerless to resist the instinctive pull. Perhaps she had developed some uncanny awareness of him, or Joseph possessed the gift of foresight. Whatever the explanation, it seemed there was no getting away from him now they lived beneath the same roof, and it was only Marina's near-constant attendance that prevented Isabelle from giving in to temptation, that morning in the gallery lighting a fuse she had no hope of extinguishing.

This is getting ridiculous. If you don't find the courage to speak to him soon you may well lose your wits altogether—and then what hope have you of anything further coming from this farce of a marriage?

Isabelle lay in her bed without moving, staring up into the gloom as her mind whirred endlessly over the question that had kept her awake into the early hours. Sometimes the answer seemed plain only to slink away again, keeping her guessing until there was no chance at all she'd be able to snatch any sleep.

Surely I'm not wrong in thinking his feelings for me have begun to change?

He'd as good as admitted it, determined to take Marina under his protection more literally than intended but pleasing all the same, and if her sister hadn't returned to the gallery at such a delicate moment Isabelle knew her appreciation would have made itself abundantly clear.

Until she knew for certain what *he* felt for *her*, however, it was doubtless best not to take that final step, such intimacy sure to cloud the water she wanted to keep as clear as possible until she knew how deep it ran. To be sure of Joseph's feelings was never going to be straightforward and she had a suspicion he might never willingly reveal them, so set was he on remaining a closed book that it would take a miracle to prise open the cover.

She sighed, that single breath the only sound in the empty room. It seemed unusually quiet, now she thought about it, and, lifting her head from the pillow, Isabelle listened carefully.

The constant beat of rain against her window had finally stopped, she realised. She'd grown so used to it over the past week that now it had gone the bedroom felt eerily still. Even the keening of the wind had gentled to a whisper instead of a shout. In the silence of the night she might have been the only person in the house, everyone else sure to have fallen asleep hours ago, and she almost allowed herself a shudder before rolling her eyes at her childish apprehension.

'Don't be absurd,' she muttered to herself sternly. 'The most frightening thing here is your utter lack of sense.'

The smallest hint of unease tried to linger, however, and as if to disprove it she sat up. The dressing gown hanging on the door of her armoire gave her a momentary jolt, looming tall and ghost-like out of the darkness, and she shook her head at her jumpiness. It seemed there was precious little hope of her settling enough to drift off: her confusion over Joseph had evidently wound her far too tightly if a simple dressing gown was enough to startle her, and with another sigh she pushed the covers aside.

Crossing to the window, she twitched open one curtain. After the violence of the storm the gardens looked peaceful, serene in the unbroken tranquillity of the night, and all at once Isabelle longed to experience their calmness for herself. It might have a soothing effect on her mind, packed too full of thoughts of Joseph and what the future might bring, and the idea of escaping just for a moment was tempting after a week of enforced captivity. If the rest of the household was asleep nobody would know if she sneaked away, slipping out through the kitchen door without being seen or questioned as to *why* she was wandering the grounds at night, and Isabelle turned away from the window before she could change her mind, only pausing to retrieve the alarming dressing gown before moving to the door.

The landing was pitch-black as she cautiously peered out. Not a soul seemed to be stirring, and on tiptoe she crept out of her rooms, hardly daring to breathe as she eased the door closed behind her and set her foot down on the first disloyally creaking floorboard. The last thing she wanted was to wake anyone and she chose each step carefully, making slow but silent progress down the corridor towards the staircase beyond.

The door to Joseph's rooms lay close to her, and for the briefest of moments she paused in front of it, allowing herself one fleeting beat to imagine him inside. They'd shared a room before, of course, but never a bed, and her heart leaped as she wondered how he slept when nobody was there to see. Would he wear a nightshirt, a scant layer of white linen the only thing covering his expansive frame as he lay stretched out on his bed? Or perhaps…he wore nothing at all…

Isabelle's throat dried instantly as an image too shameful to share flashed before her.

Stop. You're supposed to be easing your mind, not filling it even further.

The stern little voice from her subconscious was right, but that didn't make her legs feel any stronger as she groped for the wall, following it unsteadily until it brought her out into the upper hall. The garden's midnight coolness couldn't come a moment too soon while the picture of Joseph's bare chest lingered so enticingly, and she all but fled down the stairs, trying to outrun the temptation to turn back and knock at his bedroom door.

Until she had a better grasp on whatever he might be coming to feel for her she couldn't afford to indulge her desires—even if they chased her every step of the way through Winford's winding passages that led to the silent kitchen.

A pair of Marina's boots stood beside the back porch and Isabelle swiftly pushed her feet into them before reaching for the latch. It was an old door, the wood warped from years of sun and rain, and everybody in the house knew it was almost impossible to force it open from the outside. Anyone hoping to come back in again had to prop it ajar or risk being shut out, and Isabelle kicked its wooden wedge into place as she heaved the door aside and took her first lungful of cold air.

It filled her chest with ice, but she relished the freezing sensation surging beneath her ribs. After a week spent in front of fires and shut in stifling rooms it was a relief to have the cobwebs blown away, goosebumps rising on her skin as she pulled her dressing gown more tightly around her and stepped out into the night.

Behind her, only Winford's red brick façade saw her go, its darkened windows watching keenly, but she had no fear of it sharing her secret escape as she ventured down the nearest path.

The gardens had been Edwin's pride and joy, and even in the darkness they exuded the orderly calm Isabelle had been so desperate to find. Each flagged path led through an intricate maze of low hedges and borders that would burst with colour in the summer, and she didn't know whether or not to smile when she recalled how she'd pushed Edwin down to see them in his wheeled chair the previous year, neither realising then it was to be for the very last time.

For a decade the Duke had been the most important man in her life, and to think that it was now Joseph who held that honour was hard to believe, the two so opposite in every way that it seemed impossible they should both have been her husband. The only thing they had in common was that she cared for them— albeit in very different ways—and that each was a man she knew she could trust...even if Joseph was determined to hide the goodness in him that Edwin had let shine out to bathe everyone around him in its glow, the shutters around the mercenary's heart pulled down so tight it would be a miracle if she was ever to break through.

The wind lifted her tousled curls, but Isabelle paid no attention as she cut across the sparkling lawn, walking slowly and with no final destination in mind. The peace she'd come in search of was taking its time to appear, and she hunched her shoulders to ward off the chill trying to creep beneath her nightgown, her bare feet cold inside their borrowed boots. Despite the quiet shadows her thoughts refused to be soothed, and she pressed her mouth into a tight line. If she couldn't find a way to navigate their rough seas she'd be dashed on the rocks of her own uncertainty, set adrift with no way of reaching the shore. One conversation would be all it took, but to take that leap would require all her courage, jumping out into the unknown when she had no idea how far she might have to fall...

The only one with any answers was Joseph, and he was so damnably difficult to read. Out of necessity he had learned to hide any softness inside him, the loss of his family sure to have played some part in stunt- ing his emotional growth. If he had never had anyone to care for it was small wonder he was determined to keep his inner self locked away, and Isabelle was about to surrender to a wave of pity when a towering figure lurching suddenly out of the shadows made her choke on her own breath.

For one alarming moment Joseph wasn't sure whether Isabelle was going to lash out or scream. In the moonlight her eyes stretched wide and her hand appeared to have clenched instinctively into a fist, and he just had time to feel a flicker of approval at her quick reflexes before she sagged like a deflating soufflé.

'Joseph! You frightened me half to death!'

Her voice came in a startled whisper, although there was something in it Joseph didn't have to think very hard to understand. Even in the gloom he could see she was wearing only a dressing gown thrown over her nightclothes, and his already heightened awareness of her sharpened further, the tension that had stretched between them all week tautening again as they found themselves so unexpectedly face to face.

When he'd heard suspicious scuffling outside his door he hadn't imagined Isabelle to be the culprit but now she was before him, barely dressed and her golden curls falling beautifully loose around her, and he wondered if he'd stumbled into some kind of waking dream.

He tried manfully to turn his attention away from

the tantalising hint of lace peeping at the neck of her gown. 'Why on earth are you outside at this time of night?'

'I could ask you the same question. Why are you lurking about, looming out of the dark to make me jump out of my skin?'

She shot him a glance that invited an explanation and Joseph felt immediately compelled to obey. 'I heard footsteps sneaking past my rooms. They were far too surreptitious to be one of the servants, so I thought I'd investigate. I admit it didn't occur to me that you might have decided to go for a stroll at this hour.'

'Oh.' Isabelle looked away from him, carefully gathering her tousled hair over one shoulder. 'I didn't mean to wake you. I couldn't sleep, and as the rain had finally stopped I thought I'd come out to take some air.'

'At twenty past two in the morning?'

'Well, I… Yes.'

A trace of something like guilt crossed her averted face, but he didn't have long to consider it—or what might have been so important as to rob her of sleep. At that very moment something cold and wet found its way down the neck of the shirt he'd hastily pulled on beneath his coat and Joseph grimaced, looking upwards to see where to place the blame.

'You might want to cut your walk short. It appears the rain has decided not to leave us after all.'

Isabelle followed his lead, peering up at the clouds

that had darkened once again to all but eclipse the pale moon. The reward for her curiosity was a large raindrop, hurling itself directly between her eyes, and she quickly wiped her face with the sleeve of her robe.

'We should go back inside before we're soaked. Cook will be furious if she finds puddles on the kitchen floor in the morning, and I've no intention of courting her wrath.'

Another cold droplet landed on the top of Joseph's head, chased immediately by countless others as the sky began to unleash its hoard. All around them the pattering of water onto the already sodden grass increased in speed, but Joseph hesitated, drawing a questioning look from Isabelle as she held her hands over her head.

'What's the matter? Aren't you coming inside?'

'I'd like to, but…'

He glanced over his shoulder towards the house. There were still no lights at any of the windows—clearly no potential helper had been woken by two sets of creeping footsteps—and reluctantly Joseph prepared to make a confession.

'When I heard footsteps and then found the kitchen door ajar I thought someone must be trying to break in…so I kicked away the wedge. It was only afterwards that I remembered what you told me about it not opening from the outside.'

Isabelle's mouth dropped open, her fair hair sparkling now as if threaded with diamonds.

'You closed the door? You're certain?'

'I'm afraid so.'

'Then we're trapped out here!'

She stared up at him in horror, a raindrop hanging fetchingly on the very tip of her nose, and Joseph quickly shook his head.

'We'll just have to knock at the front door. I don't like to wake the servants, but—'

'We can't!'

Isabelle pulled the edges of her dressing gown together at the neck, shrinking down into the dampening collar.

'The side gate is locked at night and there's no other way to get around to the front. Edwin took our safety very seriously—you've seen how high the garden walls are, and even if you did manage to climb one, you'd find they're topped with iron spikes. You might have been an excellent mercenary, but even *you* can't bend metal.'

Cursing his stupidity, Joseph watched Isabelle shiver. The freezing rain was doing its best to soak her to the skin. He should have been more careful, damn it, but he'd been so set on chasing off any intruder that he'd acted without thinking, and now—unless he thought of something fast—there was a very real chance Isabelle might catch a dangerous chill.

He cast about him, peering through the sheeting rain that plastered his hair to his brow. The silent house didn't offer any answers, but something nagged at the back of his mind…a dim recollection from the week before.

'Isn't there a summerhouse here somewhere? I think I remember Marina mentioning one… We could shelter in there until Collins opens the side gate in the morning. I doubt you'll get much sleep but at least you'll be dry.'

To his relief, she nodded. 'Down by the back wall. It'll set tongues wagging among the servants when we appear from the garden in our nightclothes, but I don't see that we have much choice.'

Together they turned for the longest path, both squinting as the driving rain stung their eyes. Joseph only had to lengthen his already long stride slightly to keep pace with Isabelle as she hurried towards the end of the garden, an indistinct shape against the far wall growing closer until its ornamental roof and tall windows came into clearer view.

Thankfully the door opened when Joseph pushed it, and he stepped aside to let Isabelle scurry past him, her unlaced boots tracking mud onto the stone floor.

He followed her inside, shaking the water from his hair as he shut the door behind them. The rain immediately hurled itself against the wood, as if trying to break through, and Joseph ran a finger around the inside of his soaking collar as he peered about the darkened room.

'Is there a fireplace?'

'No. We only use this during the summer, when

there's no need for a fire.' Isabelle's voice was stilted, courtesy of the frozen clench of her teeth, and her arms were wrapped tightly around herself. 'I'm not sure we'll be much warmer in here, but at least we're out of the rain.'

Joseph glanced down at her. Her loose curls were more like waves now, hanging limply around her wet shoulders, and even in the semi darkness he could make out the damp sheen on her skin. She didn't strike him as bedraggled, however. Instead she reminded him of a water nymph…a naiad come to grace him with her otherworldly presence…and he had to clear his throat before he trusted himself to speak.

'That dressing gown isn't helping. It's drenched— just like my coat.'

He ran his hand over his lapel, grimacing at the cold wetness. If his coat had been any drier he would have surrendered it to Isabelle without a second thought, but it would do her little good in its present state, probably adding to her discomfort rather than the reverse.

He was just becoming uneasy when he felt inspiration strike. A chaise longue stood against one wall, with what appeared to be a fur rug folded at its foot. It might be itchy but it would be better than nothing and, crossing the room, he picked it up and shook out the folds.

'Here. You can use this.' Joseph held it out as Isabelle came nearer, still hugging herself tightly. 'Take your wet dressing gown off and wrap yourself in it. You'll soon warm up with this around you.'

He caught her glance from the rug to his face and back again, although it was with only the slightest hesitation that she undid the belt holding her dressing gown closed. Peeling it off, she lay the sodden thing over the back of the chaise, and Joseph bit down on his tongue as he placed the rug around her shoulders, achingly aware only a covering of damp linen stood between his fingers and her bare skin.

The rug hung around her like a luxurious cloak, Isabelle now resembling a queen rather than a nymph, and he made sure not to look too closely at where the neck of her nightgown showed an expanse of regally delicate white throat. Settling herself on the chaise she shucked off her boots and drew her legs up beneath her, wrapping herself more snugly before peering up at him through the gloom.

'What about you? You must be frozen too.'

'I'm fine. I've weathered far lower temperatures than this.'

Her eyes narrowed, their scrutiny stirring the hairs on his admittedly cold arms. Before he could step away, however, a little hand emerged from beneath the rug, reaching out to touch his own and sending a short, sharp shock the length of his arm.

'Your hands are like ice!'

'I said I'm fine.'

'And *I* say you're not. You could fall ill, wearing

wet clothes in the middle of the night, with no way of warming yourself for hours.'

With the determination he'd long since come to expect from her, she moved over on the chaise, loosening her wrappings and beckoning him closer.

'Come and sit beside me. This rug is big enough for two, and I won't have you catching a fever for my lack of sharing.'

Immediately Joseph's heart leaped up into his throat. The idea of sitting beside his wife while she wore only the thinnest of nightgowns was a temptation like no other, feeling the warmth of her body mingling with his until there could be no telling where his ended and hers began. It would push his self-control to its very limit and he shook his head, painfully aware of how much he wanted to accept.

Ever since that scene in the gallery he hadn't been able to stop wondering what might have happened if Marina hadn't interrupted, and now that there was little chance of anyone disturbing them he wasn't sure he ought to take the risk.

'There's really no need. I'm not some fragile creature that will keel over from a sniffle. But I thank you all the same.'

He tried to sound offhand, but he knew Isabelle wouldn't be fooled. She was far too sharp to be taken in by any pretence but still he was surprised when she looked away, an expression passing over her face that the darkness made it difficult to understand.

'I disagree. I don't think one can ever be too careful.' She spoke quietly, her voice hardly audible above the rain hammering down on the roof. 'My parents' illness began with what we all thought was some trifling cold. They were in their prime—just as you are now—and yet they were still taken from me. If it's all the same to you, I'd prefer not to gamble on losing you the same way.'

She didn't look up, concentrating on the spots and swirls of the fur, and inwardly Joseph damned his clumsiness. Of course he should have remembered what she'd told him of her parents' illness—although his self-reproach faded into the background when pitted against her final sentence.

She'd prefer not to gamble on losing me?

He slipped off his saturated coat, allowing the words to linger as he dropped it onto a low table beside the chaise. They were so unexpectedly sweet that he felt his chest tighten, her meaning confusing in the best possible way. It seemed an odd sentiment for a business partner to express—but perhaps not for a woman who was beginning to feel a certain way about a man, and for the very first time he felt a ghost of hope tentatively raise its head.

Was there a possibility—no matter how small—that Isabelle was coming to regard him in the same way he did her?

The thought shone like the brightest of stars, although Joseph scarcely dared consider it as he carefully sat down beside her, bracing himself against the flood of sensation that overcame him as he pulled the rug around them both and felt Isabelle's shoulder brush against his chest. To fully enclose themselves in the fur she would have to come even closer still, and he gritted his teeth as she did so, shuffling so near that she was all but sitting in his lap with the top of her still-damp head almost pressed beneath his chin.

At the movement of her leg against his Joseph felt his fingers twitch, itching to be allowed to go exploring. The hem of Isabelle's nightgown had risen up her thigh and the warmth of her bare skin was so close to his fingertips that he could feel it without having to move—although he couldn't think of anything he wanted to do more. The combination of her intriguing words and the heated press of her body made it hard to think, and he knew his voice must have betrayed him when he managed to force out a reply.

'I'm sorry if I offended you. I didn't mean to imply anything careless about your parents or the severity of their illness.'

For once he was glad he couldn't see Isabelle's face. Whatever she was thinking was hidden from him by the downward angle of her head and he made sure to fix his attention on the raindrops skating down the window instead of trying to catch her eye.

'You needn't apologise. I wasn't offended. Only… worried.'

'About me?'

'Of course about you. Who else?'

She shifted slightly, the press of her shoulder against his chest increasing. It had a corresponding effect on his pulse, speeding it up another notch as again her hinted sentiment fanned the embers of his new hopes, although his caution returned sharply when she went on.

'Why is it that any display of concern surprises you? Why *shouldn't* I want you to be safe?'

It was a question that came dangerously close to touching on the one subject he never wanted to broach, and the spectre of his unhappy past lurched up at once to place a skeletal hand on his shoulder, warning him to take care. If Isabelle carried on she might stumble into something he wanted to conceal, and he hoped his silence would speak loudly enough to replace the need for an answer.

It seemed, however, that his wife's curiosity was not so easily swayed, and he supposed he had to give her credit for taking so long to indulge it.

'That morning in the gallery... You said you'd never had anyone to care for.'

'Yes.'

'Does it follow, then, that nobody has ever cared for you in return? Is that why you find it so difficult to accept I might consider your wellbeing a priority? Because it's something you've never experienced before?'

Still resolutely watching the rain outside, Joseph stiffened. Somehow she had managed to neatly summarise the foundation on which he had built his entire life, and her ability to place her finger on the truth had never been less welcome. Surely now she'd want to know more? Try to unearth details of the unhappy years he had hoped to leave a mystery and he'd be forced to admit it had been by choice, not tragic loss, that he had been left all alone? If he had to explain his mother's abandonment of him in clear black and white Isabelle would know for certain what he had always suspected: that the other boys in the workhouse had been right in their taunts.

Any budding feelings for him would certainly be tainted if she discovered how he had never been wanted—left without even being given a name. She was too kind to scorn him, but it would be like a knife to his heart to see pity in her eyes—or, even worse, a flicker of regret. She'd surely wish she'd allowed a much better man than himself the honour of being her husband and he braced himself with all the strength a lifetime of solitude had instilled in him for the questions he knew must be coming to cut him down.

But he was wrong.

Isabelle didn't pry. She didn't even lift her head to try to look into his face. Instead she carried on smoothing the fur beneath her fingers, following each whorl of the pelt, and when she spoke her voice was again so low it was almost drowned out by the rain.

'You have a family again now, though, just as I do.

Perhaps in each other we can find what we were missing. At the very least, do you think we might try?'

Joseph choked back a sharp breath, although he knew Isabelle must have heard it. It appeared there was to be no inquisition after all—only the sweetest, most sincere question he had ever been asked, so simple and honest that it blew a chasm in the defences he had tried so hard to bolster.

An echo of his apprehension still hung about him, but his wonder forced it further away, too moved to pay it much attention as her quiet words cut through the clamour of his mind.

His stomach tying itself in knots, Joseph summoned his best attempt at composure. 'If you wish it—although I'd never presume to take the place of your first husband. I know you cared about him in a way I have no expectation of you feeling for me.'

A slight movement of Isabelle's head just beneath his chin sent a piercing thrill straight through him. It might have been a nod, or perhaps she was merely fidgeting, but the feel of her soft curls brushing his jaw made him bunch his fingers into fists against the desire to push them through her hair.

'It's true that I loved Edwin as deeply as I imagine any woman might love a man. But the feelings I had for him...'

He heard her take half a breath, as if about to speak again but changing her mind at the last moment. For an unmeasured stretch of time the ceaseless drumming on the roof was the only sound in the darkness, whatever Isabelle was thinking not allowed to spill from her mouth, and when she finally finished the sentence she'd started it was as if she'd just run a mile.

'They were of a very different kind from the ones I am beginning to have for you.'

The world abruptly stopped turning.

Joseph didn't move. He couldn't—not while his mind was wiped as blank and clean as a piece of slate, scrubbed of any rational thought by Isabelle's breathless rush. He found he could only sit, gazing without seeing at the storm outside, and listen as if from a distance when Isabelle carried on.

'I know you don't feel the same. I know you only married me to fulfil your part of our bargain and I'm sorry I've changed the stakes now, when there's no chance of you backing away.'

She faltered and Joseph wanted to seize hold of her, to take her in his arms and assure her that his silence was nothing to fear. His body, however, had other ideas. It was still too numbed by amazement to let him lift so much as a finger, and he had no choice but to let her obvious insecurity go unchecked.

'You needn't worry that I'll demand anything more of you,' Isabelle finished quietly, as if surrendering to her fate. 'We made a deal and I intend to keep to it—no matter what. I just thought you deserved to know the truth.'

She moved a little, the chaise creaking beneath her

uncertainty. With the rug wrapped tightly around them there was no hope of her edging away, although by the angle of her head he could tell she was desperate not to meet his eye. Probably she thought his lack of response an answer in itself, but Joseph had no idea how to contradict her when all he could think of was the same question that ran in repeated rings around the inside of his skull.

For all his cautious hopes he hadn't *really* expected her to mirror the feelings that had grown in him so gradually until he had no chance of fighting them, their tendrils growing like vines that wrapped irrevocably around his heart. He hadn't *really* allowed himself to believe that Isabelle, with her elegance and quick wit and a face that invaded his every dream, would ever truly stoop that low. She was a lady and he was nothing—a nameless bastard no one had wanted to claim.

The question increased the speed of its relentless laps until he could contain it no longer.

'What can a woman like you see in a man like me?'

It came out far more harshly than he had intended. He heard in it the years of repressed pain, the sting of rejection he had always been so determined not to entertain, and yet Isabelle didn't flinch from its bite. Instead she turned towards him, seeking him through the darkness that cast a shadow over them both, and for the first time since he had come to sit beside her she let him see the unhidden frankness of her face.

'Do you truly not know?'

She looked up at him, so close he could feel her breath on his face, and something inside him began to smoulder like a freshly lit fire.

'You truly cannot see what I do?'

'No. In truth I cannot fathom it.'

Isabelle almost smiled at his amazement. Her entrancing lips teetered on the brink of one, although the remnants of doubt in her eyes soon swept away that curve, and a searching gaze locked on to his as if she were trying to read his thoughts.

He still hadn't given her an answer, he realised. He was leaving her dangling over a precipice without knowing whether he would come to save her, and he saw her catch a breath when he slowly shook his head.

'I can't say that I understand. All I know for certain is that you have awakened something in me I didn't realise was possible—and that any regard you have for me is returned by mine for you, with a hundred times the ardency.'

He watched her expression flicker like a candle in a draught, uncertainty and elation bound together with neither willing to give way. It looked as if it was her turn to feel the creeping weight of disbelief, not wanting to accept what he was telling her. For some reason she was hesitant to trust, and Joseph's heart felt too full to function as she returned his unwavering stare.

'Do you mean that? Really?'

'Yes.'

Slowly Joseph reached out his hand. There was no need to rush. It would have taken an army to part him from his wife as she was now, wide-eyed and beautiful and clothed in little more than a scrap of white lace, and her rapt face told him she had no desire to flee either. She made the tiniest sound when his fingers traced a line up one side of her neck and began to draw her towards him, and that one breath was enough for Joseph to know he would follow her to the ends of the earth if his reward was to hear it one more time.

He almost groaned aloud when her lips moved on his, soft and sweet but determined to have their fill. To touch her now was as necessary as breathing, something he needed to keep him alive, and she didn't resist as he slipped his other hand around her waist and guided her onto his lap. Her arms snaked around his neck, pushing the rug from his shoulders to fall over the back of the chaise, but neither noticed the cold night air that rushed in to replace it.

Perhaps Isabelle's blood was as hot as Joseph's, his temperature rising with each deft movement of her tongue until he felt feverish with want, or perhaps the chill was a small price to pay to feel the heat of his hands through the thin material of her nightgown. Whatever the reason, Joseph was grateful for it, unable to stop a dark smile at Isabelle's gasp when his questing fingers found the bare skin of her thigh and were at long last allowed to savour its velvet warmth.

His heart was beating like a call to arms and he

felt Isabelle's chest moving just as fast as his own, his pulse lancing upwards as she tangled her fingers in his hair to prevent any chance of escape. His fingertips traced higher along her legs, pushing her nightdress further with every sweep, and it was only the distant recollection of their wedding night that stopped him from going further still.

She had to be the one to take the final step, no matter how much he ached to lay her down and show her what she had never known…even if his hands shook and his heart felt as though it might break through his chest. She was the purest, most precious thing in the whole of his life and he would do nothing to make her regret the feelings she had come to hold, the first person ever to want him for himself rather than the strength a bag of coins could buy. If she never felt ready to grant him the most intimate knowledge of her body then he was prepared to honour that choice— although as she leaned down to whisper into his ear, each word so suffused with helpless desire that Joseph could hardly sit still, it seemed such restraint would not be necessary.

'You know… I don't think anyone will come to disturb us this time.'

His hands tightened involuntarily on the lush fullness of her hips, his fingers digging into the skin. Drawing back slightly, he looked into her eyes, heavylidded and hazy as he knew his own must be, and the invitation in them left no room for doubt. A second glance, however, told him he'd been wrong. It was an instruction that glowed in those oceanic depths, not an invitation, and with the obedience of a man who knew when it was required Joseph traced another burning line towards the hem of her nightgown.

He felt Isabelle shiver as his hand ghosted over her skin, his breath growing uneven when she caught her bottom lip between her teeth. With a slowness the opposite of the urgency that flooded his veins he took hold of the lacy hem and drew it upwards, half expecting his body to burst into flames when the full beauty of Isabelle's undulating form was laid out before him like a perfect work of art.

He swallowed hard, unable to resist the urge to drink her in. The dips and curves of her were like a master's painting, almost too glorious to belong to one made of flesh and blood, and the alabaster of her skin shone pearly in the darkness he wished would be split by the sun. He wanted to explore every inch of her, to kiss every freckle and trace every line where laughter or sadness had left its mark, but while darkness surrounded them he would have to conduct his survey by touch instead of sight.

Her breaths were coming quickly, although he thought he caught the faintest shadow of shyness beneath the longing that held her in its grasp. It was the first time a man had seen her full splendour, Joseph remembered, and it was his honour to show her that it was a sight worth waiting for. He'd lain with women before, of course, but none like this: in both inner and outer beauty nobody could match his wife, and with fresh heat beginning to course through him he bit back a smile at Isabelle's feverish shudder as he ran his thumb over her bottom rib.

'I'm glad there will be no interruptions tonight. With your permission, I'll show you exactly how much.'

Chapter Eleven

It was still dark outside when Isabelle woke, slightly stiff from lying on the hard stone floor. The air in the summerhouse was cold, but the shape behind her was not, and without opening her eyes she smiled as she felt a warm hand slip around her bare waist to draw her closer.

Heat climbed her spine as Joseph buried his nose in her hair, his breath tickling the back of her neck, and she allowed herself to be borne away by sensation as his hand drifted lower. Wrapped in the rug, they were cocooned together, their legs a tangle neither wanted to unravel, and Isabelle's breath hitched as Joseph's gentle fingertips strayed closer and closer to the secret place so recently discovered.

The events of the night flickered against her closed eyelids like leaping flames and she arched against him, only dimly hearing his dark chuckle as she writhed in his hold. The hard planes of his body pressed insistently at her back, his skin against hers setting every nerve ablaze, and the final thought she had before abandoning reason completely was that she wished she'd allowed him such freedoms long before.

For a time neither spoke. There was no need: their instincts made words unnecessary, moving together in an unchoreographed dance they both somehow knew. Isabelle pulled Joseph closer to her, wanting to wrap herself in his heat and the deliciously masculine scent of his skin, and she gasped against his shoulder as a flood of molten bliss ran singing through every vein.

When he moved away she lay still, luxuriating in the ripples of her release as they swept over her in gradually decreasing waves. For all the stiffness in her limbs she felt better than she had in months—lighter, somehow, as if some of the weight that sat permanently on her chest had been lifted from her, and when she finally opened her eyes she at once saw the reason why.

In the semi-darkness Joseph's smile was distracting as he lay on his side, somehow managing to be soft but wicked at the same time.

'Good morning.'

'Good morning yourself.'

The grin grew a little wider. 'Did you sleep well?'

'Not at all.'

'No. Me neither.'

Isabelle felt her cheeks flush pink, although she made no move to pull the rug back up over her bare shoulders. There seemed little point in pretending modesty now, when Joseph had run his hands over every inch of her in the sleepless delight of the night and his own shirt lay in a crumpled heap near the door, where one of them must have thrown it.

'Oh, dear. Perhaps it was this poor excuse for a bed that kept you awake?'

'Perhaps...' Joseph nodded thoughtfully, bringing a well-muscled arm up to prop beneath his head. 'Or perhaps it was the person in it with me?'

Isabelle nipped at her bottom lip, trying not to look too pleased—and failing.

He reached out, her breath catching as his fingers traced the line of her collarbone. As scarred and threatening as they seemed when balled into fists, it had amazed her to find his hands could be so gentle when he chose, and his face seemed to soften likewise as he skimmed his palm along the jutting ridge.

'Last night...'

'I know. It was the same for me.'

She saw him swallow, perhaps the faintly dazed wonder that had her in its grasp holding him too. Somehow she had succeeded in breaking down the barriers Joseph had erected between himself and everyone else, her own hesitations equally powerless to deny the attraction that had blossomed into something so much more.

Now they had both finally found the courage to be honest there seemed only one question left to ask, one last piece of the puzzle to put into place, and Isabelle placed her hand on top of Joseph's to still his lingering exploration of the hollow at her throat.

'Joseph. What did you mean…?'

She paused in sudden uncertainty. Was now the best time to raise the question, both of them naked and vulnerable as the world slowly woke around them? The night had been so perfect she wanted nothing to spoil the morning following it, their newfound connection shining bright in the creeping light of a new day. With his short hair tousled and his eyes finally free of the wariness that had clouded them for once Joseph looked fallible—human instead of some handsome statue hewn from granite—and it was only the inexorable power of one dark eyebrow rising enquiringly that made her continue.

'Last night, when I spoke of my feelings, what did you mean, *a man like you*? Our ranks are different, it's true, but you must have realised by now that a title means little to me. Is that it? Or is there something else?'

For a long moment he merely looked at her, but then he turned away, rolling onto his back to examine the ceiling instead of her face. As he lay there his profile seemed made of stone, the softness of a minute before vanished without trace, and Isabelle felt cold dismay rise to drench her as she watched a frown pit his brow.

The rain had stopped. Early-morning birds had just begun to call, the pale dawn light starting to turn shadows back into tangible forms… But Isabelle was hardly aware of anything but her husband as he took a breath, apparently on the brink of something he had clearly hoped to avoid.

'No. It isn't solely the discrepancy in our social standing.'

'Then what?'

The pinch between his eyebrows tightened further. He seemed to be thinking fast, perhaps deciding which way to jump, although his natural courage was clearly winning over the temptation to back down from the truth.

'I haven't been as honest with you as I should have been. There are things…things about me I didn't wish you to know. That is what I meant.'

Isabelle's stomach tightened. What *'things'* could he be referring to? He had always been hard to read, but somehow she sensed this was different. Whatever he had been keeping from her was evidently enough to make even a mercenary uncertain, perhaps fearing the harshness of her judgement, and Isabelle's pulse stepped up as she wondered what could possibly make him so unsure.

'I see. I'd hope that now, however, you'd feel you can tell me whatever it was you thought to conceal,' she ventured carefully, making sure to keep her voice even despite the racing of her heart. 'After last night… surely you can have no doubts?'

Still Joseph studied the timber beams of the summerhouse roof. 'You might feel differently once you've heard.'

'I give you my word I will not. Whatever it is, Joseph—nothing you tell me now can alter the place you're beginning to make for yourself in my heart.'

He looked at her, the eyes searching her face hesitant yet filled with a kind of cautious hope that made her want to reach out to caress his cheek, but she made herself keep still as she let him take his time to consider.

'Do you mean that? In all sincerity?'

'Yes.'

He nodded slowly, his uncharacteristic hesitation still plain to see. Another glance seemed to help him make up his mind—perhaps something in her quiet acceptance giving him the permission he needed to open the door he had kept so firmly locked.

'Very well. If you're truly set on knowing… I find I somehow can't refuse you anything, and I know myself that you deserve the truth.'

Isabelle waited, her throat tight with apprehension. There was nothing he could say that would make her change her mind and she wished he would believe it, never faltering in that resolve even when Joseph once again turned his attention to the roof. It must be easier for him if he couldn't see her watching him, and she was just starting to wonder if she should turn away when he began to speak.

'I wasn't orphaned as a child, as I have allowed you

to believe. I don't have a family—that much is true—but only because my mother abandoned me when I was but three days old.'

Isabelle's eyes widened. Staring at that hard profile, she knew not to say a word, that any interruption would be sure to make him slam the shutters closed once more, and she watched mutely as he took a breath.

'I didn't even have a name. Where your family was lost to you because of tragedy, mine was through rejection by the person or people supposed to love me the most. I thought if you knew I was unwanted you would think the same about me as I have done for my whole life—that I am incapable of securing anyone's regard, and that there is nothing in me worth giving a damn about. To my mind, if my own mother didn't care for me, why would anybody else?'

His face was blank, any emotion that might be behind it resolutely hidden so Isabelle might not see, although that didn't stop the powerful effect his words had on her aching chest. Each one was like a knife, slicing through to pierce where he had triumphantly gained possession of her heart, and she could hardly breathe as confusion and compassion ran over her like a wave.

Joseph had been abandoned as a defenceless infant, left alone without even a name to link him to his past. It seemed unthinkable—impossible that such a strong and unyielding man should have come from such a helpless start—and the knowledge that it had made him feel so worthless was agonising. He must have been so lonely, so closed off from the world and everyone in it, and Isabelle nearly choked on the urge to gather him in her arms and never let go.

'But… Where did you grow up? Who took care of you if you had no family?'

He gave her another swift glance, taking in the disorientated surprise that must be radiating from her. Even now he was too proud to accept pity, but apparently shock and unhappiness were tolerable, as a suggestion of a humourless smile slightly twisted his mouth.

'The workhouse on Gas Street, where my mother had left me so tenderly on the steps. I lived there until I was fifteen, and every day was a torment I won't try to describe. But by the time I left I was the tallest there, even among the grown men, and I had already begun to garner a reputation as a fighter.'

He broke off to examine the healed line of scar tissue across the knuckles of one hand, running his fingers over it as though it held vivid memories.

'My first job came from a local gentleman. He wanted me to threaten a man who had cheated him at cards, and I found I was good at providing menace for money. I learned to trade on my strength and never looked back, not expecting anyone to care for me or intending to show any care in turn—until, of course, I met you.'

Joseph rolled over, coming to rest on his side so he could face Isabelle directly, and she felt a little of her compassion give way to a fluttering sensation. The hard-edged smile was still there, hinting at far darker recollections he had no intention of sharing, but he reached out his hand, his fingers finding hers and taking hold of them with gentle firmness, and Isabelle found she couldn't answer as he slowly brought them to his lips.

'I don't know by what means you got under my skin, a woman the perfect embodiment of everything I thought I could never hope for, but you're there now and I wouldn't have it any other way.'

The fluttering grew stronger as he kissed her fingertips, the slight prickle of his stubble sending delightful friction across her skin. The air around them was still chill but his kisses stoked a fire in her blood, raising her temperature as if it was a summer day outside and not the aftermath of a storm, and made it difficult to focus on the thoughts running riot through her mind.

Sorrow and sympathy threatened to spill over, and she struggled to find the right words, wanting to offer comfort to this man who must have grown coolly accustomed to finding none.

'Joseph...'

She faltered when he quietly shook his head, as if already guessing what she was going to say.

'There's no need to say anything more. I'd rather not speak of it now. If I'm right, and I've somehow become the luckiest man alive, we will have years to talk of the things I've never told anyone else.'

Again he trailed his lips across her knuckles, and Isabelle knew when she was beaten. It would have taken a far harder woman than she to withstand the assault of that clever mouth, and her breathing grew a little faster when he lifted his eyes to meet hers in a look that made time stand still.

'Of course. That's up to you to decide.'

The heat beneath her skin was building and she felt a pang of vivid disappointment when Joseph let go of her hand, pushing himself up to lean against the side of the chaise. The rug slipped down as he moved, barely covering his waist, and Isabelle couldn't look away as he stretched, the taut ridges of his muscles clear even in the dim dawn light.

'As much as I'd like to stay here with you all morning, I think perhaps we ought to return to the house. The servants will be up by now, and I can't imagine you'd like to be found like this.'

He ran his eyes over her, as if to emphasise his point, and Isabelle shivered with something very different from cold as she saw the desire there, his gaze lingering on the pale smoothness of her bare shoulders.

'Indeed not. With any luck Cook will be in the kitchen now. She'll have propped the door open and we might slip inside without too much fuss.'

Reaching out, she retrieved her nightgown from where it had slipped to the floor and pulled it over her head, watching out of the corner of her eye as Joseph stood. He had no shame at all in letting her see him naked, it seemed, and a hungry darkness returned to his gaze as he pulled on his trousers, a thrill skittering sharply down the back of Isabelle's neck when he stood before her, half dressed and smiling like a man with things on his mind.

'Don't look at me like that.'

'Like what?'

'As if you know how much I want to take that nightgown right off you again.'

She flushed, a rosy tint crossing each cheek. 'How dare you? I would never think such vulgar things.'

'Of course you wouldn't. Just as I would never act on that desire.'

Buttoning his waistband, Joseph cast her an ironic bow, the gleam in his eye brighter than ever.

'Just to be on the safe side, however, I think we had better go back to the house quickly...before I change my mind.'

By the time Joseph came to sit opposite her at the breakfast table Isabelle was once again a picture of demure elegance. Not a single hair was out of place, her pale yellow gown neat and perfectly pressed, and only the tell-tale hint of colour along her cheekbones betrayed that she wasn't quite as serene as she appeared.

It was Marina's presence beside her that required such composure, as Joseph well understood, although he couldn't quite manage to stop himself from brushing her fingertips as she handed him a teacup, secretly pleased when he saw her shiver in response.

Thankfully oblivious to the unspoken connection playing out before her, Marina smiled. 'Good morning, Joseph. Did you sleep well?'

'Not especially, I'm afraid.'

'Oh, dear.'

She looked at him with a sympathy he knew he didn't deserve, and he was careful not to catch Isabelle's eye.

'Perhaps tonight will be better.'

'I'm not sure it will. I have a feeling I won't be able to sleep very much for many nights to come.'

There was a sound suspiciously like someone choking on their tea and Marina patted Isabelle's back as her sister's face disappeared into a napkin. When it reappeared Isabelle's cheeks were rosier than ever, but Joseph didn't have time to admire the effect before Collins entered with a discreet knock at the door.

'The morning post, ma'am.'

As Isabelle was still spluttering, Marina reached out instead. 'Thank you, Collins. I'll take it.'

She began to flick through the handful of letters and Joseph took advantage of her preoccupation to glance across at his wife. Isabelle had managed to compose herself, and the glare she shot him might have made him fear he was in trouble if it hadn't been accompanied by a curve of her lips that she hid behind her napkin.

She looked so different from only a couple of hours before, when the dawn light had made her bare skin gleam and her tousled curls had spread like a halo around her, and he marvelled at how she could be two people at the same time. On the one hand was the woman who had been a duchess, dignified and re-fined and impeccably polished, while on the other...

An untamed spirit, bound by nobody's wishes but her own. And both versions of Isabelle, against all odds, have come to care for me.

He could still hardly believe it. She knew every-thing now, every shameful secret he'd tried so hard to hide, and still she hadn't turned away. It seemed too good to be true that she would appreciate him for what he truly was, and he could scarcely tear his eyes away as she sat before him, half fearing that if he blinked she might somehow slip away.

After so many years of the loneliness he had tried to pass off as indifference it had almost been a relief to destroy the final obstacle between them and fully let down his guard, the warmth of Isabelle's accep-tance melting the frost he had always thought he had to endure. When she'd first asked the question he had been dreading he had instinctively wanted to run from it—but he hadn't, drawing on the nerve that had kept him alive through all his adventures, and now he was gladder than he knew how to express that he had finally let her in.

Now they could build a new life, the two of them together, with nothing left to hide. He would have to accustom himself to living with her and Marina, to having a family to replace what he had lost, and doubtless she would need to exercise patience of her own; but Joseph had never been one to flee from a challenge and it was one that he knew, without hesitation, he was ready to begin.

'Oh!'

Both Joseph and Isabelle started at Marina's cry. She was holding one of the letters, her face alight with excitement, and Isabelle's eyebrows rose enquiringly.

'What is it?'

'We're invited to a ball at Colonel Lockhart's house on the eighteenth—all three of us!' Marina pushed the letter across the table towards her sister, who picked it up with a trace of hesitation. 'We'll go, won't we? You find Mrs Lockhart pleasant company, and you know their youngest daughter is my most particular friend. Joseph hasn't met all of our acquaintance yet, and there are sure to be people there who wish to offer their congratulations.'

Joseph watched a wary shadow creep over Isabelle's face. He hadn't been wrong: she'd definitely paused before reading the invitation, and now a crease had appeared on her smooth brow as she ran her eye down the page. He had an idea of what she was thinking, but evidently Marina did not. She seemed only aware that there didn't seem to be an enthusiastic acceptance forthcoming and was preparing to make her case.

'Please, Issy…'

Marina's voice was so plaintive it might even have softened Joseph's resolve if he'd been on the receiving end.

'We haven't been anywhere in so long. Not since…'

'Not since Edwin died. I know. Nor even before that, on account of his health.'

Isabelle didn't lift her gaze from the invitation, and Joseph knew he had indeed guessed correctly what was running through her mind.

A ball meant people coming together. It meant Marina wearing a pretty dress, showing off her youthful face and figure to their best advantage as she danced, and it meant young men would flock to watch her. It would take only one of those young men to have dark intentions, Marina's vast dowry a siren call for other creatures like Hart or Lewis.

The near-miss of the previous debacle was not one Isabelle had any intention of repeating. While Marina was too trusting to guard herself properly, Isabelle was clearly intent on doing it for her—although to keep the girl locked away was sure to breed only resentment that would cause both sisters pain.

Isabelle laid the invitation down, carefully smoothing it with one hand. She seemed to be trying to buy time before having to answer, and Joseph could feel her reluctance as she leaned back a little in her chair.

'I'll think about it.'

'Oh, Issy!'

Marina was on her feet at once and flinging her arms around her sister she hugged her tightly, almost unbalancing them both in the process.

'Thank you. I knew you would agree!'

'I didn't say yes!'

Isabelle's voice was muffled by the clumsy embrace, but Marina didn't stay to hear it more clearly. With a beam at Joseph she danced away, her footsteps tripping prettily towards the door, and with the whisk of a rose-pink skirt she disappeared from the room.

'Marina!' Isabelle called after her, half rising from her chair. 'Marina! *I didn't say yes!*'

For a moment she stood, staring at the empty doorway, before slowly sinking back into her seat. Marina's exuberance had knocked over the saltshaker and Isabelle reached for it, setting it upright with a weary sigh.

'Well… That'll be all she talks of now, whether I intended to accept or not.'

'And you didn't.'

It wasn't a question. Joseph watched her from over the rim of his teacup, disliking the worry that now dared tinge her happiness, and Isabelle quietly shook her head.

'No. I confess if I'd seen the invitation first I might

not have told her about it.' She sighed again, fiddling with the saltshaker's silver lid. 'I know that isn't fair. I know I ought not think of keeping things from her. It's just... You've seen yourself how vulnerable she is. I'd never been so scared as when I thought I might lose her, and I don't ever want that to happen again.'

Joseph put down his cup. None of Isabelle's fears surprised him. She'd been terrified the first time, left with nowhere to turn—but now things were different.

He leaned forward, reaching across the table to gently take hold of her hand, and immediately she stopped fidgeting, allowing him to trace his thumb over her clenched knuckles.

'I understand that you want the best for her, but you can't keep her locked away until she's an old maid. The reason we wed—to begin with, at least—was so I could help you keep her safe while she lived her life. I fully intend to keep that promise. You have my word that I won't let anything bad befall her again.'

Isabelle's eyes narrowed briefly. She seemed to be wondering whether to accept his reassurances, and trying for a small smile that didn't quite convince.

'You would go to a ball to watch over her?' she enquired doubtfully. 'Even though you detest the *ton*?'

Joseph hesitated. The idea of spending an evening immersed in the world he loathed wasn't one he relished, it was true. He'd never been a ball before, of course, but it was bound to be everything he despised, with gaudy shows of wealth and privilege everywhere he looked, and he'd be surrounded by people who had never lifted a finger for themselves in their entire lives. It would be an ordeal he never would have chosen to undertake if Isabelle hadn't looked so tired, her face drawn and unease written in every line, but he made himself shrug.

'If I have to. If that's what it will take to wipe away your frown.'

Her face softened. 'Truly? You'd go so far?'

At his short nod she gently disentangled her fingers from his and pushed back her chair. Joseph watched as she came around the table towards him, his heart starting to beat more quickly as she stood beside him, and something stirred embers inside him when she placed a cool hand on each of his cheeks.

'You're a good man.' Bending down, Isabelle tilted his face up to hers, dropping a tantalisingly soft kiss on his lips. 'I can't imagine now how I didn't see it the first time we met.'

She drew back a little to look into his eyes, her own eyes widening when he abruptly swept her into his lap. He wrapped his arms around her waist so she had no hope of wriggling free, but she didn't seem to want to, leaning against his chest so he could smell the scent of her freshly washed her hair.

'Probably because I was inexcusably rude and more concerned with my tankard than with you. Hellfire, I was a fool!'

Isabelle laughed. Some of her worry had clearly

lifted at his promise and he treasured the sound, more dear to him now than he ever could have imagined.

'That might have had something to do with it. How glad I am for second chances.'

Chapter Twelve

Her prediction was indeed correct. For the next two weeks Marina spoke of little but the upcoming ball, and Isabelle found she didn't have the heart to check her after so many months of sadness and change.

Novelty played a large part in Marina's excitement: the Lockharts' ball would be her first, and not even the prospect of Isabelle watching her every move was enough to dampen her enthusiasm. Her prettiest gown had already been selected, and many serious discussions undertaken about how she should put up her hair, and as the time drew nearer Isabelle was mildly concerned that her sister might burst with anticipation.

Not everyone, however, was quite as thrilled by the idea of their first real *ton* gathering.

For all his earlier assurances Joseph didn't look entirely at ease as Isabelle descended Winford's grand staircase on the evening of the eighteenth. Unaware he was being observed, he fiddled with the collar of his new coat, unnecessarily adjusting the pristine lapels as he waited by the front door, although he lowered his hand the instant he realised he wasn't alone.

He turned, and Isabelle felt her face warm slightly at the change in his expression as he watched her come towards him. He shook his head as he surveyed her, from the feathers in her hair to the hem of her coral gown, his eyes lingering over the low neckline for a second longer than was strictly polite.

'How do you manage it?'

'Manage what?'

'This. Just when I think you couldn't get more beautiful, you prove me wrong.'

The colour in Isabelle's cheeks deepened and she felt her lips lift into a smile she couldn't have prevented if she'd wanted to. She was still getting used to the change in her husband since they'd finally found the courage to be honest, and even now it seemed hard to believe how far they had come. If anyone had told her, after that first disastrous meeting at the Drake, how much he would come to mean to her she would have laughed or thought they were deranged; and yet it was true.

'You're too kind. You look very handsome yourself.'

'Hmm…' He glanced down at himself doubtfully. 'Thank you. I almost didn't recognise myself when I first looked in the mirror. I suppose it was inevitable there would need to be changes.'

Isabelle ran an admiring hand over the expensive fabric of his sleeve. 'It's only your clothes that we might alter slightly. *You* don't need to change one bit. Knowing how little you want to be there tonight, I simply imagined you'd prefer to avoid drawing attention to yourself...blending in with what the other gentlemen will be wearing will help.'

Privately, she thought he stood very little chance of going unnoticed whatever he wore, and when he smiled Isabelle felt herself stir. He was easily the most comely man in all of Bishops Morton, and probably in the county, and the crisp clothes of a gentleman did nothing to put him at a disadvantage.

For the first time since she'd known him he had shaved right down to the skin. Even on their wedding day a trace of stubble had remained, but now his face was clear, his jawline displayed so sharply Isabelle wondered vaguely if she might chip a tooth on it. There was a pale scar on his chin she hadn't noticed before, shining like a tiny crescent moon, and she was about to reach up to touch it when Marina came barrelling into the hall.

'Are you ready? Shall we go?'

Her face was glowing with excitement, and despite her reservations Isabelle couldn't help but laugh. In her haste Marina was trying to put her gloves on the wrong hands, and Isabelle gently took them from her, swapping them over before giving them back.

'The ball will wait while you put your gloves on correctly. It isn't going anywhere.'

'I know. I'm just so excited!' Marina beamed at both

her sister and Joseph—who, to his credit, attempted to appear marginally more enthusiastic. 'Georgiana Lockhart said there's to be real pineapple in the punch and dancing till dawn. Think of it, Issy—pineapple!'

It crossed Isabelle's mind that the youngest Miss Lockhart was possibly stretching the truth, but she didn't voice her cynicism. Marina's joy was a pleasure to see and she was careful not to let her apprehension show as they left the house and crunched across the gravel driveway to the carriage, the evening's chill compensated for by countless glittering stars. The Colonel's impressive home wasn't far away, and Isabelle resolved that by the time they arrived she would have put her worries to one side, determined not to spoil an evening about which her sister held such high hopes. Surely no young man would be fool enough to dare anything improper under Joseph's nose?

But as the carriage jerked forward Isabelle tried to ignore the little voice in the back of her mind that queried whether she was making a mistake.

Joseph's foreboding increased as he stepped down from the carriage and looked up at the imposing house before him. The front door was open, candlelight spilling down the grand steps and flickering in the tall windows, and the sound of music and laughter drifted on the night air. Colonel Lockhart's home wasn't quite as magnificent as Winford House, but it was still a sight more impressive than the residences he'd been

accustomed to for the first thirty-something years of
his life, and just because he now lived in splendour
himself didn't mean he felt any more comfortable
about what was to come.

For anyone else he wouldn't even have considered
coming. For nobody but Isabelle would he endure such
a disagreeable evening, the anxiety she was trying so
hard to hide setting his protective instincts alight. He
didn't *want* to be there, rubbing shoulders with people who wouldn't have given him a second glance if
he'd been lying in the gutter, but for Marina's safety
and his wife's peace of mind he was prepared to do
whatever was necessary.

He was a husband, a brother-in-law, and a man
with a purpose bigger than himself—a position he
had never dreamed of holding but would now protect
with his life.

He felt a hand settle in the crook of his elbow. Isabelle was likewise gazing up at the house's façade
with a tinge of worry, but she smiled encouragingly
when she met his eye.

'A handsome house, is it not?'

'Yes. Though I think I'd feel more at home going
around the back to the tradesman's entrance...'

She suppressed a laugh, dipping an elegant curtsey
to a well-dressed couple making for the steps.

Other guests were arriving thick and fast. This colonel was evidently fond of a large gathering, and Joseph found his shoulders had tensed. It seemed as if

they were coming from every direction: men with their gleaming buttons and silk cravats exiting crest-emblazoned carriages with women so bedazzled and bedecked with jewels they almost hurt his eyes.

Steady. You've faced far worse than this.

He could feel Isabelle's attention trained on him and he deliberately dropped his shoulders, squaring them as if he were about to march into battle. He might have some misgivings, but he would *not* have her thinking he was in any way afraid, and he even managed to find a smile for Marina when she took his other arm.

'Why are we waiting? Let's go in!'

She seemed ready to drag him if he didn't move, and Joseph mounted the first step, pushing his reluctance aside with a firm hand. With every forward pace the music and buzz of voices grew louder, and setting foot inside the door he felt as though he'd entered another world.

Servants came forward immediately to relieve them of hats and cloaks and he allowed Marina to lead— or rather haul—him towards a set of open doors beyond which the dancing had clearly already begun. On his other arm Isabelle sailed with all the serenity of a swan, first greeting their hosts and then nodding and smiling at passing acquaintances with a grace her sister might have done well to copy.

The three of them made slow but steady progress through the crowds until they reached the far end of the room. Above them candles blazed in gilded chan-

deliers, their light glancing off silken gowns and sparkling jewels, while mirrors hanging from every wall
made the space seem even bigger and more packed
with luxury than it already was. The floor was so
highly polished that Joseph could almost see his reflection, and despite his unease he had to be careful
not to stare, the wealth and extravagance all around
him so striking he hardly knew where to look.

'Marina. Listen to me.'

Clearly the bustling opulence had captured Marina's
attention as well as Joseph's. Her eyes were wide and
she seemed barely to notice that she was being spoken
to, only dragging her gaze away from a woman in a
particularly sumptuous gown when Isabelle placed a
cautionary hand on her arm.

'Remember what we talked of. You must stay where
I can see you and you are not to wander off alone. Do
you hear me? I want to be able to see you at all times.'

'Yes, Issy. I know.'

'You're here to enjoy yourself, not to find a husband.'

'Yes, Issy. I know.'

'So if any young man tries to impose upon you—'

'Yes, Issy—*I know*!'

Marina looked desperate to be spared another lecture, and with obvious reluctance Isabelle let go of
her arm. No sooner had she relinquished her claim
than a young lady appeared from out of the crowd,
falling upon Marina with the kind of enthusiasm only

sixteen-year-old girls in a great state of excitement could manage.

'You're here at last!'

Joseph watched with mild bemusement as the two embraced with the fervour of friends who had been parted for years, rather than a single day. It seemed Miss Lockhart had no more intention of letting the evening go to waste than Marina did, and with only the barest of curtseys in his and Isabelle's direction their youngest hostess linked her arm and began to draw her away, the two girls' heads close together as they whispered about who knew what.

'Marina... Remember...'

Isabelle let her warning tail off as her sister was borne rapidly away. Her face was tight with anxiety, and Joseph gently laid his hand on the small of her back, meaning only to comfort her but unable to stop a flicker of appreciation at the subtle warmth beneath his palm.

'Try to relax. You'll be in for a long night if you're so tightly wound the whole time.'

She was craning her neck to follow Marina's progress through the crowd, but at his words Isabelle sighed. 'I know. I'm behaving like a fussy old hen, worried that a fox might get too close to her eggs.'

With one last glance towards where Marina and Miss Lockhart were now huddled with a gaggle of other young ladies against the opposite wall, Isabelle gave him a wry half-smile.

'Come on. We may as well go to stand with the other old hens.'

She took his arm, a now-familiar tingle spreading beneath his skin as her gloved hand settled at his elbow. A group of older women sat on various sofas and comfortable chairs in one corner of the ballroom and Isabelle guided him towards them, their advance hampered by seemingly the whole of Bishops Morton coming to offer their good wishes. There were introductions to weather and smiles to fake, and by the time Joseph dropped onto one of the vacant sofas he felt as though he had been battered by a storm.

Isabelle arranged herself demurely beside him. She didn't seem in the least perturbed by the flurry of interest that had eddied around them, and under cover of brushing a fleck of dust from Joseph's shoulder she whispered into his ear.

'You're doing extremely well. Nobody will have any idea how little you're enjoying yourself. That last bow to Lady Fitzgerald was especially convincing.'

The feeling of her breath on his neck was far too pleasant for such a public setting, and he steeled himself against the urge to turn his head. It would be easy to catch her lips if he moved, but he managed—just—to resist.

'Thank you. I'll be fine so long as I can sit here and mind my own business. I assume I won't be expected to dance?'

'Not by me. It isn't considered fashionable to dance

with one's own husband. You'll be safe while you sit among the chaperones—although if you go wandering about you might have to do your duty if there are those without partners.'

He glanced around, nodding politely when he made accidental eye contact with a matronly-looking woman on the next sofa. 'Is that who these ladies are? Chaperones?'

'Yes. It's our job to make sure nobody enjoys themselves.'

There was amusement in Isabelle's lowered voice, but it couldn't entirely mask her lingering uncertainty. Her eyes flitted constantly towards Marina, her attention never wavering for more than a moment.

'Really, though…we all just want the best for our charges. The way we go about it might seem strange from the outside, but that's how it is—and how I imagine it will always be among the *ton*.'

Joseph followed the direction of her gaze to where Marina was taking her place for the next dance. Her cheeks were flushed and her smile lit up the room, and when the band started she leapt forward with a delight even the coldest of hearts couldn't ignore.

Her partner took her hand and Joseph frowned, ready to spring to his feet if Isabelle gave him the word. 'Is that allowed?'

Her nod put him a little more at ease. 'He's the Colonel's son. A pleasant boy with no ambition and still very much tied to his mother's apron strings. Marina is in no danger from him.'

Joseph watched the youth turn the colour of a beetroot as Marina skipped around him. Anyone with eyes could see she was a pretty girl, and would become an even prettier woman, and for the first time Joseph felt a glimmer of understanding. It must have been bittersweet for Isabelle to watch her sister growing older, having to loosen her grip on the girl she'd mothered since she was a girl herself. She was proud of Marina while being fearful for her too, and he wished the *ton*'s damnably stiff etiquette would allow him to take a reassuring hold of her hand.

'I suppose even among these good families there will always be young lads looking for ways around the rules. I've lost count of the times I was paid to act as go-between for some star-crossed couple. I even escorted a girl up to Gretna once—although that isn't something I'd ever repeat.'

Isabelle turned to him with startled speed, but Joseph shook his head.

'Don't look so worried. It's *because* I know all the tricks that I'll be able to protect Marina. An old poacher makes the best gamekeeper, after all.'

She hesitated for a moment, still looking more alarmed than he'd meant to make her. Her gaze flicked yet again to her sister, apparently drawing some small comfort from the sight of Lockhart Junior tripping over his own feet.

'You still think I'm being over-cautious?'

'No. But perhaps you needn't worry *quite* so much. You've done all you can to guard her from unwise matrimony—even going so far as to enter into it yourself. And look where that got you!'

He'd meant to lighten the mood, but Isabelle didn't smile. Her silk-gloved fingers were laced together, and although she was far too well bred to grimace in public he could tell it was a struggle for her not to.

'I know she'll have to marry eventually,' she answered, her voice carefully quiet. 'And I *want* her to. Just not while she's still half a child…and certainly not because she's been backed into a corner by some scheming brute only after her dowry. She deserves a love match, and I intend to watch out for her until the right man comes along to offer one.'

Joseph's desire to reach for her was beginning to become unbearable. If she didn't stop looking so anxious he thought he might not be able to resist taking her fretful face in his hands and kissing away her fears, and hang any member of the stuffy upper class who might be offended.

'I know that. You want a love match for Marina because you couldn't have one for yourself.'

'Perhaps not in the traditional sense, although Edwin and I did truly love each other in a way. And as for you—'

Isabelle stopped, the end of her sentence hanging unspoken between them. He saw her glance sideways quickly, as if wondering if she'd said too much, and then his heart turned over as she turned away, her face hidden but the tip of her shell-like ear turning suspiciously pink.

He watched her, waiting for her to look back, but she seemed to be focusing on one of the chandeliers, and the back of her head gave nothing away.

What was she about to say...?

Joseph's chest tightened. Had Isabelle been about to say that she *loved* him? Perhaps stumblingly, perhaps wandering into a confession she was now too shy to own, but the meaning of her silence saying more than any impassioned speech?

His insides felt as though they were locked in a fist of disbelief. He knew she cared for him—the past weeks since that night in the garden had been the most wonderful of his life—but for her to go further still...

Those three little words were something he had never expected to inspire in anyone—something he hadn't known how much he wanted until Isabelle had come crashing into his hard, cold existence, and even as he tried not to be swept up in a tide of breathless hope he realised he already knew his own truth.

If she says it, I'll say it back. And even if she doesn't I'll tell her anyway.

The ballroom seemed to have grown quiet around him, its colour and vigour dimmed. All he could see was Isabelle. The golden sheen of her hair with its crown of feathers made her look even more like the queen he considered her to be, and he felt as though he ought to kneel before her instead of lean forward to murmur into her ear.

'What about me…?'

He heard her take a sharp breath at the nearness of his lips to her skin, perhaps a thrill tingling at her sensitive nape. She half turned, her eyes seeking his, and Joseph had to bite down on a snatched breath of his own as their gazes locked, hazel on greenish blue, to send a bolt of pure lightning through every one of his nerves.

For all the bustle around them they might have been the only two people in the room, the unwavering connection of that powerful stare linking them so intimately it belonged more in a bedroom than anywhere else, and Joseph was about to throw caution to the wind and lean in to kiss her when a shadow falling over them shattered the moment like a rock through a pane of glass.

'Well, Mrs Carter. What do you think of our poor arrangements?'

Mrs Lockhart was standing beside them, thankfully too wrapped up in the rigours of being a hostess to notice the tension she had broken with her ill-timed interruption, and at once Isabelle snapped back to her ladylike self. Only a slight flush betrayed her, and Joseph had to marvel at how smoothly she could make the transition.

'There's nothing poor about them. Everything looks wonderful. The musicians are particularly good.'

'Thank you. I do like to see my guests enjoying themselves.'

Their hostess looked pleased, surveying her kingdom with modest satisfaction.

'Your sister's enthusiasm has been especially gratifying to watch. But does she not intend to dance any more this evening? I don't see her taking her place.'

Immediately Isabelle's sharp eyes swept the room, darting to the place where they had last seen Marina. Her partner was still lingering near the spot, as if hoping she might return, and Georgiana was giggling up at some smiling young man, but it was true that Marina herself was nowhere to be seen.

Isabelle rose swiftly to her feet. 'I'm certain she does. Dancing is all she's spoken of since your kind invitation arrived.'

Joseph stood likewise, making sure to keep his own wariness in check. Isabelle's was far more obvious as she looked around, lifting her chin to peer over the heads of the people around her, her palpable unease growing with every second.

Mrs Lockhart was casting about too, although with far less urgency. 'How strange… I watched her in the quadrille with Georgiana, but now I can't see her. I much prefer it when the girls are together—Miss Marina is such a sensible influence, and my youngest is a goose at the best of times.'

It was much easier for Joseph to take a survey of the ballroom than it was for either of the women, and he did so with rising apprehension. He was taller than everyone else there, towering a good half a head over the rest of the men, but that didn't help him to spot the person all three were searching for.

Isabelle looked up at him, her expression almost pleading. It was as if she was begging him not to say what she most feared—although it was Mrs Lockhart who delivered the unwanted truth.

'No, I don't see her lining up. In fact... I can't see her anywhere in this room at all.'

Chapter Thirteen

Isabelle stood still, trying to maintain some semblance of composure. At her side she could sense Joseph taking another swift scan of the room, but she already knew it was pointless. Marina's golden hair was just as distinctive as her own, and easy to pick out in a crowd. If he hadn't seen her on his first sweep he wouldn't have any more luck with the second—something he acknowledged with a subtle shake of his head as Isabelle's heart railed against her ribs.

Try to stay calm. Things may not be what they seem.

She clung to that hope as a parade of horrors danced before her and fear tried to take her by the throat. Just because Marina wasn't in the ballroom, it didn't mean she'd disappeared, and with a monumental effort Isabelle managed to find a smile to plaster over her suddenly cold face.

'How strange… If you'll excuse me? I'll go and ask Georgiana if she knows where Marina might be.'

She gave her hostess as polite a curtsey as she could

muster and moved away, slipping through the throng of people that now seemed far too thick. It would have been better to send Joseph ahead, his broad form cleaving through the crowds like the parting of the Red Sea, but all Isabelle could think of was getting to Miss Lockhart before the next dance began.

If Marina wasn't there to take up her place in the set then there had to be a reason, and as Isabelle bore down on Georgiana she was dimly glad to feel Joseph's silent presence at her back.

If something has happened at least I won't have to weather it alone. If there's anyone in the world I'd choose to have with me at this moment it would be him.

She'd been about to tell him as much when Mrs Lockhart had unwittingly intervened. The words had teetered on her tongue, wanting to spill out, but some accursed shyness had held them back, and now they would just have to wait.

It was hardly the time for her to make that most intimate of confessions now. There was no rush, after all. Her feelings had shaped themselves into their final form, like a sculptor putting the finishing touch to a masterpiece, and they would never now revert to unmoulded clay. She loved her husband, and the passing of a few more minutes would make no difference to the name carved into her heart that was more convinced with every beat that he was the only man who could have won it.

Georgiana's face was aglow when Isabelle reached her—whatever her partner was saying was clearly very agreeable indeed. She could hardly drag her eyes away from him, and Isabelle had to repeat her question twice before she could gain any kind of answer.

'Marina? Oh… I think she stepped outside to get a breath of air.'

Isabelle felt something inside her shift, although whether with relief or apprehension remained to be seen. 'Alone?'

'I—yes… I suppose she must have been.'

Isabelle seized Joseph's arm.

'If she went to take some air she should be on the terrace. Can we go to her?'

Her pulse was still jumping, but a little of her initial alarm receded as Joseph cut a path for them through the other guests, making for the double doors standing open at the end of the room. Beyond lay the moonlit flagstones of a patio, and Isabelle took a deep breath as she and Joseph stepped out into the night, the air cold but welcome after the cloying heat of the ballroom's too many bodies.

'Do you see her?'

In unison they looked around, straining through the darkness which the candlelight behind them didn't do much to lift. The terrace stretched away towards a wide and sloping lawn, Greek statuettes dotted about casting long shadows over the level slabs, and it was only a movement at the corner of her eye that made

Isabelle turn towards one standing at the very furthest end.

'Over there!'

Relief flooded her as she saw Marina's ghostly form emerge from the gloom, moving away from the statue that had concealed her. Isabelle started towards her at once, a reprimand leaping to her lips, but a second spectral form made her falter, materialising from behind the same statue as Marina to send Isabelle's stomach plummeting down to her feet.

The darkness made it difficult to see the man's face. All she knew for certain was that Marina was trying to pull away, leaning backwards as she tried to haul her arm free of the stranger's unrelenting grip. He seemed to have no intention of releasing her, however, no matter how much she tugged, and a blinding haze of anger swept over Isabelle from head to foot as without thinking she surged forward.

But she was not the first to reach them.

Joseph had closed the space between himself and Marina's unwanted admirer faster than a bird in flight, and Isabelle was still too far away to stop him when she saw him reach out to grasp the other man's collar.

'Wait!' Her cry was strangled, a half-hiss, half-whisper that those inside wouldn't be able to hear, but it was enough to bring Joseph up short. 'Don't touch him! There are too many people—'

She knew instinctively what would happen if Joseph caught hold of his prey and it made her blood run cold. If anyone stepped onto the terrace to witness either a tussle or Marina being manhandled it would be an unrecoverable social disaster, and she prayed she wasn't too late to avert it as she drew level with Joseph and saw the gut-wrenching fear in her sister's eyes.

'Issy—'

Again Marina tried to break free, but the man's grip was firm. He was smiling—actually *smiling*—as if he didn't understand that he was a hair's breadth from becoming acquainted with a scarred fist, and Isabelle could feel the cold fury radiating from Joseph as he kept himself under commendable self-control. Now she was close enough to see it, the young man's face was vaguely familiar—one of the eldest Lockhart son's friends, she realised, and clearly so drunk he hardly knew what he was doing. He was swaying slightly, but his hand didn't falter on Marina's arm, and Isabelle's anger rose again to battle against her desire to avoid a very public disgrace.

'What is the meaning of this? Let go of my sister at once!'

She kept her voice low, but hard as diamond, and she sensed Joseph moving closer to her side, deliberately shielding her and Marina from view. If anyone were to look out of the ballroom doors they wouldn't see anything untoward, and for that she was grateful as the intoxicated young man shrugged, too far gone in drink to know how close to the wind he was sailing.

'I saw Miss Marina outside all alone. What kind

of gentleman would I be if I hadn't gone over to talk with her? She looked as though she'd welcome the company.'

He peered at Marina, a horrible attempt at an ingratiating smile still on his lips, and Isabelle's ire reached new heights at her sister's immediate and vehement shake of her head.

'I only came out to take some air before the next dance. I never intended anyone to follow me—'

'I'm more than worth her notice.'

The man cut across her as if she hadn't spoken, his fingers biting deeper into Marina's arm. Even in the darkness Isabelle could see how he was pinching her skin, and it took all her resolve not to allow Joseph to knock the wretch to the ground.

'I'll have almost a thousand a year when my grandfather finally takes the hint to die…but then I suppose you two ladies know all about waiting around for an old man's money…'

He laughed, a ridiculous inebriated giggle that made Isabelle's skin crawl, but it was the jibe against Edwin that cut her down to the bone. She saw Marina gasp, hating the hurt and confusion that leapt into her eyes alongside her distress, but Isabelle hadn't time to reply before a strong hand moved her aside.

'Joseph!'

For a sickening moment she thought he was going to fell the drunken man with one blow. Joseph stepped forward, leaning so close to the other man that he must have been able to smell the drink on his breath, and with more restraint than Isabelle had realised he possessed he used his words, rather than his fists, to make his point.

'You are drunk, *sir*, and not behaving in the manner befitting a gentleman. Let go of the lady's arm and remove yourself at once.'

If she had thought his voice was like gravel before, then now it was chips of granite, cold and hard and sharp enough to slice through any amount of alcohol. The younger man squinted upwards, appearing belatedly to realise that a giant towered over him, and for the first time his hand loosened a little on Marina's arm. He was still reluctant to surrender her completely, pride or perhaps port making him more obstinate than was wise, and Isabelle's breath caught again when he lifted his chin to try and meet Joseph's eye.

'What if I don't wish to? What if I've no reason to do as you say?'

Joseph gazed down at him, his face a perfectly blank mask that was somehow more frightening than any glare. 'That would be your choice. But I would make you regret it.'

It wasn't a threat. It was a promise: delivered so simply and honestly that even the drunken youth didn't doubt him. The unsteady fingers at last relinquished their grip on Marina and she fled at once into Isabelle's waiting arms, trembling so hard it seemed her legs were on the brink of giving way beneath her.

The young man scowled around at the three un-friendly faces, his gaze sliding past Joseph's with un-derstandable speed. 'I can't be blamed for wanting to speak to the prettiest girl here,' he slurred resentfully, jerking his head at Marina and setting her shaking all the more. 'Everybody knows she isn't allowed to walk a step without her sister watching. The old Duke was the same—why bother even letting her out if she isn't available?'

Revulsion spread through Isabelle like wildfire. He spoke as though Marina was a vacant cab or a horse for sale, not a person at all, and she turned, placing an arm around Marina's waist as she began to guide her away.

Behind her she heard the man start to call after them, her worry peaking sharply at the prospect of him making a loud, attention-grabbing scene, but a glance over her shoulder showed him change his mind. Apparently whatever Joseph muttered into his ear was enough to make him think the better of it, his face losing its port-induced ruddiness to turn the colour of ash, and the final thought she had before turning round again was how glad she was to have a husband on whom she knew, without question, she could al-ways rely.

Nobody spoke much during the short carriage jour-ney back to Winford House, and that suited Joseph very well. He wanted to be alone with his thoughts and he kept his face turned to the darkened window, looking out without noticing the moonlit streets and houses passing by, and it wasn't until Isabelle came to the parlour after settling Marina into her rooms that she finally broke the silence he would have been happy to continue.

For once casting aside her usual elegance, she dropped heavily into the fireside armchair opposite his own, drawing her bare feet up beneath her. She'd pulled the pins out of her hair and it rippled around her shoulders, slightly dishevelled, but gleaming like spun gold when she pushed it back from her face. In the firelight she was prettier than ever, and Joseph found himself staring into the flames, unwilling to look in her direction as she heaved a weary sigh.

'Well… It seems the evening took the very turn we were hoping it wouldn't.'

It was exactly the thing he had been thinking, and to hear Isabelle voice it was like a dagger thrust into the most vulnerable part of him. She spoke with no reproach, but it made little difference to the bitter knowledge that sat inside him like a fist.

You failed.

He nodded, his chest too tight for him to make any reply. The incident on the terrace played yet again through his mind and he had to fight the desire to sink his head into his hands, raw disappointment in himself and burning regret impossible to ignore.

I had one job. One role to play. One single task. And I let both Isabelle and Marina down.

He should have been more careful. He should have protected Marina in the way Isabelle had relied upon him to. If they hadn't found her on the terrace there was no telling what might have happened, and the fact that Isabelle's precious faith in him had been so poorly repaid made him want to curse out loud. For the first time in his life somebody had placed their trust in him for a purer reason than money and he had shown himself unworthy of it, Isabelle's belief in him coming so near to ending in disaster that it tore him to shreds. Mere hours before he had balanced on a precipice, with the world at his feet and more happiness than he'd ever dared dream of spread out before him, but now he had taken his chance and destroyed it, and any hopes for the future were like dust beneath his boots.

She was speaking again, her voice barely louder than the crackling coming from the grate. 'I'm beyond grateful that you were there with me. If you hadn't been I'm not sure how the situation would have been resolved.'

Out of the corner of his eye he saw her cast him a tired smile and his heart gave a painful squeeze. Her gratitude stung: it unwittingly twisted the knife further into an open wound, his guilt magnified by the sweetness he no longer felt he deserved.

'You have nothing to thank me for.'

Making himself face her, Joseph watched Isabelle's smile fade. Immediately he longed to restore it, never wanting to be the reason for her brow to crease, but he couldn't allow himself to touch her. Only a man who had done right by his wife deserved to feel the warmth of her skin, and after the Lockharts' ball he could no longer count himself among that number.

'It was inexcusable how close Marina came to being disgraced when it was my duty to protect her. That man should never have been able to lay a finger on her, and if you hadn't been there to stop me I would have made an already bad situation ten times worse. I failed you tonight, and I wish more than anything that I hadn't.'

Surprise crossed Isabelle's face. 'What? What are you talking about? It was because you intervened that Marina was able to get free. Why are you being so hard on yourself?'

'Because she shouldn't have been in that position in the first place. That is *my* failing and nobody else's.'

Isabelle's frown returned, but Joseph gave her no time to argue. She was too generous to rebuke him so he would do it himself, part of his penance to look his mistake in the eye and see how far from the mark he had fallen.

'Her innocence is shattered. She knows the real nature of the world now, and the darkness in it you had hoped she would never see. If I'd watched her more closely…'

He didn't know how to finish. Isabelle stared at him, confusion and unhappiness clear in her wide-set eyes, and he loathed himself for causing it. It would be gutless to back away from the truth, however, and it was the truth that she should have, anything less showing a cowardice he could never entertain.

She leaned towards him, shifting forward in her chair as if to try to see directly into his face, and despite the ache in his throat Joseph made sure he didn't break away from her earnest searching gaze.

'You're taking too much on yourself. It was foolish of me to dream I could hide the unpleasant aspects of life from her for ever. She knows now how dangerous some men can be, yes, but knowledge is power, and she's seen what she must guard herself against. In the strangest of ways, this evening might even have been a blessing in disguise.'

Joseph exhaled, slowly shaking his head in disbelief. How could her faith be so unshakable when he had proved so clearly it had been misplaced? He looked at her, at her kind, cherished face, just starting to show the first signs of dark circles beneath tired eyes, and his ribs felt as though they might crack beneath the lead weight that settled on his chest.

Isabelle was the most precious person in the world to him, and his feelings towards her were growing day by day, like an ocean fed by a narrow stream. They had deepened, reaching down into his soul to light corners he didn't know he had, and that he loved her was now beyond any doubt.

'I'm not taking on any more than I should. We married so that I might help you keep Marina from harm, to carry on the legacy of your late husband, and instead I let some drunkard get his hands on her. If someone else had come out onto the terrace instead of us your sister's reputation would be in tatters by now.'

His head felt heavy, and again he suppressed the urge to drop it into his hands. It would be self-indulgent to let his torment show when the potential for Isabelle's was so much greater, and he drew on the stoicism he had always shown before she came into his life to help him keep his emotion in check.

'It seems I'm not the man you thought I was after all. The only thing I had worth offering you was my protection, and tonight I have showed even that has questionable value.'

Isabelle was already almost on the edge of her chair, but now she leaned further still—although Joseph moved before she could touch his hand. He stood, drawing away from her, and he saw the dismay in her eyes. If he allowed her fingers to so much as brush against his he might not be able to hold back the desire to gather her into his arms, and a man with so little to offer had no business even being in the same room as one so hopelessly above him in every respect.

It was as the boys in the workhouse had always said, Joseph thought dimly, too consumed by the hurt in his wife's expression to think of much else. There was something wrong with him—something defective that his own mother hadn't been able to accept—and now even the single talent he'd been dubiously blessed with wasn't enough.

'Why are you doing this?' Isabelle demanded, bewilderment lending a sharp edge to her voice. 'I don't understand. Why are you pulling away from me? I thought…'

Her unhappiness was like sharp teeth tearing into his gut, ripping and pulling, but he made himself stand firm. 'You gave me more than I ever dreamed possible and I have repaid you with broken promises. Surely you can see why I don't deserve your acceptance now?'

Isabelle stood. With her chin up and shoulders squared she was suddenly the proud Duchess again, just as determined as that first time he'd set foot in her house and realised there might be more to her than first appeared, and he had to stop his mind from casting back to revisit that day.

Had that been the moment he'd begun to feel something for her? Or had that come later, when he'd caught a glimpse of the woman beneath the polish and been struck by a hidden side to her he never would have believed existed?

Either way, the outcome was the same, and he wished he could turn himself to stone, uncertain whether his willpower could outlast his wife's.

'Don't you think it's for me to decide how I feel about you? After everything we've shared?'

Her eyes searched the shadows in his, looking for some gleam of surrender, but Joseph made sure she found none. Any weakness, any hint of light escaping from beneath a locked door would beckon her onwards and he might not be able to resist. His mind was made up, but the agony of it was no less for knowing he was right.

'Not this time. Not when you've already made that mistake once before.'

She flinched back as though he had physically pushed her away. For a moment she looked at him, the pale set of her face something he would never forget, but then she swallowed, the subtle movement of her throat catching his eye in the otherwise still room.

'I see.'

She nodded—a single dip of her haloed head. Without another word she turned away, rustling across the parlour towards the door, and all Joseph could do was watch as she took hold of the handle and pulled it open. He wanted to call out, to stride after her, to stop her and imprison her in his arms; but he did none of those things. Instead he stood and felt his soul crumble as she disappeared, only able to murmur after her so quietly that there was no chance she could have heard.

'Yes. Now you see...'

Chapter Fourteen

The frost crunched beneath her boots as Isabelle walked slowly down the path cutting through Winford's manicured grounds. Even wrapped up against the wind she was still cold, although that seemed a small price to pay to escape the house itself.

Three days previously Joseph's appearance in a room would have sent a shiver of excitement through her, but now the sight of him made her shoulders tense, the aftermath of the Lockharts' disastrous ball affecting more than just Marina.

At least her sister was just beginning to seem like herself again. She had been subdued at first, but was now recovering swiftly from the ordeal that had taught her such a harsh lesson in the ways of the world, and Isabelle wished she and Joseph could mend their rift as quickly. Since that moment in the parlour when he had wrenched open a new gulf between them everything had changed, the connection she'd thought so secure now hanging by a thread, and more than anything she longed to be able to return to what they had endured so much to find.

It was fortunate, then, that she had an idea of how to do just that.

He had meant what he said—of that she had no doubt. It was less that he didn't *want* her regard and more that he felt he didn't *deserve* it, and it was up to her to cut through his damnable stubbornness with the truth. If she could just help him to see he had value beyond the strength of his arm he would surely come to realise what she already knew: he was a man of honour and capability—not just some nameless orphan abandoned on the workhouse steps—and his poor opinion of himself was in no way shared by anyone else.

But he's so accursedly sure he's right—as if he knows my mind better than I do myself. If I could only be sure my plan will work...

The sound of footsteps behind her made her turn, her heart leaping painfully until she saw who they belonged to. Boots stamping through frost-hardened grass had immediately made her think of Joseph, and she wasn't sure whether to be disappointed or relieved when instead Collins greeted her with a bow, respectful even when the tip of his nose was blue with cold.

'You shouldn't be out here without a coat. You'll catch your death.'

'Thank you for your concern, ma'am. I only came to give you this.'

The butler held something out to her—a white shape in his hand that made her stomach curdle abruptly.

'You said you wanted to know at once when the morning post came, so I brought it without delay.'

Isabelle glanced towards the house, scanning the empty windows before she took the proffered letter. 'Did my husband see this arrive?'

'No, ma'am. I was discreet, as per your instructions.'

His modest pride in his subtlety might have made Isabelle smile if she hadn't felt as though the letter was burning her hand. She'd been awaiting its arrival, but now it was in her grasp apprehension rose within her, and she was strangely hesitant to break it open even as she longed to know what it said.

'Thank you, Collins. You did very well.'

The butler bowed again and turned back to the house, walking a little more quickly than usual as the freezing wind nipped at his heels, and Isabelle waited a few moments before she followed. She wanted to be alone when she slit the seal holding the paper closed, and she was careful to conceal it beneath her cloak as she reached the back porch and passed through the kitchen.

Until she had read whatever was inside she wanted nobody to question her about it—not Marina and *absolutely not* Joseph, the thought of him becoming aware of her plans before she was ready to reveal them making her wary.

That could ruin everything—assuming, of course, there's anything to ruin.

There was nobody in the parlour when she cautiously peered around the doorframe. Marina must still be in bed, a reluctant riser on cold mornings, and where Joseph might be was anyone's guess. They hadn't shared a bedroom since that fateful night, and he kept his distance as much as possible during the day, clearly determined to enforce the chasm between them which he had wrought with his misguided words.

The essence of him lingered, however, unseen in every corner of Winford House, and Isabelle made sure to double-check the parlour's emptiness before settling into one of the chairs beside the fire.

Her heart was far too loud as she turned the letter over, tracing the embossed wax of the seal. Whatever was contained within this one piece of paper could be the answer to her prayers—or it could make fresh ones urgently necessary. The happiness she had found with Joseph was too precious to be allowed to slip away without a fight, however, any timidness on her part possibly meaning the difference between saving their bond or surrendering to its destruction, and she gathered all her courage as she took a deep breath, dug her nail beneath the wax and prised it free.

For the next few minutes the house around her ceased to exist.

Isabelle's eyes flitted down the page, leaping from line to line like a squirrel in the branches of a tree. Reaching the bottom, she paused to take in the scrawled signature, her heartbeat setting up such a tumult now that she worried it might bring the servants running. She read it again—slowly this time, drinking in every word—and then had to take a moment to fully absorb what she had seen.

But this is wonderful. How much better could it possibly be?

It was exactly what she'd hoped for, and she hardly dared believe it could be true. One single piece of paper had made all the difference in the world, illuminating the darkness like a lighthouse in a storm, and with a little more luck she and Joseph might not be dashed against the rocks as she had feared.

He still had his doubts, but now she had a card to play that might just persuade him he was wrong, and wild hope leapt inside her—a snatch of silvery optimism where once there had been despair.

But she had little chance to revel in her newfound faith. For the second time that morning the sound of footsteps set alarm ringing, far too distinctive to belong to anyone but the person she most definitely did not want to see.

Hurriedly she folded the letter and slid it between herself and the padded arm of the chair—but not quite hurriedly enough. With exquisitely bad timing Joseph appeared in the doorway at the very moment she shoved the paper out of sight, his gaze flickering from the cushion to her face, and Isabelle felt a sharp twinge of fear that her expression might betray her completely.

'Good morning.'

'Good morning.'

He hovered on the threshold, his hesitancy strikingly at odds with his towering frame.

'I'm sorry. I didn't realise you were in here. Did I interrupt you reading something?'

Instinctively Isabelle stiffened, convinced the shake of her head must look like jerky clockwork. 'No. I was just sitting…enjoying the fire. It's so cold today.'

She was sure she caught something flitting through Joseph's eyes, but it had vanished before she could tell what it was. He didn't look convinced, however, lying never one of Isabelle's talents, and she wished with sudden intensity that she could cross the room and pitch herself into his arms. It was unnatural to be within a few paces and not touch him, to be breathing the same air and yet feel the invisible barrier between them he had felt the need to build, and she twined her fingers together so tightly her knuckles turned white.

Joseph cast about the room, evidently not wanting to meet her eye, and she felt pain lance through her to see how uneasy he was in her company. Only a few days ago he would have greeted her with a kiss, making her shudder with delight as his hand strayed down to trace the line of her collarbone and dip—just the tiniest fraction—beneath the neckline of her gown, before retreating with a dark chuckle when she gasped against his lips. Now he was like a different man, and the contrast made her ache, the hollow feeling growing until she could stand it no longer.

I have to act now. I have to be the one to save what we had.

Abruptly she stood, deftly sliding the letter behind her back. With Joseph's eyes turned away from her it was easy enough to reach the door without him seeing it, and the tightness in her throat increased as she saw how quickly he moved out of her way. He was resolved not even to brush her hand and she tried not to let her earlier hope die, guarding the fragile embers that might so easily turn to ash.

'I'm going out. I have an appointment and I'm not sure when I'll return.'

If he wondered where she was going he hid it well, only the tension in the set of his shoulders a wordless giveaway that he was suffering every bit as much as Isabelle herself.

'Very good. I shall see you whenever that might be.'

He inclined his head in his usual approximation of a bow and Isabelle sailed past him, endeavouring to exude more poise than she felt. Her chest was bursting and her heart thundering like a galloping horse, and her legs were worryingly shaky beneath her as she called for her carriage.

With nerveless fingers she fastened her cloak and

pulled on her bonnet, pausing only for a second to look in the glass hanging in the entrance hall.

She was pale. Her eyes were shadowed through lack of sleep and the planes of her face were drawn, the skin pulled tightly over the bone to echo the tension inside her. It was the countenance of a woman with everything to gain but just as much to lose, and she turned away from her own apprehensive gaze to throw open the front door.

Her coachman bowed as she neared him, too well trained to show any curiosity at being so hurriedly summoned.

'Good morning, ma'am.'

Isabelle attempted a smile in response, although her mouth was reluctant to obey. 'Good morning, Monroe. I'd like you to take me to—'

She broke off as the coachman glanced over her shoulder towards the house. Clearly something had distracted him for a fleeting moment, and Isabelle half turned to see what it was, her heart turning over when a figure at one window caught her eye.

Joseph was standing quite still, looking out at her with such immeasurable sadness in his face that Isabelle's breath clawed at her throat. The instant their eyes met he drew back from the window with the speed of a man who had not intended to be seen, but the image of his haunting misery stayed with her as she climbed the carriage steps, ducking inside as if the safety of the cabin would erase the memory of that terrible sight.

'To Gas Street, please, Monroe. As quickly as you can.'

The morning passed with agonising slowness as Joseph sat in his study, attempting to read the book he had pulled blindly from one of the shelves. He was at least four chapters in by the time he finally threw it aside, realising he hadn't registered a single word, and he screwed his eyes shut as he leaned back in his chair.

Damn you. Look what a mess you've made of everything.

If it was just his own suffering he had caused then he could have borne it, but seeing the change in Isabelle was far worse than anything else. The way she'd looked at him when he had stumbled across her in the parlour wouldn't leave him alone, constantly reminding him of how obviously she hadn't wanted to see him, and if that wasn't enough...

She was receiving letters she not only hid but lied about getting? Going off to mysterious places without a hint of where they might be?

Where once she had shared everything with him Isabelle had now withdrawn, keeping her own counsel rather than letting him in, but that was his own fault. He was the one who had withdrawn first, severing the intimacy between them like an executioner delivering a fatal blow, and he would be the worst kind of hypocrite if he felt hurt that she had taken him at his word.

Putting some distance between them had seemed the best way to avoid disappointing her again, but so far all he had achieved was causing them both pain, and Joseph pressed his fingertips against his closed eyelids as he wondered how the hell he could fix what he'd destroyed.

He stood, pacing across the room with frustrated energy. How could he have been so idiotic as to throw Isabelle's acceptance of him back in her face? Turning away as if it had meant nothing? She'd told him he was wrong but he hadn't believed her, too blinkered by self-doubt to see she that knew her own mind. For all he thought he didn't deserve her regard she had been determined to bestow it regardless, and his heart sank as he realised the full extent of his mistake—as well as how much he ached to utter those three simple words.

When she comes back I'll tell her. Even if she doesn't feel the same, even if I've spoiled everything once and for all...she ought to know the truth.

She might reject him. He wouldn't blame her if she did. After his behaviour he hadn't earned a second chance; but then, Isabelle's generosity was one of the things he had grown to love so fiercely. If anybody was likely to be merciful it was her—and when the door of the study swung suddenly open to reveal her standing in the corridor beyond, it felt to Joseph as if divine intervention had held out its hand.

Framed in the doorway she was like a painting, bringing with her the fresh, crisp scent of the air outside, and at once the clamour of Joseph's mind fell silent. There was something in her eyes that cut through the turmoil, flying straight as an arrow to lodge deep in his chest, and he forgot to wonder why she should be in such a hurry to see him that she hadn't even stopped to take off her cloak.

'Joseph. There you are. I've just this moment come home. I have something…something to share with you and I can only pray you'll want to hear.'

Her voice was strange. Half nervous, half excited… Joseph felt his own hopes and apprehension rise to follow its lead. What she could have to tell him that would make her so agitated he couldn't begin to guess, and gesturing awkwardly to one of the chairs standing beside the fireplace seemed wiser than trying.

'Of course. Will you sit?'

She accepted his offer, busying herself with removing her cloak as he sat down opposite. Out of the corner of his eye Joseph saw her hand was unsteady as she undid the ribbons of her bonnet and pulled it from her head—more evidence, if it was required, that something was most definitely amiss.

Isabelle arranged her skirts around her, tucking them prettily into place—but then the next moment she was on her feet again, sweeping away from him to pace the room. It was the same restless striding that she had interrupted him undertaking himself, and Joseph half rose from his chair, watching with growing bewilderment as she wheeled round to stand beside the hearth. Tapping her fingers distractedly on the mantel, she looked away, her eyes flitting to the corners of the room as if seeking inspiration, and the drumming of her fingertips reached a feverish pitch before abruptly she ceased.

'I'm going to tell you everything, and I don't want you to speak until I've finished. Do you accept?'

Caught off balance by the sudden change of tack, Joseph hesitated. 'What? I mean, if that's what you want… But—'

'It is. If you stop me at any point I might not be able to find the nerve to continue.'

A fleeting glance in his direction made sure of no further questions. It was a gaze that managed to be firm as well as anxious and Joseph closed his mouth, the queries wanting to spill forth dying on his tongue. Intense curiosity assailed him, but he made himself sit quietly as he waited for her to break the suspense.

She was clearly gathering her courage and she reminded him of a rider about to take a dangerous jump, perhaps afraid she might fall beneath the horse's hooves. He wanted to reach out for her hand, to tell her that she could speak openly without fear of his reaction, but she began before he had the chance to move.

'What you said three nights ago hurt me deeply, but

I realised what pained me the most was how poorly you viewed yourself. You were so sure in your low opinion that I knew unless that changed you would never allow me closer.'

'Isabelle. I—'

A stern look was his reward for interrupting and he fell silent—although beneath the cover of his shirt his heart had begun to jump.

'As I was saying… I thought about it for some time, wondering what I could do to help you see what I see, and that's when I realised. I had to start at the very beginning.'

She cut her green-blue eyes in his direction, as though suspecting another disruption, but this time Joseph kept his peace.

'Your mother's abandonment of you was the catalyst for everything that followed. You imagined yourself unworthy of love, of compassion, of anything good and pure, and I could see that until those scars were given the chance to heal you would never think anything else. So… I wrote to the workhouse.'

The last five words were delivered in a rush, a tinge of colour blooming in her cheeks, and Joseph felt as though he had forgotten to breathe.

He hadn't had any real idea of what she'd been so hesitant to tell him, but nothing could have prepared him for *that*. A hundred different thoughts rose like a flock of birds, wings clattering in a confusing din so loud it made rationality impossible, and Isabelle took advantage of his mute surprise to hurry onwards.

'I asked about you. I asked for details of the day you were found—if your mother had left any information…anything that might help me to help you. I wasn't sure what reply—if any—would come, but this morning I received this.'

With a shaking hand, she drew a crumpled letter from the folds of her skirt.

'It seems my position as the widow of a duke still wields some influence. The governor of the workhouse wrote back to me, asking if I would care to discuss the matter in person—and so that's where I've been.'

She let out a ragged breath. Perhaps she was relieved to have got so far in her explanation without him setting up any resistance, although in truth he wouldn't have known where to begin. It was so unexpected, so far from anything he might ever have imagined, that all he could do was stare as she crossed back to where her cloak lay, flung over the back of her chair, and dug into one of the pockets.

'He gave me this.'

Isabelle held out a folded piece of paper that quivered slightly in her quaking fingers. The movement made it look as though it was alive—a stark contrast to Joseph's immobile shock that wouldn't let him lift his hand to take it, sitting still as he struggled to understand what was happening before his eyes.

Isabelle had been to the workhouse. She had used her position to make the governor speak to her and found out…what, exactly? And why? Why, after he had treated her so poorly, had she still found it in her heart to try to help him when he deserved no such kindness?

Perhaps I haven't ruined everything after all. Perhaps there might be some hope left.

The thought occurred distantly, seeming to come from far away, as at last he took the letter between numb fingertips. Without meaning to he brushed Isabelle's hand, the warmth of it darting through him to light a match in his stomach, and it meant everything in the world to him that she didn't pull away.

'I haven't read it, obviously, but I understand that it contains a written account of everything he told me. What you choose to do with that information is up to you.'

He nodded mutely, looking down at his own name scribbled in a familiar slant. The old governor must be in his seventies by now, but the prospect of tormenting his charges had clearly kept him young enough to remain in the cracked leather chair Joseph recalled so well. That cold, pitiless man wasn't his concern, however—not while Isabelle stood so near, the swiftness with which her chest rose and fell telling him more than any words when he finally managed to lift his eyes to look at her.

She watched him anxiously, searching his face for

some clue as to what he was thinking. If he was any judge she was worried about his reaction, and her lips twitched when he gently held out his hand.

'Have you finished? Can I speak now?'

A wordless nod was her only reply. A shadow of something horribly close to apprehension had darkened her gaze and he ran his thumb over her knuckles, wanting more than anything to make sure she never looked so worried again.

'Before I read this—before I learn what you already know—will you answer a question?'

There was another nod of that golden head, this time a little more determined. 'Anything. You need only ask.'

'Very well, then. Answer me this.'

She took half a step back when he stood, lifting her chin to look up at him. Her hand was still in his, its softness the perfect counterpart to the violence-roughened palm of his own, and he longed to keep hold of it and never let go.

'Why did you do this for me? It was no mere idle curiosity on your part. There must have been a reason, and I would know what it was.'

Her eyebrows twitched together briefly and Joseph had the sudden feeling that he had asked the most obvious question in the world.

'Why do you think?'

At his shrug, her eyes narrowed, the uncertainty in them chased out by exasperation. In one beat of his pounding heart she was the old Isabelle again, forthright in the face of what she clearly felt was his dimwittedness, and he could have pulled her into his arms there and then when she reached up to touch his stubble-dusted chin.

'Of all the… Because I love you, you stubborn, wilful, *frustrating* man. And I believe that, despite your terrible way of showing it, you love me too.'

The light pressure of Isabelle's fingertips against his skin was like a benediction, but Joseph couldn't fully appreciate their warmth. Her words resounded inside his head, reverberating and echoing like the peals of a bell. It was the first time in his life he had ever heard them and their power almost felled him where he stood.

He felt as though he'd been consumed by a roaring flood, elation and amazement buoying him up to keep his head above the surface. Isabelle spoke so plainly, concealing nothing, and her honesty set his final barrier ablaze until nothing stood between them but the ashes of his mistakes.

For more than thirty years he had been alone, determined to fool himself into believing he preferred it that way, but his wife had pulled down the walls of his deception and reached out to hold his heart in one gentle hand.

His throat felt as if it was filled with ground glass, his voice little more than a hoarse murmur. 'You're right. I do. I love you…'

Isabelle let out a tiny breath—one he hadn't realised she had been holding. Her hand still lay against his face and he felt it quake, the last thing he was aware of before he bent to lay claim to her trembling mouth.

The letter almost fell from his fingers as he took Isabelle in his arms and held her tightly against him, sinking the fingers of his free hand into her hair. He had almost lost her but she had come back, guiding him onto the right path when it had been he who had taken the wrong turn, and now they were together he would make sure they never parted again.

Isabelle's arms were around his neck and he shuddered to feel her body fit against him as seamlessly as if they were two halves of a whole. Perhaps they were, he thought, in the one tiny corner of his mind that hadn't yet been swallowed up by hopeless joy...

But then he felt Isabelle smile against his mouth. The curve of her lips was so precious to him that he could see it even when his eyes were closed, and that final corner of rationality surrendered to the same blissful state as every other.

When he at last drew back Joseph saw the same dazed wonder in her face as he imagined must be present in his own. Letting go of her was out of the question, and he brought her with him as he collapsed into a chair, gathering her against him as a willing captive to her soft weight in his lap.

'I was such a fool. I told you—'

She cut him off with the flick of one effortlessly

regal hand. 'Did you truly think I would stop loving you just because you implied I shouldn't? Of course not. When have you ever known me to do as I was told?'

Carefully Isabelle lifted his closed hand from its place on her thigh, turning it over to reveal the paper crumpled in his palm. He'd kept his grip on it quite unconsciously, and even now it seemed far less important than Isabelle being curled against him, their breathing falling into time with each other's as she gently unfolded his fingers.

'Are you going to read this?'

He glanced down. 'Do you think I should?'

'I believe you'll be glad you did.'

Privately, Joseph doubted Isabelle's hesitant optimism, but he would have rather never spoken again than disappoint her. She'd gone to so much trouble on his account that the least he could do was read a few scribbled lines, even if he held scant hope that they might say anything worthwhile. The workhouse was behind him now, the false lessons it had taught him about his value now lying in the dust, but he settled his other hand more tightly around Isabelle's waist as he broke the seal and began to read what he knew was to be his final link to a past he now intended to forget.

He felt Isabelle watching him as with every scrawled word his disbelief grew, gathering pace like a hare running full tilt. Twice more he read the contents, their meaning not fully penetrating the haze—until he turned blindly to Isabelle, seeking her loving gaze to help him understand.

'I don't— This letter can't be right.'

Joseph stared at it once again, the scratchy black shapes shifting until they were indistinct smudges instead of real words.

'My mother... This says she *didn't* abandon me without a backward glance. But how can that be so? How can that be when all my childhood I was told she didn't care?'

Isabelle leaned closer against him, placing the palm of one warm hand against his neck. It was calming, to a point, but not quite enough to slow his racing mind, darting in so many directions it felt as if it were being pulled apart.

'It's the truth. She was very young, unmarried, terribly afraid... She left you at the workhouse because she had no other choice. As much as she wanted to keep you, she knew she couldn't give you what you needed. Your mother left you because she loved you— not because she didn't.'

The swarming in Joseph's mind grew more intense, his thoughts milling like hornets around a nest. He could hear what Isabelle was saying but he couldn't make sense of it, a lifetime displaced in seconds by one piece of paper...

'It says here that I wasn't left on the steps. She paid—she actually *paid* them. Gave them the very last of her money to take me in so that I might be safe.'

'She must have been desperate if she believed that was the best place for you. Her life must have been grim indeed if the workhouse was preferable to what you would have endured elsewhere.'

Joseph dropped the letter onto Isabelle's lap, passing a hand over his bewildered eyes. A maelstrom of emotion battered him and his insides gave a wrench as he thought of the woman he had always tried to disregard. She must have battled with her decision, and Joseph felt a surge of pity rise within him for the mother he had never known, faced with a horrifying choice and damned no matter which way she jumped. It was startling, unbelievable and it turned the entirety of his world on its head, although of one thing at least he knew he could be sure. Isabelle was still in his arms, the lavender scent of her perfume just as enticing now as it had been when they'd first met, and her steady presence was like a harbour as a storm raged inside him.

'I can't believe it. My whole life I believed she didn't care…and now I find it was all a lie. But why? Why would they tell me that if it wasn't true?'

Isabelle's mouth tightened. 'Cruelty. Plain and simple. I believe the governor wouldn't have told me if he hadn't been so elderly and ill. I imagine he wants a clean slate before he has to answer for his sins.'

Joseph exhaled harshly. *That* at least sounded right. The damage that lie had done was immense, and unforgivable, and at one time Joseph would have demanded vengeance—but now he was a different man. Isabelle had shown him a way to be better and he would hold on to that, striving every day to prove her faith in him was deserved.

'It gives me two other revelations.' He tapped the letter with a forefinger, watching Isabelle's brows raise enquiringly. 'She named me. My mother named me Joseph. Not them. And her name is here too.'

Isabelle's eyes widened. 'You have her *name*? That means... Do you want to try to find her?'

He traced the embroidered pattern on Isabelle's skirt, feeling her shift slightly as his hand drifted over her leg. 'I might... It's been over thirty years, though, and I wouldn't want to raise my hopes too high. I need some time to think.'

His fingers skimmed higher, circling round to rest against the warm dip of her lower back. The heady mix of differing emotions still simmered within him, but with Isabelle pressed against him they felt more manageable somehow, and her quiet strength was more than a match for his own.

'Even if I don't find her, or if she's passed on some-where I can't reach her, I'm glad that I know the truth. She did her best and that's enough for me.'

Isabelle nodded, her face very close to his. It would be the easiest thing in the world to lean forward and kiss her, and Joseph had just decided to do exactly that when she drew back a little to look into his eyes.

'You know she loved you now. Just as you know I love you, too.'

He gazed back at her, hazel locking on to greenish blue to make Isabelle's cheeks flush pink. Of its own accord his mind reeled back to revisit the first time he had seen her, so proud and haughty that the love he felt for her now seemed like something from a dream.

'Something I would never have predicted. If you hadn't been so determined to walk back to your carriage alone we might never have come to this place.'

Isabelle's laugh changed into a gasp as his mouth came down on hers, cutting off whatever she'd been about to say with a passion that held them both willing prisoners. Her hands tunnelled through his hair, and she made a soft cry of protest when he broke the kiss to murmur against her lips, revelling in the knowledge that they had both finally found what they needed to make them whole.

'It'll take me a lifetime to learn how to thank you for that lapse of judgement… *Your Grace.*'

* * * * *

COMING SOON!

We really hope you enjoyed reading this
book. If you're looking for more romance
be sure to head to the shops when
new books are available on

Thursday 20th
July

To see which titles are coming soon, please visit
millsandboon.co.uk/nextmonth

MILLS & BOON®

Coming next month

A LAIRD WITHOUT A PAST
Jeanine Englert

Where are my clothes? Why am I naked?

What was going on?

A dog barked, and Royce lowered into a battle stance putting out his hands to defend his body.

'Easy, boy. Easy,' he commanded.

The dog barked again and nudged his wet nose to Royce's hand. Royce opened his palm, and the dog slathered his hand with its tongue and released a playful yip. Royce exhaled, his shoulders relaxing. He pet the dog's wiry hair and took a halting breath as his heart tried to regain a normal rhythm.

A latch clanked behind him followed by the slow, creaky opening of a door, and Royce whirled around to defend himself, blinking rapidly to clear his vision but still seeing nothing.

'Who are you?' he ordered, his voice stern and commanding as he felt about for a weapon, any weapon. His hand closed around what felt like a vase, and he held it high in the air. 'And how dare you keep me prisoner here. Release me!'

'Sailor's fortune' a woman cried. 'I think my soul left my body; you gave me such a fright. You are no prisoner,' a woman stated plainly. 'By all that's holy, cover yourself. And put down the vase. It was one of my mother's favourites.'

Light footfalls sounded away from him, but Royce stood poised to strike. He stared out into the darkness confused. Where was he and what was happening? And why was some woman speaking to him as if she knew him.

The door squeaked as it closed followed by the dropping of a latch.

'Then why am I here?' he demanded, still gripping the vase, unwilling to set it aside for clothes. Staying alive trumped any sense of propriety. She might not be alone.

'I cannot say. You were face down in the sand being stripped of your worldly possessions when I discovered you.' A pot clanged on what sounded to be a stove. 'Care to put on some trews? They are dry now.'

'Are you alone?' he asked, shifting from one foot to another staring out into the black abyss.

'Aye,' she chuckled.

He relaxed his hold on the vase, felt for the mattress, and sat down fighting off the light-headedness that made him feel weak in the knees.

'Could I trouble you to light a candle if you do not plan to kill me? I cannot see a blasted thing, and I would very much like to put on those trews you mentioned.'

Continue reading
A LAIRD WITHOUT A PAST
Jeanine Englert

Available next month
www.millsandboon.co.uk

LET'S TALK

Romance

For exclusive extracts, competitions and special offers, find us online:

- **f** MillsandBoon
- **𝕏** @MillsandBoon
- **📷** @MillsandBoonUK
- **♪** @MillsandBoonUK

Get in touch on 01413 063 232